blue
hour

By Sarah Schmidt

See What I Have Done
Blue Hour

blue hour

SARAH SCHMIDT

TINDER
PRESS

First published by Hachette Australia

First published in Great Britain in 2022 by Tinder Press
An imprint of HEADLINE PUBLISHING GROUP

1

Cataloguing in Publication Data is available from the British Library

Hardback ISBN 978 1 4722 5062 9
Trade paperback ISBN 978 1 4722 5063 6

Typeset in Adobe Garamond Pro 12.25/19.12 pt

Printed and bound in Great Britain by Clays Ltd, Elcograf S.p.A.

MIX
Paper from
responsible sources
FSC® C104740

Headline's policy is to use papers that are natural, renewable and recyclable
products and made from wood grown in well-managed forests and other
controlled sources. The logging and manufacturing processes are expected to
conform to the environmental regulations of the country of origin.

HEADLINE PUBLISHING GROUP
An Hachette UK Company
Carmelite House
50 Victoria Embankment
London EC4Y 0DZ

www.tinderpress.co.uk
www.headline.co.uk
www.hachette.co.uk

For my daughter

MY WORLD OF BLUE

Many birds of prey do not hunt near their nests. A neutral zone. It is thought this arrangement developed so birds of prey don't accidentally hunt their own offspring.

Sarah Sentilles, *Draw Your Weapons*

Eleanor

Present (1973)

STAND. WALK. AND she does, moves down the hall to their
bedroom, and when she's by his side, Eleanor leans into her
husband's mouth, waits for warm breath on lips. Breasts are full;
the warm drip of herself down her stomach, down between her
legs. There is no way to stop the flow of yourself once the body
accepts release.

Eleanor quiets to the bathroom, switches the light on, lifts
her top, wipes herself clean: right breast and stomach and water
between her legs gives her the urge to urinate and so she does,
a slight sting from having held on overnight.

All quiet in the house, all quiet in the blue hour. Move quicker,
Eleanor.

1

She heads back down the hallway, opens the door to her daughter, the blue lava lamp in shadow play on walls. Eleanor goes to the cot, scoops up Amy, scoops up blankets, and the sight of her daughter's mouth brings a drop of milk, the way all feeds do. Eleanor, leave now so you can get to safety before nightfall, and she whispers, 'Everything will be better soon, Amy.'

There in the first yawn of daylight: dishes stacked by the sink, pumpkin soup splatter on the wall near the telephone, broken chips of the earthenware bowls from Kitty. Mother's wedding gifts. There: a baby rattle in the middle of the lounge room floor, an open cupboard door. Last night's leftovers, never tidied.

Things are the same until you're not, she thinks.

Eleanor feels her way along the walls, navigates past dining chairs, through the obstacle course of day-in-day-out. The smear of dried pumpkin soup on the wall, the phone cord, cold wallpaper, the humming fridge. Open it, Eleanor, and she does, lights up the room with artificial light. Be quiet. On the kitchen counter: her husband's black box, brought home from Vietnam. She holds Amy closer, kisses and kisses.

Artificial light allows you to see what you want to see and so she sees a home filled with the passion of a husband and wife, of two people magnetised hip to hip, moving a body as one through the night, the way they tell each other things that only make sense when whispered in an ear, at just that sonic frequency. Like birds, like whale song: language of like-like species; the taxonomy of family. There: George standing in the lounge room holding his granddaughter Amy, his smile gate-wide, speaking about how in the summer they will camp up at the blue mountain just like old times. There: Kitty laughing along to a story Eleanor has told her. There: Badger with his children.

But there is no existence like this. Out the front door into darkness: colder than she expects. She wraps the blanket tighter around Amy, keeps her warm. A streetlight glows fog from the opposite side of the street and in the distance is a car, another car, rolling towards early-morning shift work. Down the front steps: flowers graze her calves and she is at the gas meter in the front yard, the small ticking like night crickets hiding in grass. Letterboxes rise like field mushrooms, grey in the streetlight. Up above: powerful owl sound, the skitch of a possum running overhead on the electric wire. A goat hangs from the Burgesses' porch, night dew fur, swings in time with tree movement. The smell of the goat. The last hunt was two days ago. There is no disguising death. It sticks to skin, sticks to clothing, sticks to memory. Often you have to look past it to keep going on with life, on with the day. She sniffs her skin, her jumper, hopes the winter air will take away the smell.

Eleanor carries her daughter to the midnight blue 1968 Belmont station wagon filled with a few of their belongings, the emergency items they will need for their journey, straps Amy into the back seat. 'I'm just going to do one last thing.' She kisses her daughter, goes back into the house.

Inside, she leans against the closed bedroom door; uses wood for a spine. Listens. She opens the door, holds her breath, and he's limbed out like a tree, the giant way he takes up space. I just need to make sure he's not awake. Everything is quiet and her heart races to her throat. Eleanor, leave. It's time to leave, he will wake any minute.

She closes the door and rushes to the kitchen, snatches the black box off the counter, runs out of the house to her daughter.

Automatic pulses push Eleanor through Wintonvale streets, car tyres smooth on tar. Ahead of her a crow scamps around the base of a tree and wind sweeps through feathers; a black sea. Eleanor and her birds: makes her smile. Wind swims hair, messes into face and eyes. She smoothes her hair away so she can see, winds the window up, blasts the car with heat. It's always so cold everywhere. Eleanor reaches over the driver seat to Amy, palms her daughter's pudgy legs. 'Are you ready for a long drive, bub?' The journey to the blue mountain will take a while.

Outside the car: houses beam light; people fetch newspapers from yards, burrow down into neighbour talk.

Inside the car: a small piece of lapis on a thin strip of leather swings from the rear-view mirror. Kitty had given it to Eleanor, an unexpected gift she's never been able to bring herself to get rid of.

Eleanor, tell your daughter a story to keep yourself awake. And, an eye on lapis, she does, says, 'Did you know the sky is blue but once, a long time ago, humans didn't have a word for such a colour? Blue isn't as common in nature as you would think. In old books the sky is described as apocalyptic blazes of purple, something to fear. Those people didn't realise how many ways a human eye could detect shades of blue and so they didn't always know what colour they were looking at. Isn't that amazing, Amy?'

The idea of it makes Eleanor cry. Stop it.

'Amy, wouldn't it be wonderful to see something that's rarer than blue?' And she watches the lapis swing, thinks of the blue mountain, her favourite place. 'We're going somewhere we will be safe. We never have to come back here.' Her foot on the accelerator takes them out of Wintonvale, takes them towards the highway to the mountain. She eyes the rear-view mirror, keeps a lookout for headlights, keeps a lookout for him.

Kitty

1940

HOW TO MAKE a woman:

Kitty watched men, watched them sit, watched them tie fingers into fingers, tongues, lick around lips; the search for something sweet, for something more. Maybe they're looking for the peach kiss of a woman, of a man, of something warm and comforting from the past. Who knows what anyone is looking for.

In the dining hall at Wintonvale Repatriation Hospital, Kitty winced at the splotch noise of too-cooked porridge as she ladled it into shallow white bowls. 'This will fill you up.' Summer-voiced. You're at your best when you're the sun. She kept filling bowls, kept smiling.

When she got to Paul, to his broken middle-aged body, his groin full of warm and stench, he shifted in his chair, his hand to trousers, patted himself, looked at his fingers then sniffed them. Sobbed.

'What's happened?'

'I've done it again. I've done it again.' His voice: aged child. She half-expected him to say, 'Don't tell Mummy.'

'It's alright. Just an accident.'

'I didn't know I needed to go.' Forgetting how bodies worked. This man like so many who had returned from the Great War.

'It doesn't matter. Let me fix you.' Kitty cupped her hands around his, sticky and warm, and she smiled, tried to be sympathy.

He shook his head. 'It just keeps happening.'

'Lucky you have me to help you.'

And they walked out of the dining room, down a corridor, into his room, where Kitty sat him down on the bed. She pulled his trousers down, tried not to stare too long at anything she shouldn't.

'Let's get you dry and comfortable.'

Paul nodded, cried, kept crying.

Kitty sponged him, tried not to focus on the shrapnel wounds along his middle-aged thigh, looked away from his chest, which had been opened and reopened so many times that the scars now looked like prehistoric fossils, his torso a small history of the earth.

Afterwards, Kitty helped him into dry clothes and somewhere outside in the hospital grounds two patients argued like punches. This sound of men living among each other; she wished it would stop.

Kitty hooked her arms under Paul, lifted him up, felt his snot drip onto the back of her hand, wiped it off on her uniform, and walked him back to the dining room.

'Thank you, Sister.'

Kitty patted his hand, the smooth shape of knuckle, imagined the shapes his hand would make around a hip, a breast, around the butt of a rifle. 'I've still got a few months left before you can call me that.' She patted his hand again. How many people had he shot in the war? She stopped smiling. How long can I last in a place like this? What's the difference between commitment and duty?

'Thank you, Sister. I feel better now.' Paul cleared his throat, spooned cold porridge.

'Would you like me to reheat it for you?'

'No. I'll just eat what I was given.'

I'll stay for as long as I can be good at being good, at being sunshine.

———

Three years earlier: no idea what awaited her as she boarded the train from suburban Melbourne to Wintonvale, a little bag packed with hard-earned belongings, bumped along the track all the way to womanhood. She'd been told to be careful. 'Those people in psychiatric hospitals have soft brains, Kitty. They're likely to do God knows what.' These neighbourhood warnings, all those fearful ways of thinking about other people. It had begun to make her feel as if choosing to do her nurse's training at Wintonvale Hospital meant there was something wrong with her, that she was brain-soft too.

She didn't like people thinking that of her. She had just wanted a guaranteed job, wanted a new life away from her mother and father.

'They might be harmless,' Kitty would say. 'They're just people who need help.'

'Still. A young girl like you.'

'A young girl like you.'

'A young girl like you ought to be careful.'

'Young girls like you.'

'You're foolishly idealistic.'

A chorus of warnings to a nineteen-year-old. All those people constantly telling her how to live her life made her feel stuck, like she couldn't breathe. At her last meal with her family Mother said to her, 'Sit up straight, elbows off the table. How can you be delightful if you can't even hold yourself?' Then Mother said, 'Men don't like ladies who have no neck! Lift your chin and show that lovely neck of yours.' Then Mother said, 'Compliments are kisses, Kitty. Don't go looking for the real thing.' Mother said, 'Just remember now that you're bleeding you will get pregnant.' Mother said and Mother said and her father only ever raised his eyebrows. Though she had done nothing, her mother already accused her of wrongdoing, of failing.

'Mum, I promise I will be on my best behaviour.'

'I know, darling. I'm just trying to look out for you as much as I can before you leave us.'

'I'm not leaving you! I promise to call all the time.' But Kitty knew promises would be hard to keep.

Later that night, her father stood at Kitty's door as she readied herself for bed. 'I know your mother and I have gone over this, but I just want to be sure you're leaving us with a clear head.'

'I am.'

'What do you do if you make a promise to someone, Kitty?' This man, the way he kept her a perpetual child.

'You keep it.'

'What are the promises you've kept in particular?'

She knew what he meant. 'That I'll never do anything to embarrass you.' He'd said it to her and her sisters many times: virginity was a virtue.

He nodded. 'Just keeping you in check, Kitty. It's a different world out there.'

'Yes, Father.'

'Well, you'd better get your rest. You've got a big day tomorrow.'

And when he left, Kitty stared at herself in her dressing-table mirror, brushed her hair. 'I've got a big life ahead of me.' She considered what that life would be, how it might include boys, include secrets. She lifted her chin like Mother had said, grew her long neck longer. Keep your promises, Kitty.

———

Every Friday night was the same: trade in your uniform for a night-out dress, figure out which shoes would work best with the new blisters from the week.

Kitty and three other nurses, Carol and Jude and Betty, made up faces, made up bodies, made up lives and went out for the night.

The Wintonvale hall was a few kilometres away from the hospital, close to the army barracks. It was white, terracotta-templed, with a small mission bell on the highest point of the roof that meant it could double as a church hall. A place for dance and love and sex and prayers; walls for all seasons. The small foldout doors to the basement of the building were usually locked, but when they arrived at the hall on this night, Kitty saw that they were open. Carol said, 'You should go in. There might be some hidden treasure.'

'What could possibly be under there?'

Carol shrugged. 'There's always something hidden somewhere. I bet it's buried. Top secret. Wasn't there some guy who saw something flying in the sky t—'

Kitty waved her hand at Carol to be quiet. The idea of things that go bump in the night, of things that couldn't easily be explained, made her shiver.

Carol grinned at her, grabbed her by the arm. 'Come on, you big baby.'

Music snaked from windows, from the solid wooden door chocked open with a small black doorstop. Big band swing and voices of men; Kitty stopped thinking about hidden things then.

She said to the other three women, 'If I don't find someone tonight I'll scream.' She felt a pulse in her groin, closed her eyes momentarily, imagined someone between her legs. What would that feel like in real life? The idea of it made her giddy. Her mouth parted sea-wide at the thought of a tongue making her warm and Carol said, 'Bloody pull yourself together, Kitty.'

The others laughed at her like they always did, and they walked together towards the entrance, a four-headed mythological creature, their smell a punch of Aphrodite, rising from necks, from wrists, from inner thighs; made the mission bell toll. Just outside the door were soldiers from the barracks and local men with cigarettes hanging over the side of lips, smoke rising from them like ectoplasm. They stepped back and the women closed in, dresses brushed against uniforms. Kitty decided that tonight would be the night she would finally have fun, finally explore who she could be.

Music played: Kitty lifted her chin, pulled her shoulders back and knew she was catching the eyes of them all. They could eat out of my palm, she thought. They could have a feast. But then she heard her mother in her ear, her voice speaking of the danger of being *that* girl. Why couldn't she go through life without her mother's voice in her mind? Would it ever stop? If Kitty ever had her own daughter she'd make sure her voice never left a mark behind. To do that to someone else: she would never.

Dancers made patterns across the room: music, bodies swayed in slow time, heads on shoulders. Those not chosen for dances circled the edge as they waited for their turn, like animals surrounding their prey. Kitty went to the small bar in the corner of the room, said to the bartender, 'I'll have a beer.'

'Please,' he said, smiled, winked.

'Please.' She put her hand out, waited for her reward, then went to find Carol.

Together they stood against a wall, watched over the crowd of people trying to impress people.

'Most of them will die.' Carol took a swig from her beer bottle. 'That's morbid.'

'It's true. War means someone dies and a whole lot of people are going. It's simple statistics.'

'What do you know about statistics?'

Carol looked at Kitty. 'A bloody hell of a lot more than you do.' She bared her teeth in a smile. Kitty poked her finger into Carol's cheek, all its round smooth flesh. 'It's still morbid.'

Carol sighed. 'I know.'

Drinking beer, watching lives go by. The room felt brighter than it should and Kitty said so.

'Just wait. Another hour and everything will be dark enough.' Carol was right. The dark came, the night began, the hall lit only by small candles on tables.

———

His name was George Turner. They collided as they weaved through gaps between the tables. 'I'm sorry. I hope I didn't hurt you.' His voice the way a psalm sounds read out loud: solitude. It made her smile. He put his hand on her shoulder. His touch warm; sun on skin.

'Not at all.' Like she was made new. They held each other's gaze and she smiled. 'You'd be surprised at how strong I actually am.'

She liked him immediately, liked the idea that he was a soldier and if they hit it off she would be with a future hero.

It was as simple as that. He asked her to dance, excusing his clumsiness, and she enjoyed that he couldn't take his eyes off her, that he seemed unable to speak much in her presence. Hours spent dancing, drinking. She told him, 'I'll be a qualified nurse in a few months,' and he said, 'That's impressive. You should be proud of yourself. It takes a lot to care for someone like that.' No one had ever complimented her like this before.

'What do you do in the armed forces?'

'I'll be a navigator.'

'When do you go?'

'Five weeks.'

The way he couldn't take his eyes off her. How could it be she had finally met someone, only to discover they wouldn't be here for long?

'Let's have fun then!'

Loud at each other against the music. She pressed against his ear. 'You should kiss me.' All the ways she wasn't herself, like he was magic, was turning her. He obeyed and then he told her, 'I haven't been with many girls before.'

This time she kissed him. The band played and they danced and she prepared to keep a secret.

———

Love hits fast when you're young and the possibility of death is near. They left the dance early, walked arm in arm through the streets of Wintonvale, saw feral rabbits hanging from verandahs. 'Do you think it's weird they just hang them all up like that?' she asked him. When she'd first arrived in town she was shocked at the openness of death.

'I grew up in the country so it's not unusual for me. I like that people here are willing to eat what they kill.' The sense he made to her. What else could he explain about the world?

They sipped from bottles of beer stolen from the hall, talked the talk of strangers getting to know each other. There was an ease that came from speaking his name, the easy roll off her tongue. 'You know, George is my new favourite name,' she said, made him blush. She wanted to keep saying it. When he told her about his farm-boy life, labouring on the land, she imagined all that earth on her skin, how it might be to have him uproot her from what she once knew. They stopped by a park and George said, 'I can still hear music in my head. Will you dance with me?'

Swooning made her nod. Keep yourself together, Kitty. Into arms: George and his dancing, George and his shy smile. His mouth hummed next to her ear and he whispered, 'I worry I'll die.'

'Shhh, don't think that.' Something she'd say to any of the patients at the hospital to soothe them.

'What if I don't get a chance to live a full life?' A small boy's voice.

They swayed together, this natural movement that seemed to be between them, and she said, 'Live a full life with me.'

He hummed next to her ear, said:

'I'd take away your worries.'

'I'd make you feel safe.'

'We would make children who were one part you, one part me.'

'I'll watch you grow old.'

His promises. She wanted them; felt that if she had them she would be closer to happiness, this thing she'd been after since leaving home. Where did this man come from? It felt greedy to ask for more but she said, 'If you came back, what then?'

They danced and George carved out a life for them:

'And we'll have a house together.'

'And I'll sing to you at night.'

'And we will travel.'

'I'll make love to you all the time.'

'I'll be your best friend.'

'I'll never leave your side.'

These promises; atoms of love. She absorbed them, let them enter her blood, let herself fall into the future. She kissed George, this man who would leave soon, and her mouth filled with him. I want more, I want more, I want more.

———

Kitty crept back to the dorm room, to bed, thought of George. All the ways he had already made her feel good: she couldn't stop thinking about it. She was disappointed that he didn't ask her to do more than kiss that night. She wanted him and now she felt empty, sad, like something was missing. She lay in her bed listening to Betty snore and the pulse between her legs from earlier that night came back. She spread her legs, stretched her inner thighs, was surprised at the heat that came from them. I could start fires. She thought of putting her fingers inside herself, just to feed the pulse, to stop sad feelings, and she thought of what her father would say. 'This is filth.'

But filth is an invitation to live and she planned on living. Kitty put her hands on her stomach, smoothed her skin. Maybe just a little bit. Betty snored and Kitty dropped her hands to her side, closed her legs, let out a sigh. Tonight was not her chance to feel something more than an ordinary life. She'd have to wait to find herself.

———

The next day their courtship of birds, of mountains, of walking together began. They only had a few weeks before he would disappear. George introduced Kitty to all the things he loved, told her, 'There's so much pleasure in sitting back and watching nature do its thing. Don't you agree?'

She didn't. It bored her. But she'd never met anyone who was passionate about anything, never met someone who only spoke when he had something important to say, something thoughtful. She could really love a man like this. Eventually I'll enjoy his things, these things, too.

George opened doors, gave her compliments. 'I love your mind, Kitty. You're beautiful.' He'd wait for her by the hospital gates after her shifts, always with a gift: flowers, a poem he'd written for her, a feather found on a walk, a cake he'd made. She was so used to taking care of others that she'd forgotten you could receive care too. She liked the way he looked at her, as if he needed her, desired her. When they walked through Wintonvale, Kitty knew people watched them in awe, as if they were bodies of gold. The way their eyebrows raised, a jealousy.

'I hate living in Wintonvale,' she said. 'There's nothing to do here.'

'When I come back from the war we can move to anywhere you like,' he promised.

'I want to live by the sea!'

'Then that's what we'll do.'

When you let love in, the future rushes towards you whether you're ready for it or not.

A few days before he left for war, George picked her up early in the morning, told her, 'I hope you like long drives.'

She couldn't stand them – they made her car sick – but she wanted to be with him. 'Where are we going?'

'I want to show you my favourite place.'

They drove all day, talked about childhood dreams, their pasts. George described how caring his mother was when his father came back from the first war.

'She was so gentle with him. I used to wonder if that's how they'd always been together. I liked seeing it.'

This is how I will be, too, Kitty told herself. I will be this woman: I will be your mother, I will be your lover. I will be.

They drove past muddy dams, hay bales stacked in paddocks, and she said, 'I want to be happy all the time just doing things with you.'

'Whatever you want, I want that too.'

Every two hours they stopped the car and kissed by the side of the road.

'You're the most beautiful person I've ever seen. You're so special, Kitty,' he said in her ear, then he licked her neck, traced fingers underneath her skirt, inside her body, and she said, 'Never stop touching me, George.'

'Whatever you want, I want that too.'

The smell of him. She was done for.

When they reached the blue mountain, they inhaled the scent of eucalypts, breathed in air that was milk and honey. He took her by the hand and led her up the track for as long as she could handle the climb. They stood on a ledge and he said, 'You make me feel like this. You make me feel at peace.' He pointed to an expanse of never-ending blue and green. The sight of it overwhelmed her, made her feel as if she would fall out of her body onto the rocks below. 'Kitty,' he said, 'I want to marry you.'

'Yes. I want that too.' The taste of potential vows; her voice caught in her mouth.

'Can we get married when I come back? It'll give me something to live for.'

'I promise. I don't want to be without you.'

'I love you.'

'I love you.'

The mountain took their love, made plans for it. Later that night they read to each other sitting on the edge of her bed then exchanged the kind of stories couples shared under sheets: low-toned in the ear. Finally Kitty asked, 'Are you scared of going?'

'I don't think I'm allowed to be.'

This too was a story they were telling each other. She kissed him, tried not to think about Carol's statistics: they were living decades of marriage in the time they had together because chances were George wouldn't be coming back. And she would eventually have to move on, like all young women should.

———

She called her mother about the engagement, to ask her how she should get on with life without George. 'Kitty, men leave and if they return they are never the person you expected. So just tell yourself it's over.'

It wasn't what she wanted to hear but she tried to take her mother's advice because that was what she was expected to do.

The mass exodus of men from Wintonvale was happening again. They left the barracks, left Australia, left for a country hard to find on a map. George had asked her not to see him off with all the other wellwishers. 'I don't want to think about anything other than the time we had together.'

She agreed and they kissed and as quickly as he came into her life he was gone. Kitty wrote letters to George, hoped that they would bring him comfort. She told him of small things – what she ate for breakfast (porridge), what she ate for lunch (creamed corn on toast), told him dinner was a meal that she wished she could share with him. She hoped her banality would reassure George, didn't want to remind him that while he was at war, she was still able to have fun with her friends. So she told him that when she thought of him she touched herself (a lie), that she missed him, but after a while she wondered how true this was. Can you really miss someone you have only just met, that you don't have full knowledge of?

George responded with descriptions of what it was like to navigate planes over enemy lines, flying through dark and fire-blast. 'One big mechanical bird, Kitty!' Details were scant, but he'd tell her he loved her, couldn't wait to see her again.

Eventually the letters stopped and she assumed he had either died or met someone else.

Work is useful to take your mind off life, to take you into day after day after. And so Kitty completed her training and worked and lived and played, and met others, lots of others, and they helped to take her sad feelings away, to fill her emptiness, and in time thoughts of George faded.

Kitty

1941

THERE IS A certain freedom to be found in days that mimic each other: no need for thinking, for second guesses. You wake up, dress yourself in your uniform, eat with the other women, chat about this and that, check your teeth in the mirror for leftover life and walk out the door, onto the hospital grounds, see a patient or two under wide-fronded palm trees, a promise of tropic healing, and they will wave and you'll wave back because that's the done thing.

On her way to day shift on ward six, to the men with physical injuries, Kitty spotted a notebook filled with drawings of naked women and bullet holes; saw a man rubbing his cock against the hind legs of the work horse, Country Kettle; found a single black sock under a sun-bleached cane chair, a wet cigarette stub, a false tooth, a scrap of bloodied bandage; spied a patient headbutting a brick wall, screaming for someone, anyone, to stop the ringing in his ears. The way people were: it was becoming too much. 'I need to get out of here,' she muttered.

Kitty's conversations with patients were the same now.

'Did you manage to write a letter to your friends? I'm sure they'd love to hear how you're progressing in here.'

'I bet you'll have all the girls lining up for you once you go home.'

'Look at you! You are much better.'

All the poor bastards, so grateful to have you near, so grateful that someone was paying attention to them, so grateful that you didn't mention their missing limbs, missing faces, missing minds, so grateful that they had a pretty face to stare into, so grateful they hadn't perished over there like their brothers in arms, so grateful their bodies were healing, so grateful they didn't have to talk about what war was like inside their head, only had to talk about good times and weather, so grateful that they would eventually leave hospital and pick up their old lives, assume the shape they'd had before.

Last week, when she went to the butcher to satisfy a craving for meatloaf, she saw Max, a man who had lived at the hospital on and off for almost twenty years, buying sausages. He waited for change to be dropped in his palm, took stock of the meat cabinet, that raw flesh, burst into tears, said, 'Don't you smell them? God, can't you smell them?'

Kitty went to him, arm around shoulders. 'Come on, Max. Let's go, eh?'

Was any of the care they were giving their patients helping at all? Maybe it was time to leave Wintonvale, take a position at a different hospital.

At handover she checked over the new patient list. George Turner. He appeared as he had when they first met: out of nowhere, something sent. Heart flipped and breath caught in her throat. He was awake when she went into the room, head half-covered in bandages, was still a regimental soldier in bed. His height, like ghost gums, controlled shoulders, all weight into brass bedframe, all the things that prop you up, let others believe that nothing is amiss. Her breath caught in her stomach as Kitty was dragged back in time to the night they met. Like most Wintonvale patients, the worst of his injuries had been fixed overseas. Her finger followed the words across his chart, like reading fiction: back to Wintonvale for physical rehabilitation and a facial prosthetic. The left side of George's face had been blown apart, and he was missing fingers from his left hand, missing a piece of upper arm muscle, missing, missing, missing. His chart said to note any other signs of trauma, and Kitty knew they were looking for what war had broken inside, where they couldn't see.

This man now back from the dead. She couldn't bear him. But her eyes met his eyes and there was no looking away.

'Kitty?' He still sounded like a psalm.

She nodded. 'Hello, George.' It was the best she could do. 'I have to wash you. I hope that's alright?'

'Of course. You need to do your job.'

Close to him: night musk under his gown, like when they had slept side by side, fully clothed, pretending marriage. Being close to him made it harder to be professional, harder not to ask him what had happened, how he'd survived, why he'd stopped writing.

She concentrated on his body, all the pieces that were just as they once were, gently pressed on skin as she wiped him clean, and she remembered his poetry, his bird-warble mimicry, the way they danced. Now he was her patient.

He said nothing to her as she washed him and it was like listening to a stone drop through the well of her. This feeling of not being acknowledged; an echo, empty. She nursed as if giving a baptism; water lapped from the bowl, lapped at skin. If I keep washing will it take us back to before? I just want you to speak to me, George. She washed the blue vein lake under his wrists, over his temple, washed his blood, his heartbeat, nursed his pulse. And then George reached for her, held her hand and stroked her skin with his thumb, and water dripped onto sheets. 'I didn't think I'd see you again.' Like reading minds; now she knew she could materialise thought into action. Poor bastard. He still wants me. She removed her hand from his, smiled politely. 'I've just been here in Wintonvale.'

———

Weeks were born and close proximity allowed them to get to know one another again. There were glimpses of the man she'd begun falling in love with before he left. When someone comes to you missing half of who they were, you want to make them complete. Kitty doled out medication, doled out herself, and they chatted about Europe, chatted about weather, chatted about anything that blocked out what she didn't want to hear, that noise about war and death and reality. She handed over clean pyjamas and mentioned a trip she had taken to the Great Ocean Road with her girlfriends. They tried to carve out a shared life from hospital routine and he made her laugh and she made him sigh.

When they were outside together, when his skin wore sun, when she could see his carotid artery drum against his throat, she entertained the idea of sex with George, what it would be like to know him from the inside out. But what was the point? Eventually she would move on from Wintonvale and they wouldn't see each other again and that would be that. And yet.

Kitty always insisted on taking George to Dr Fleischmann for his check-ups and prosthetic fitting.

'This is ridiculous, Kitty. Patients don't belong to you.' Betty had become a real pain.

'He trusts me and that's worth honouring. You'd do the same. Everyone needs to feel safe.' She couldn't explain that she was using these excursions as a way to understand him, was attracted to the idea that she was helping him. She'd listen to the way George spoke to the doctor, his assertive tone, the way he spoke in facts that hid any raw emotion. In these appointments she could see that George had grown out of his shyness and had stepped into the uniform of war. This was what he must have been like over there. The surety that comes from facts and figures, from life and death.

'How is everything else?' Fleischmann asked.

'How do you mean?'

'Any nightmares? Intrusive thoughts? Feelings of being on edge? Anything like that.'

Kitty had seen the night nurse's scrawled note: they had to sedate him once, twice, for thrashing about. What was unusual about that? We all thrash about.

'Nothing completely unusual,' George said, wiped his fingers along the side of his mouth.

Kitty nodded along, made it easier to believe that his injuries were all on the outside. He wasn't like the others, wasn't that sick.

Fleischmann measured wounds, calculated the angles and proportions for George's new face, and said, 'Don't worry. We'll have you looking close to your old self in no time. Then you can get on with your life.' He patted George on the back and George leaned into him, a small child consoled by parental warmth.

George tilted his head towards the ceiling and she saw the edge of bone, wanted to look inside his cavity, see how far down he went. If I go hunting will I find what I'm looking for?

———

Kitty called it making love but she knew what it really was: a way to lose yourself. The solace that comes when you explore someone else's body entwined in yours, explore different versions of yourself. You can be anyone you please and I please myself. But there was always a voice telling her she was doing the wrong thing. But what was right?

She was with George walking through the hospital gardens when they stopped to watch a couple of men playing cricket with a coconut and George laughed, that way he had when they were at the blue mountain. Nostalgia made her ache for something she didn't understand. The urge that came. I want that George. The past made her feel good inside, like she had something to look forward to, something that could be the present.

She whispered, 'Come with me,' took him by the hand, led him into the hospital block. The change of voices, of yelling across rooms, across corridors, voices that painted murals of interior thoughts on bare white walls. They entered a small room to the side of the dining room. Just enough light. Kitty guided his hand underneath her dress, and although he smiled, he hesitated at her underwear.

'What's wrong?' she asked.

'I've not been with anyone before.'

'You can be with me.' Lips on cheek, lips on eye.

He whispered, 'Do I disgust you?' And she took his hand and pushed him finger-length inside her before pulling him out. She sucked on his fingers, moulded them to trigger points and she said, 'Close your eyes.' She licked his lips, then teeth, as she pulled down his pyjama pants and he said, 'I don't know what to do.' Kitty ran her hands over his stomach, over pubis, over penis, and he let out a small cry, writhed hips into patterns. If this is how I could shape his body I could shape his mind too. They kissed and he hardened and she said, 'Now all you need to do is let me sit on you,' and she straddled him, slipped him inside. Here he finally is.

It was not earth-shattering but it shattered George. He smiled, looked at her as she rocked her hips; a swing. He gasped for air and she covered his mouth with her hand, felt his jaw clench, and she tried to push herself as deep as she could, her thighs around his narrow body, leaned towards him. George was in her ear, cried, said, 'You're warm,' said, 'I thought about you all the time,' said, 'Is this love, Kitty?', whispered, 'I want you to keep fucking me,' and she dug her fingernails into his shoulders, made him whimper. 'Say it again, George.'

'I want.'

The voice of a lover is a trick; you mistake it for your own. Is this what I want too? Him against her: it made the day disappear, made her feel like she was someone else, could bring someone to themselves. And yet. She felt as though she had slipped away, hadn't felt a thing, had missed the moment she'd been waiting for.

A man howled in the dining room, men called out to one another, but when George came inside Kitty he was silent.

'Have I not been good enough? Are you alright?'

'Yes.' He kissed her forehead and his body relaxed; electrical pulses that had been generated switched off. She wasn't going to be able to finish. And yet. There was the smell of him rising from underneath. I want to eat him all up. He smiled at her and she climbed off him, cleaned herself with the inside hem of her uniform.

I don't feel relief, only that emptiness again.

But you can return to this moment later and find your own relief.

And she nodded to herself and they kissed and they left the room.

———

Tender breasts, bloating, cramping, sore skin, nausea: Kitty misread the signs, waited for a period that never came. A month, two months. They tried to make up for the war years and occasionally they had sex together and through it all she kept checking her underwear for blood. After three months a test confirmed intuition: she was edging closer to motherhood. She cried, punched herself in the stomach over and over, hoped the force of herself would dislodge the thing inside her uterus, break what was to come.

She took George to the hospital gardens and told him what was happening.

Silence, the way it was with him so often now. It was as if he'd disappeared into a twin of himself: George before and George after. The longer he was quiet the louder she heard the memory of her father. *Don't embarrass me.*

Anger claimed her. 'Fucking say something!'

'Are you happy about it?' Like he was hopeful.

'It's not ideal.' It would not be easy to be an unwed single mother. She weighed the cost of living a life with a man who would need fragments of her own in order to survive; daily transplants. She kept searching for the version of George she'd met at the dance. Sometimes he was there when she took him walking through the bushland just beyond the hospital boundaries. The next day she'd find him in the dining hall, book in hand, staring at the wall.

He moved towards her, his prosthetic lopsided, and she went to fix it for him, stopped. She counted the missing fingers of his left hand as he rearranged himself, wished he would tell her what it had been like, what he had seen when he was over there. If I can just know a little bit more of him it may not be so bad.

He said, 'Those things I told you before I left – I meant them.'

'That wasn't real life, George.' She could wound. She wanted to take it back instantly.

'I meant them.' To hear his voice; like a heartbeat, the way it rises when you run to a lover. He took her hand, said, 'We should get married.'

This was no mountain love. This was the reality of logic. 'We should.'

He nodded. 'I do love you, Kitty.'

How can you be sure love is enough? It had been easy to love him before. I could make this work.

———

The ceremony was small. When she introduced her parents to George, Kitty told them they'd be grandparents.

'I see,' her father said.

'Isn't this wonderful?' Her mother rubbed Kitty's stomach. 'You won't know yourself once you become a mother. You'll see.'

Kitty hoped so.

Eleanor

1955

THEY WERE ON their way to the mountain. Eleanor and Badger were in the back seat of the car and she watched her parents' shoulders magnet towards each other, watched Kitty pull away to look out the window. Push and push, push and pull; their little dances made Eleanor grin.

'I think it's time for a singalong. What do you think?' Kitty looked over her shoulder into the back seat.

'Okay!' Eleanor said.

'Make sure you sing loud, Badger,' Kitty said. 'Your sister has a habit of drowning you out.' Kitty smiled, touched George's lap, and George nodded, squinted in the rear-view mirror. Eleanor reached for Badger, stretched her fingers so far and long they felt as if they'd break. Why does he always sit so far away? Maybe this is what happens when you get older. Things don't stay the same. 'Badger, did you see the hawks outside?' She must've spoken too loudly because Kitty turned, said, 'Eleanor, leave him alone,' and Eleanor made sure she was good, lowered herself in the seat, stared into the back of George's head and shoulders. She liked the scars at the back of her dad's neck; they made him wrinkled, like cracks in the pavement to skip over. As if her mum could read her mind, Kitty stroked the back of George's neck, long fingers, red nails. Eleanor smiled. She and her mother, it was like mind-melding; she felt warm inside and her angry feelings towards Badger disappeared.

Kitty turned the radio dial, broke static with music, and George whistled along for one, two, three beats, stopped so that he could concentrate on the road. But he looked sad. Eleanor summoned her animal voice, deep in her throat, sang loud and wild: out came the sound of a dog on its hind legs, out came a fish underwater, a wolf barking bubbles. She turned to her brother and smiled, kept singing the song of creatures.

Kitty was full glory: she belted out the high notes, took George's hand for a few seconds before he pulled away and held on to the steering wheel.

'Mum, are we all going on the climb in the mountain?'

Kitty took forever to answer. 'I don't know. Maybe.' Maybe she was afraid it'd be too windy. Kitty didn't like going to the mountain when it was windy. She said it made her nervous.

George cleared his throat, banged his hand into the car horn as if he was angry at her mother. The radio played and the car drove along the road and everyone went quiet and Eleanor watched the sky for birds.

———

They arrived at the mountain and all the car talk between her parents was replaced with silence. They all got out of the car and the family separated: Kitty and Badger sat under a weeping willow tree, outstretched legs, her mother's eyes to the sky. George and Eleanor left them, walked along a narrow path a few metres away. Eleanor found a dead lorikeet.

'Dad! I can see its insides.' Blood and heart, soft red. 'I don't like it.' But she couldn't look away.

'It's alright, Eleanor. This is what happens when things die. It's decomposing. There's nothing to be afraid of.'

'Do all things decompose when they die? Even people?' She looked over at her mum and brother, shook her head.

A wave in George's throat. 'Not always like this. When anything dies it begins to decompose. Sometimes it's not always obvious.'

'But where does the life go?'

'Nowhere. It already happened. This is like the next part.'

Eleanor crouched by the lorikeet, wondered if she should touch it. 'How do you know all this?'

'Well, I saw it growing up on the farm. I see it when I'm on my walks.'

'Did you see it in the sky?' She knew she shouldn't ask about the war but she couldn't help herself.

'Not exactly. But I did see people die in the war, yes.'

'That's really . . .' She patted her dad's hand, kept looking at the bird. 'So where will this bird go now that it's dead?'

'It will likely just stay here and eventually it'll disappear. Some of its bones will stay behind.'

'So it won't get buried?'

'Not everything can be buried, Eleanor.'

'I want to bury this bird.' She stood up, went to the edge of the path, picked flowers, picked leaves, picked sticks, carried them back over and laid them on top of the bird; pagan piles. 'It looks much better!'

George nodded. 'It's very colourful.'

'Can we walk up the mountain now?'

George put his hands on his hips, looked down at the ground. She knew that's how he stands when he thinks too many thoughts. 'Wait here.' He left her with the bird, walked over to Kitty and Badger, and she could hear her parents talking but she couldn't hear what they were saying. Then her dad tried to hug her mum but she pushed him away, screamed, 'I'm not ready. I told you this before. I'm not going!'

Eleanor licked her finger, put it high in the air, tried to figure out the direction of the wind. The wind seemed quiet today. 'Maybe it's too scary for her,' she said to the lorikeet.

Eleanor sat on the ground, dragged sticks along dirt, waited for her dad to come take her up the mountain.

But when her dad came back he said, 'Come on. We're going home.'

She pounded fists into the ground. 'Why? We didn't even go walking! We drove *all* day.'

'I know. We can try again another time.'

'Is it because I made Mum angry in the car?'

George shook his head. 'Let's go.'

They all headed back to the car. Kitty slammed the back door after she buckled Eleanor in, slammed the front door, and Eleanor looked at her brother, whispered, 'What's going on?'

George reversed out of the car park, and they drove to the Kellerman's Motel to rest overnight before heading back to Wintonvale.

'Can we have a singalong?' Eleanor hoped she wasn't being too naughty for asking.

'No.' Her parents; unison. She sank all the way down into her seat, turned to Badger and stuck her tongue out at him.

Eleanor

Present

THE SKY GROWLS rain and Eleanor watches grey clouds muscle together. 'Sweetheart, see above us? That's a nimbus forming.' Her father had told her things like this on a similar trip when she was a teenager, this weatherman talk to fill in time. Eleanor glances in the rear-view mirror, sees Amy's feet move with the sway of the car. This baby, my happy baby. And to think just a few short months ago Eleanor was convinced this wouldn't be possible: the endless cycles of crying and sleeplessness and non-feeding and not understanding the needs of another human quick enough had made for hard night after hard night; had made it hard to believe there would be any good days to come. But then things changed.

The sky growls again and Eleanor imagines future days of her and Amy standing in the rain, splash of puddles, soaked boots, wringing out water from socks, from clothing.

A crow flies above the eye line of the car, makes Eleanor smile. 'Did you know Mummy studies birds?' This attempt to make the journey less frightening for herself, for Amy. 'Did I ever tell you crows pass on their memories? They pass all their collected thoughts and knowledge down the generations for survival.' For love. There is no telling what has been passed down to me, to us.

Eleanor notices the needle hovering above empty on the petrol gauge. 'Great.' She'd forgotten to refuel days ago, just one of the many things she forgot to do lately; the small ways living becomes hard. She releases the accelerator pedal to preserve what little she has left in the tank, checks the rear view, keeping an eye out for anyone following. 'Amy, we should always be aware of what's around us.' She checks the rear view again, feels panic rising. What if Leon has woken up, has started searching for them? The fear of him when something gets away. The way he'd been with her last night when she pulled the black box from a kitchen drawer, put it on the countertop.

Dark went his eyes. 'You're a fucking bitch.' Venomous. He went to snatch the box but she was too quick.

'I don't understand why you won't let me see inside it.'

And Leon came for her as Amy cried from her bedroom. 'If you go to her, I will make you sorry,' he said, and then he grabbed her arm, made it burn.

In the car she tells Amy, 'My body always bruises.' There on her arm: her husband's mark, a weight. She keeps an eye on the fuel gauge, an eye out for Leon. But no one is behind her and so she relaxes for now.

She sees Amy in the back seat, that small warmth of skin that is half him, half her, and tells herself that we are not the sum total of our past, that we all have our own history waiting to be made.

'Did you know in the natural world there is something called "selection" that describes the strongest match to continue the species?'

All the things you'll need to know, Amy. It had never occurred to Eleanor that she would want to have children. And then one day she woke up pregnant and her mother was happy, and in that moment Kitty held her daughter in a way that meant their hearts were finally beating against each other. For the first time they shared a closeness.

'But I'm here to tell you something, bub. Some surprises end up being good.' Always these whispers to Amy when they are together in the car, waiting for sleep to crawl up from the road like a passenger, sit alongside her daughter and soothe them both to peace. Together and together.

Eleanor didn't have the heart to tell her daughter that, at first, she wanted the baby out of her body, out of existence, because it meant having to stay with Leon, meant that a part of her own life would have to stop when it was only just beginning. She was petrified of making the mistakes of her parents, petrified that she *was* her parents, petrified that one day Amy would discover who her mother really was and not love her.

Eleanor was halfway through her PhD in animal behaviour, studying crows, when she became pregnant. *I study animals and nature to understand people,* she would say if asked why she was doing it, though that was rare. She had been accepted to travel to New Caledonia to research whether crows could learn how to make tools to better their chances of survival. But that was then, this is now. Sometimes things are paused. But her body didn't pause and it grew a child, grew a different version of life.

Eleanor thinks of Leon coming home from Vietnam, the bandages around his wrists, the attempted suicide in the base bathroom that brought him home. The lie of it. A genus of human that wears masks.

Powerlines perimeter the road, guards of honour, and the car jerks slightly. She's been down this road many times, knows there's a petrol station coming up on the left. Aching hands, arched fingers: the giveaway she's been gripping the steering wheel too tight for too long. She lets go, stretches her neck side to side and the car veers left, heart runs to her throat, the loss of control frightening, and Eleanor holds on to the steering wheel tight again.

There the petrol station, bowsers like lighthouses in sea fog. She stops the car, gets out, and legs welcome the stretch. She lifts the petrol hose into the tank, takes in the fumes, and a petrol attendant walks towards her, holds himself by a smile, his skin made leather from too much sun, too much standing: the body of a man who enjoys small talk.

His hand on her hand, his shoulder angling her away. 'How much you needin'?'

'I was doing a full tank.'

'Where ya headin' to, love?'

Why do men always want to know where you're going? And *love*, that grating word.

She almost tells him, 'We're running for safety,' but she is trained to always be polite and she can't help but respond with a lollied mouth. 'A little trip to the mountains.'

He taps the Belmont's roof, laughs. 'In this thing? It won't make it.'

'I've done it before.' She can do it again.

He whistles, shakes his head, looks the car over. 'What about your tyres?'

Eleanor looks down. There is evidence of wear but the treads are still good. There is nothing wrong with the tyres of this car. Nothing to stop me from reaching the blue mountain. 'They're fine.'

'Reckon we might need to check that radiator for ya.'

Eleanor glances towards the road, can't stop looking for Leon's car, can't stop looking for what follows her. Why is this taking so long? She shakes her head, he drops the subject, the bowser clicks to full and she says, 'That's probably enough now.'

He takes out the hose, shakes it off, hangs it back in the cradle. 'Need anything else then?' A bit angry this time.

'We're good.'

'We?'

Eleanor points to Amy and the petrol attendant smiles. 'Nice to take your kids out. Mine like camping.'

She smiles, nods, hands over the twenty dollars, then takes a squeegee from a bucket of water to wash the windshield. The attendant comes at her, hand over hers, takes the squeegee from her. His touch makes her jump; his smell of morning sweat, of Juicy Fruit gum, of taking over, makes her dry-retch.

He peers through the back window again, nods at Amy. 'Good sleeper?'

'Not in the beginning. But we got there.'

He turns to Eleanor. 'I hope you make it up there. Hell of a time with her if you don't.'

'We'll be okay.'

Eleanor squeezes her eyes, the only thing she can think of doing to stop herself from crying.

Before he can say another word she opens the car door, slides inside, closes the door on him. End of discussion.

She starts the car, rolls away, leaves the petrol attendant in the gravel. Eleanor readjusts her rear-view mirror, catches sight of Amy. 'Sometimes you need to end things quickly, even be rude, so you're not stuck in a place you don't want to be.'

The shape of her girl in her seat makes her smile. The car picks up speed.

———

Lapis swings from the mirror. Tyres over black bitumen, that vinyl whir: that's the sound of sifting through thought. Now comes the smell of apricot skins, shrunk and putrefied, the dead-sweet scent of ingested mother's milk and vegetable matter rising through cloth nappy. Amy needs to be changed. The sound of the car moving, everything seems such a long way from her. The morning hours feel like they happened a decade ago.

Eleanor, hands on the steering wheel, stares out the windscreen and it's there in front of her: last night. Leon at the kitchen table, slunk mouth. She told him, 'I can't do this anymore.'

'You're not leaving.'

'Leon . . .'

'You'd be that callous, to leave me after all this time?' This way of men manipulating.

Fist, table, thump; his anger across the table, made her teeth hurt, made her want to throw up. 'I'm taking Amy,' she had told him and she spat in his face. He hit her across the cheek, as he had done before. And then she waited for him to go to bed.

Have I done the right thing? These thoughts like needles. I should turn the car around, go back to Wintonvale, go back to the house, go back to the room, go back to Leon, go back to the night before, go back to the moment when I decided to leave him. To go back means that nothing ever happened; to go back means that you can change the direction of your actions, undo them all. As she drives, she clears her throat, the heavy feeling of whatever it is that she's been holding on to, the taste of something from the bedroom as she left Leon to sleep. He always was a heavy presence in her mouth, in her body.

———

How long does the scent of a child last on mother-skin? How long does it take to fully exit the womb, for you to no longer have any memory of how you once fit inside it? Eleanor is roadside, half hanging out the back seat while changing Amy's nappy. She wipes away the smear of her daughter, wipes at the small blisters on her buttocks with zinc cream, calculates the remaining hours versus miles to go, throws the nappy into a plastic bag, into the boot of the car, leans into her daughter to try to find herself. Almost a year of watching Amy grow without Kitty, without Leon. Eleanor found herself in the undergrowth of Amy's neck: the smell that came from between her legs after she pushed her daughter out, had been left to rise, that lingered for months, like something too warm. It was intoxicating.

The smash of kookaburras startles her and thoughts wander to her own mother, how lately when Eleanor speaks to Amy she imagines Kitty speaking to her too, as if for once we share a tongue, share a common interest. We say: My little one. You still look the way you did at birth, so peaceful and yet. The shock of having to join this world. I see it, I understand it.

What is this place we have come to?

Little one. Once we are here there is no going back and yet so often that's all we want to do. I watch you sleep and I remember your face from before, that first time we met, and I wonder what right time has to exist. What right it has to drag us into the future. But then. Without time, without a future, you can't build a life.

We say together: I want to go back but I don't know what I would be returning to. I want to go back to a history that never happened. How different it could've been. I want to go back to a time when my mother wasn't a mother. I want to hold the hand of a girl who woke up every day with a smile on her face. To hold the hand of a girl, a young woman, who laughed, who hadn't yet learned to turn away from the world, to turn away from herself. I want to hold the hand of the girl who hadn't yet learned to hate me. Who is the woman who existed before me? Which version of woman was I when you emerged from me?

Eleanor, stop these circular thoughts, and she shakes her head, knows nothing about this will help. 'Amy, it turns out your mummy doesn't have an answer for everything.'

She places Amy back into her car seat, shuts the door and settles back behind the wheel. The car eats bitumen and Eleanor knows that she has invented a person, a mother, who was never born. If Amy knew everything I'd done, would she want to reinvent me too?

'Amy,' she says, looks to her daughter before eyes return to the road, 'I don't know if I should say this out loud to you, but I became a mother when I didn't want to be one and now I never want you to leave me. But I constantly fear I'll become Kitty.'

When you cut off your heart to someone after a lifetime of telling them you loved them, even when you didn't, the heart attempts to mend by convincing you that grief is guilt.

Because guilt doesn't let you say out loud that when you were around your mother you couldn't breathe. Guilt doesn't let you say out loud that every time you failed to make your mother happy she would tell you she wished you were dead and you accepted it without question because this was your first language. All the ways a thing like that can change you. Guilt won't let you say it out loud.

But grief. It lets me tell you that if I had to look my mother in the eye one more time and forgive her, forget the past, I was going to disappear completely. And I don't want to do that now I've met you, Amy. I want to hold on to all the remaining parts of me that are still alive and give them to you. How much more of my life was I prepared to spend hating myself because I wasn't good enough for Kitty?

Grief lets me tell you that I hope I am good enough for you.

'Little one, I'm afraid of myself because I know what I am capable of.'

I am the person who walks away. I am the person who ends things. I am the person who wishes death on her mother, her spouse. I am the person who is your mother.

Eleanor glances over her shoulder at Amy as she speaks. My child. A lump in Eleanor's throat. Amy is still and Eleanor returns her attention to the road.

Kitty

1942

MARRIED NOW. A MOTHER now. In the dark of their bed George crushed his hands together as if he were building fires, tinder sticks alighting. All the heat of him spread to Kitty in her dreams. The way it woke her, as if she were fleeing burning buildings. Kitty switched on the lamp to kill the dark: George stared into the ceiling like he wasn't there.

'George! George, come back.' The earthquake of her voice didn't move him. Why didn't he warn her that this was how he would leave her?

In the morning she made him coffee, made him eat, made herself watch her husband; hours trapped in the thick black of molasses movement. He hadn't been like this before the baby arrived. 'I'm feeling so good,' he'd told her. 'I haven't had a nightmare since the hospital.' She'd believed him. But she'd come to realise that nightmares don't need sleep to come alive. He screamed into the bathroom wall when the shower was too hot, as if bathing in poisoned water. He screamed into backyard grass, screamed into the shed, his hands, his legs. 'I'm losing my mind, aren't I?'

'No. No, you're not.' The ways she tried to convince him, convince herself.

George was often so tired he slept for days and Kitty was duty, sponge-bathed him so she wouldn't have to keep smelling night terrors leaking out from him into the room. Days, a week, and then he'd come back to her, from the dead, as if it had all been in her head.

Some nights he refused to eat dinner, claimed there was no room in his body. His nightmares started with spinal jolts, tunnelled into murder screams, a strange lullaby for their infant son. But he never spoke to her about any of it. He'd pick at his prosthetic like a scab and she would have to wrap his fingers with bandages, teach him to care for his face.

'You must think I'm a child.'

'I don't think anything.'

'How can you bear it, Kitty?'

'I made a vow.' She hated herself for not saying she loved him. Some responses don't come quick enough. What did she really feel? But she couldn't think about it; could only tell herself that they had a child now and that things would get better. She would make them get better.

A few months after giving birth to Alfred, Kitty joined a group of new mothers whose husbands had suddenly gone to war on them. The great metamorphosis. They met at the hall, sat around lemon linen, tumblers of old fashioneds in hand.

One said, 'He keeps saying that he hasn't changed, that he's the same old, same old.'

They all nodded. The way war changes a man isn't always quantifiable.

'Mine still doesn't eat much. Says the smells make him sick.'

'He's always mowing that bloody lawn. Doesn't he have any idea how hard it is to get twins to sleep every afternoon?'

'He punched the wall and told me it would be my face next.'

The way they opened their secrets, like being sucked into the black hole of their marriages; the wonder of being inside something so cavernous you forget you're falling to the end of yourself.

Kitty shifted in her seat; the wood underneath a landing, that thud, made Kitty say, 'Mine can't work at the moment because he won't stop sleeping. And when he is awake he gets so jumpy. The only thing that calms him is fixing clocks in the shed.'

The women nodded, told her, 'You're doing the best you can.'

'Am I? Because it doesn't feel like it. It's almost like half of me has walked out the front door and left him while the other half doesn't know how to unlock it. I don't know how to be around him.' The way she slipped out of herself with these women; she couldn't stop. She gritted her teeth. So she said, 'I'll stay, of course. It's just a thought I have sometimes.'

One said, 'I'm glad we've got each other. I can't talk to my friends about this.'

They nodded. They said, 'So glad.' They said, 'I just want to know what he's thinking. What it was like.'

They said, 'He barely says anything about it.'

'He barely says anything.'

'He barely says a thing.'

'He said I wouldn't understand.'

They sipped along and their children lay on sheepskins on the floor, a flock. Kitty cut a ginger cake she made, the dark syrup heart. The shock smell of fresh spice hit them and they pushed their plates towards her. Kitty served, and compliments came flowing. She ran her index finger along the cake knife, collected crumbs and licked herself clean: warm, a little sting on the tongue. I am still here if I can feel something.

'I slept with someone else.' It came from the new woman, Pamela. 'After the baby. He wouldn't touch me. I just wanted . . .'

They all nodded their heads but Kitty couldn't commit to the movement. Pamela should be ashamed of herself. There was no excuse not to be a good wife. And yet. It wouldn't take me much to do the same, just to be desired. Kitty licked cake from the knife.

Often she would lock herself in the bathroom for hours at a time, crying over George, over the stress of having a small child, over living. Sometimes she'd lie in the bathtub with her baby, the weight of his head against her arm, his head to breast while she sobbed. Just his mouth around her, small gum bites, was enough to remind her that there was something outside all of this, that she wasn't a failure at everything. Close your eyes, Kitty. Think of where you might take this baby. The bath an adventure: sail away, sail away.

When she woke up to the sound of a fist against skin, to the sound of blunt teeth echoing from the kitchen, to the sound of George whimpering, she ran from the bathroom through the house to where she could see the light flooding George with too much brightness.

'George, no!' Kitty tore towards her husband. He had removed his pyjama bottoms, was there with a paring knife, digging at his thighs like he was trying to remove rotten muscle. 'What are you doing? George, stop!' She screamed at him, woke the baby. But he looked at her, said, 'Just a little bit more and I'll be alright.' He stabbed his thigh and he cried and the sound of him breaking open made her vomit on the floor, made her reach for his hand, take the knife away. Someone save me. Their son cried and Kitty sat George on the floor, wrapped his pyjamas tight around his thigh. 'I'm going to call the hospital.'

George was gone by daylight, gone for just a little while, and Kitty rocked her son for comfort, sang into him, made a life within a life just for the two of them. Her child sank into her chest, nuzzled her neck, beat his hands into her as if trying to break her open and take shelter. 'The littlest of badgers,' she told him. 'That's what you are.'

By lunchtime Kitty tried to force the day to make sense, had put her son down to nap, had cleaned blood from the floor, had put on make-up, her blue-red lips were jewels, gave her no choice but to smile. For a moment. I can smile for a moment.

A knock at the door and she went to it, obedient to neighbour-hood demand. Now is when all the women come, tell me they had no idea how bad things were, how well I do to hide it all. But it was her over-the-road neighbour, Charlie, who filled the doorframe. 'Diane sent me over to see if you needed anything fixed. I know George wanted the back porch lights changed.' Charlie pulled at his ear, smoothed his neck.

'That's very kind of you both.' They looked one another over, spoke to each other with eyes, the way they had started to do a few months before. Charlie looked over her shoulder into the house, like he'd been sent to spy, to report back if anything was amiss. She followed his line of sight, saw how everything was in its right place, chairs straightened, food canisters lined in a row.

'I'm sure he'll be home soon.' His polite way.

'Yes, of course.' But Kitty knew what was likely. It would be months. Months of her alone with a baby, of working to keep everything running, a roof over their head. Charlie touched her shoulder; the shock of it surged through her body, made the hair on the back of her neck spike. Proof that I can't be gone if I can still feel.

'I'm sorry, Kitty. We're all sorry.'

Nodded, held her hand over his, both of them at her body. To have this kind of touch. It had been so long. 'Thank you.' In the past they had winked at one another as they played couple-games at card night. It hadn't really been anything, just a reflex of the body, then a kiss on the cheek for goodbyes. She'd occasionally thought about Charlie while she masturbated. The things she wanted him to do to her. But she tried not to think about it, especially when Diane had knocked on her door with a casserole and promises to look after the baby when Kitty had to work. This woman who was always good to her. She had to be good in return.

'Would you like me to come in and fix something?' He smiled at her, kind eyes.

'I don't know, Charlie. I just want . . .'

She widened the front door, stood aside, let him in. When the door was closed Kitty cried and Charlie held her hand. 'What if he keeps doing it, Charlie?'

He held her, told her, 'It's alright.' But it didn't make her feel better, didn't stop that falling feeling. Charlie kissed her forehead, then he kissed her mouth and she licked his lips, a need to taste something that didn't remind her of the morning. Kitty undid his belt, stopped herself from going further. But that pulse between her legs: a magnet. Her hands pulled him undone, traced over his stomach, over pubis, and breast milk leaked. Kitty, what are you doing? She kissed him again, said, 'Please touch me,' and Charlie licked his finger, went under her dress, found the place that made thoughts stop.

Kitty

1944

DAYS BEGIN LIKE days do. Outside: the sun rose, birds called in trees, telephones trilled background noise, dogs barked, a neighbour's front door opened, slammed shut. Morning sounds. Inside: cold floorboards whined, refrigerator hummed, kitchen clock was seconds full, sore dry feet tangled under sheets, rubbed together. Another day, Kitty. Another day has arrived.

Kitty and George sunk down into their brass bed; pillows: mountains, hugged tight. Unison breathing; this good morning. His hands crawled knuckle then fingertips over her skin, made her arch, coaxed a moan from the centre of her body. These tender touches. The first time in a long time George isn't crying, is not anything except welcome heat against her. This is the marriage

I was meant to have. His fingers between her legs, gentling them open, fingers inside. Her body to his; latch, key, lock.

Kitty heard the elephant-clump of boy cross the floor of a room, a slide of books dropped to the floor, little grunts. 'What is he up to?' But George kissed her neck, licked, and Kitty warmed her hands along the base of George, watched his face stretch in and out with the fever of her, and she tried to forget about her son down the hall.

George craned to the ceiling and Kitty eyed his throat, the way it submerged, surfaced like driftwood when he swallowed. This sight of him when he couldn't bring himself to look her in the eye. Is it something about me he can't bear to face? She reached towards him, pulled on his neck, anchored him, his eyes closed, and she said, 'Look at me, George,' and he opened them, and she thought she saw a tear. I can soothe you before it becomes anything. Kitty kissed him, wet lips, tongue to tongue, her body a throb, the sound of George pulsing, a sweat. Kept going, kept going until they were just a shared breath.

What a way to start the morning, the follow-up of a peaceful night.

Almost a year without nightmares, without having to unhook his hands from an imaginary lever, to whisper into him that everything would be alright, that he wasn't in the air, wasn't in the plane, wasn't in the hospital, wasn't anywhere he didn't want to be. A year without the need to be a nurse, a caregiver, to be alert, the family guard. Just Kitty Turner, sleeping wife. It's been so peaceful I've barely thought of being with anyone else. She'd been such a good woman, just like her mother was. Her mother who brushed her hair one hundred times each side, brushed teeth until gums bled, who made sure casseroles were dispatched to needy neighbours, who never complained about illness. And yet something mechanical about her, the way she knew her limits because God, her husband, had created them for her. A boundary keeps a flock from straying and her mother never strayed. This was Kitty now.

She didn't think about alternative wife versions of herself, didn't think of other men. This was something else altogether. This was how it could always be if George was normal, if the past was erased from him. If he was erased from himself, had never been to war, never decided to go up in that plane. This was George before.

When she looked at Badger she could see the younger version of her husband. At what age would he become his father, show trace elements of him? To fall in love with your son's face, to see your husband's past through your son; a future haunting. Kitty reached out and stroked George's forehead, a comfort for herself. God, how she loved him like this.

They listened to Badger play and they played themselves. Eventually their son waddled into their room, climbed into bed and crawled between them. Badger said, 'I'm still sleepy,' and Kitty leaned into him, smelled bed in his hair and skin, a night of thumb-sucking, boy saliva, smiled. 'You can snuggle with us.'

They three; lying like lovers together. I want this to be forever. But nothing is forever. She tried not to think about Badger's tantrum the day before: she'd struck him across the face, had pushed him in the chest, snarled at him. 'Stop it! Stop it at once.' Every part of her body with that feeling of hammers, wanting to pound, pound, pound right out of herself and take off. *I am a good woman, a good mother.* She couldn't remember what had set her off. Kitty didn't want to be like those women who came into the hospital from time to time, frightened eyes, some demonic twist in the cheek, their spitfire tongues. Betty said they put it on. 'Seen it all before. Wouldn't you do it if your children were rotten? I'd want a break from them too.' If it were true, what an act, to dare show that side of yourself. But Kitty had seen enough patients to know what was real. And those women were not figments of imagination. She took her son in her arms, told him she was sorry, that sometimes she forgot who she was, and he said, 'Alright.'

There were three in the bed. Kitty tapped her foot against George's, grinned at him over the top of Badger's head. George and his knowing face, that love for it. *If I had to relive a moment for the rest of my life it would be this.* Badger patted his hands along the patchwork quilt cover, said, 'Is it time to get up yet? I'm bored,' and George pushed away from Kitty, pushed the bedding off. 'Let's go.' He clamped Badger's hands, pulled him along, made pyjama bottoms slide down, expose bare skin, made Badger laugh. 'I can see your bum, Badge. I might take it from you.' George, rare singsong.

A shriek. 'That's *my* bum-bum, Daddy. It won't fit you.'

What would I need to renounce to have mornings like this for the rest of my life?

George and Badger left the room, backs of heads soft-tilted to the left, this strange little tic passed from father to son. Down the hallway, Badger giggled from his room, made Kitty grin. But on her own she couldn't help her thoughts slipping into other possibilities, other versions of herself, other types of happiness. Why is it that what is in front of us is never good enough?

George started the record player, big band swing, whistled along, danced around, made the record skip and scratch, this thing he always did, gave Kitty that sharp shrill feeling along her teeth, made her shiver. Couldn't he be more careful, more considerate? She sighed too loudly, could feel the morning slipping away. While George got coffee ready, she went to Badger's room, hand on the doorknob, and before she turned the handle, she imagined what was on the other side, how she might find her child: a jump on the bed, a sprawl on the floor playing with small wooden blocks, a boy grinning, waiting for her, perhaps a boy magically turned into a man. In she went and it was dark inside the room and she turned on the light. In front of her: a half-constructed blanket cubby held up by stools covered half the bed. Inside the cubby: stacked hardcover books, a pair of dark green children's binoculars, Teddy, Floppy Rabbit. 'Badger, you in here?'

A shuffle behind the blanket cubby, underneath the bed. A secret hiding place. Kitty crept close. 'Badger? You in here? Hello?' She made her voice weep, played up worry.

She heard her boy giggle and got on her hands and knees, crawled close to the bed and said, 'I'm going to put my arms underneath here and see what I can find. I hope a monster doesn't get me.' Reached deep, felt for Badger, caught his hand, made her boy shriek.

'My goodness, what's this?' Pantomime surprise.

'I'm the swamp monster and I'm going to kill you.' Badger soft-toothed into her skin, growled a giggle.

Kitty pulled him towards her till she recovered her boy's head and shoulders. 'What are you doing in there?'

'I tucked myself up into tiny pieces so you couldn't find me.'

'But what if I didn't find you? Would you stay in pieces?'

Badger hands-and-kneed to standing. 'Maybe. I like that you sound worried when you can't find me. It's funny.'

'I don't think it's very funny. What if I really couldn't find you?' Kitty studied his face, his mischievous grin, tried to hide her own smile. 'Maybe I'd have to get a new son and pretend it was you.'

Badger chewed his lips, considered. 'You could, but it wouldn't be me.'

My precious, precious. It was not enough to look at him. Kitty lunged for her boy, kissed across his face, made him squirm, wriggle, tickled Badger, breathed him in, let it all go quiet. They hugged each other and Badger ran his hands along Kitty's back, said, 'You're the best in the world.'

In the lounge room, big band swing, whistling George, the smell of coffee. Him and them. Two things existing at once.

———

That night Badger crawled into their bed, pushed Kitty into the middle, a bridge between two versions of a man. The older Badger got it was as if George was reborn, had grown inside Kitty with all her love and attention; a good mother. I wouldn't let you go to war, wouldn't let you go up in a fighter plane, near the worst part of you that feels like it will never leave. I wouldn't let you.

She wrapped her arm around George, around Badger, and her heart beat double time, too quickly against her chest. She caught her breath, waiting in the feeling that comes before everything crashes down. 'I should've made you stay,' Kitty whispered into the half-lit dark, whispered to her husband. 'I should've known bad things would happen.' War doesn't need its fortune told. Its future is always present.

She looked at George, saw the undergrowth of skin under the ill-fitting facial prosthetic. Stared at all the things that remained. 'I need to tell you something,' he said. I'd give anything to hear all your somethings.

'What is it?'

He was quiet for the longest time and she thought he'd fallen asleep. And then, quietly, 'I keep thinking about how it's hard to be here.'

'What do you mean?'

'Sometimes I wake up and I think I've died and in that split second it's so peaceful.' He said it matter-of-fact. It was not what she was expecting, and in that moment she wanted to rage at him, wanted to hold him. What was he telling her? She'd tried so hard to make things better. 'So you'd rather be dead than be with your family?'

'That's not what I meant.'

'Well, how do you expect me to take it?' She imagined coming home from work, discovering him dead in the bed, how she'd have to raise their son on her own, all things on her own. But she knows this truth like the back of her hand. It feels like this now.

George came out from under her arm, sat so they faced each other. 'I want to be here. I love you both.'

Badger stirred, flipped himself over to his other side.

Fear got the better of her. 'If living is so awful . . .' Kitty wished she could take it back, wished she had simply said, Thank you for telling me, wished she had said, I am so sorry this happened to you.

'It's just a thought. Not even that. I just wake up and I'm surprised that I can't feel or hear anything. Because inside it's so loud all the time.' He took her hand, played with her wedding band. 'I like to think that it means one day peace is coming, because I can make it stop for a little while.' He smiled.

'What about us and our peace?'

George got up, hit his leg with his palm. 'I can't make it sound right. Everything is coming out wrong.'

She wanted to throw up. 'George, I'm sorry.' She kneeled on the bed, reached for him. 'I didn't handle that as well as I should. Come back. Tell me more.'

He shook his head. 'It'll only upset you.'

Discussion over. Doors shut like earthquakes and her body measured the magnitude of this new movement.

Eleanor

1958

ELEANOR HAD COME home from school early, was licking a Granny Smith apple core when she heard a knock from Badger's room where there shouldn't be any noise. 'Badger?' The knock again, blank and full all at once, and she ran down the hallway, still holding the sticky apple core, and when she burst through the door George was in front of Badger's wardrobe, blood and dust on his forehead, the way you bleed when you've hurt yourself but your body hasn't decided how much yet. He was still wearing the light brown suit and white shirt he wore for his job interview that morning. 'You look handsome, Dad,' she'd said and he winked at her. It felt like a million years ago.

'Daddy!' She didn't mean to throw the apple core at him but she wasn't sure how else to get his attention.

George hit his head again and he didn't do it really hard but it looked like it hurt and Eleanor ran to him, tried to push him over. She bear-hugged arms around his waist, tried again to push him over, and George's legs collapsed beneath him and he fell to the floor. He had been crying and he said, 'It's right here,' and he pointed to his heart and she didn't know what to do and just wanted to hide under the bed and wait for someone else to come and make it alright, but Kitty was still at the hospital working so Eleanor would have to get a grown-up neighbour and tell them what had happened. She knew that George wouldn't like that, because he hates fusses and she's not really allowed to let people know that sometimes things go wrong at home. She held George's hands and they were really soft and she wondered if it was true what he told her: that when he was born his hands were softer than soft and his mum thought they were made of rabbit fur and that's how she knew he would be a cuddly baby. But if that was true, how come he didn't have fur on his hands now instead of blood? She hugged her dad, said, 'It's okay, George. Everything will be alright,' because that's what she'd seen Kitty do and he always seemed better after a little while. But when she said it he didn't answer her and she worried that she'd done something wrong and she'd get into trouble. The room spun like the washing machine and her dad started crying so loud that it went all the way through the middle of her body and she screamed out, 'Help me,' as loud as she could. Hoped that someone had their windows open for once and would hear her. She wished she'd stayed at school with Susan and Ruth, wished she'd played elastics instead of wanting to go home and be by herself for a little while to draw pictures in her notebooks. But if she'd stayed at school her dad would've been all alone and stuck in his head, so maybe she has a little bit of a special power to know when her father needs her. Eleanor stroked George's head and he stopped crying and she told him, 'I'm going to get help,' and she ran out of the house, across the road to the Nelsons', knocked on the grey front door, heard their dog Pepe-pom-pom yap near the lounge room window, and she called out, 'It's Eleanor. Dad's hurt his head in the house.' Someone please come.

Mr Nelson opened the front door and she said, 'He's bleeding in Badger's room,' and he said, 'Shit,' and then Mr Nelson sprinted towards her house and she noticed a little square of toilet paper under his boot, and then Mrs Nelson came and held her hand and said, 'You just stay here with me, darl.'

Eleanor nodded and she thought crying was probably not a good idea right then so she squeezed Mrs Nelson's hand and Mrs Nelson said, 'Let's go have a slice of pineapple upside-down cake.'

———

A few days later she heard her mum soft-giggling on the phone. Eleanor liked her mother best when she was full of laughter and playmate games. Maybe when she's off the phone she'll come into my room and play dollhouses with me.

'I like the idea of that,' Kitty said, quieter. Was she speaking to George? Maybe he was going to come home from the hospital early.

Eleanor put her dolls away, made like a small animal and crawled along the floorboards and tried not to let her knees pound too loud as she went down the hallway. *Meow*, she felt like saying. This was a little game. *Meow. Woof. Neigh.* Ghost pets: her favourite game to play with Badger. There they'd be, crawling along the ground whispering *meow, woof, neigh* into the house to see how long it took for their parents to tell them to be quiet. They hadn't played for a while, but it was easier to play ghosts when you needed to be invisible. Her fingernails scratched the floor like kitten claws and when she opened her mouth she could taste dust and aldehydes and heavy grease of the blue-red lipstick her mother wore. Kitty was a trail of scent from the lounge room and Eleanor licked the side of her mouth and pretended to gag. She whispered, 'Blagh. *Meow.* Humans taste yuck,' but she opened her mouth wider. The way her mother came wafting down the hall; it was a comfort.

She peeked around the corner, smudged her cheek against the wall and there was Kitty: back resting against the red velvet sofa, black phone cord in her hand. Just like walking a dog.

'Why not? I need you to touch me and make love to me.' Kitty sounded spiky. She bent her entire body forwards and for a moment Eleanor wondered if Kitty was going to fall all the way into the floor.

These things adults said; she'd heard them before. It was how you made people love you. She could hear Kitty was sad that whoever she needed wasn't making her happy.

'I could make love to you, Mum,' Eleanor whispered. She could look after Kitty, could touch her to make her feel better. Eleanor could feel the floor underneath her hands, knew how strong she was becoming. *I can help her, make her smile.* She imagined crawling over to her mother and pulling herself up into her lap, tickling Kitty's neck to show just how happy Eleanor could make her.

Make love. What was it like when I was inside her tummy? Did I make love inside there, too? I could do it again.

'But we *are* having this conversation now.' Kitty's voice lowered, was like thunder in walls.

Who was she talking to? Eleanor crawled further into the lounge room, crawled until her knees hurt and she had to stop. Bony knees, her dad had told her. *You and your brother and your bony knees.* What she wouldn't give for Kitty to hang up the phone, come to kiss her. *I love you very much, darling. You're a gift.* Eleanor smiled at the idea of being a present. She hoped she was.

Eleanor held her breath, waited for her mother to end the call. Instead she heard Kitty cry. Eleanor jumped from the floor and ran to Kitty, ran her fingers over her mother's face to soothe her. Her cheeks were smooth like clouds. 'It's okay, Mum.'

Kitty's lipstick had smudged, her face dropped. 'Why are you looking at me like that?'

'I'm sorry,' Eleanor said. 'I just wanted to make you better.' All the quick words she knew to make things right.

'How long were you watching me? You're a little spy, are you?'

Eleanor shook her head. 'No. I promise.'

Kitty threw the phone on the ground, massaged her temples. The way she breathed, like she'd been running for days.

'Mummy, are you alright?'

Kitty scrunched her face into small pieces. 'What do you think?'

Her mother's voice, harsh, frightened her, and Eleanor crossed her legs so she wouldn't wet herself.

Kitty's shoulders curled into her chest, made her skin look as if all it wanted to do was break open and sink back into her body, suck Eleanor inside. 'What do you want?' Her breathing, the way wind sucks winter air into the mountain at night, swirling like the end of the world.

And Eleanor searched for something to calm her, to stop her from being angry, but she couldn't think of anything good. 'I was just going to ask if Ruth could come over.'

'*I was just going to ask if Ruth could come over.*' Her mum sneered, curled her lips, brought her fingers to temples, looked like a witch who could start fires with the click of her tongue. Eleanor tightened her mouth.

'I'm sick, Eleanor. And I'm all by myself with my children.' Her mother's voice trampled down the hallway, hurt her insides. Kitty didn't look like Kitty anymore. She looked like the lady Eleanor sometimes saw at night in her bedroom, the one who cried on her floor, told her that she was lucky to be alive. A hag. Just what Ruth had told Eleanor. 'She's gonna curse you too.' Eleanor was glad to have Ruth to confide in. Sometimes her mother scared her.

Kitty cried, was quiet, and then she bumped past Eleanor, went to her bedroom and shut the door.

———

The next day Eleanor made baked beans on toast with loads of cheese on top, made a glass of Milo, carrot sticks. To be fancy, she put a grevillea picked from the garden in a small red vase, placed it at the head of the table and sat where George would normally be. His chair was much comfier than hers. Look at me being fancy! Eleanor had opened the kitchen windows so that the conversations from the neighbours' backyards came inside, made her feel like the whole neighbourhood was standing around her.

'Did you hear me, Neil? I said do you want two sausages or three?'

'I don't want none!'

'I've cooked these bloody sausages and you're eating them. Two or three?'

'I said I don't want none!'

Eleanor ate her beans. All those voices outside, like imaginary friends. She laughed to herself, thought of all the things she could say back. It was fun to live in your head. The life in there was gigantic and ferocious, sounded like a million bird wings flapping all at once. Take me away to a time when I am older and living all by myself, Eleanor thought. She could come and go as she pleased, wouldn't have to ask permission to have friends over. Maybe I could travel around the world?

After lunch she tidied the kitchen and then she decided to tidy the lounge room, so that when Kitty eventually came out from her bedroom she would have a lovely house to relax in. Eleanor dusted the bookshelves, all the photos over the fireplace, and then swept the floor as best she could. Afterwards, she lay down on the lounge-room rug to rest. She tried very hard to tell herself not to go into Kitty's bedroom and check on her.

Eleanor rolled over onto her side. Don't go in.

But she tiptoed to her parents' bedroom door and opened it wide enough to fit her body through. All the curtains were closed, the lights off.

She sat on the chair by her mum in the dark, listened to her sleep, listened to her teeth grind. Eleanor hugged her knees to her chest. Waited. Her eyes adjusted to the dark, powerful like an owl's, and she could see the shapes of her parents' lives all over the room: the photos of her and Badger next to a photo of Kitty and George on their wedding day, next to votive candles next to the bottle of hand cream her mother kept on her bedside table. The room smelled like sweat, like tears, and just then Kitty's deep breaths stopped for a moment before starting again. Is she dying? I don't want her to die.

She slipped from the chair, made her way across the floor to Kitty, careful not to make a sound, careful not to make any sound that would hurt in her mother's head.

Eleanor carefully moved onto the bed, leaned close to her mother and there, underneath Kitty's soft hair, the smell of honey-suckle shampoo: mother sounds. This faint music she had heard all her life. Strings, drums, piano key, a light howl from the cave of her mouth. At school that week they had been shown cave drawings from thousands of years ago, tiny child drawings of the moon and stars and animals at night. Eleanor leaned closer to Kitty, wanted to draw the night sky for her mother. 'Just to let you know I was here and I visited you and I love you,' she whispered.

She wanted her mum to wake up, wanted to tell her that the sun was shining outside, that this morning she had seen a caterpillar crawl up the side of the fence, that she might now have sunburn. She wanted her mum to wake up and for her headaches to stop and for her mother to be normal again and not scary. She wanted her kind mum back.

'Mummy,' she said. She always had something to say, always something she needed to tell Kitty, even if it wasn't the right time. 'Mummy, can you hear me?'

Kitty stopped breathing.

'I just wanted to see if you're okay and to see if maybe I'm allowed to go out the front and play?' All the time it took for an answer; like waiting for morning to wake you from a bad dream. She thought she heard Kitty grind her teeth, thought she heard her say hello. She waited and waited and waited but Kitty gave her nothing. The last time this happened Kitty had let her sit on the bed, had even smiled at her.

'I'm going now, Mum. I'm going to go outside for a bit. Out the front.'

Eleanor got up from the bed, headed to the door, and as she opened it Kitty said, 'I told you to stay out of my room.' It was like a wolf with a furred voice had dug inside her mother and howled through her tongue. The sound of her: tears coming. Eleanor cupped her hands over her eyes, pressed hard to stop tears. You're not very nice, she wanted to say to her mother.

'You're a bad girl for not listening.'

I just wanted to help you.

Eleanor opened the door, hoped Kitty could see her in the light as she left.

———

She got the idea to go and look for birds. She got the idea that she would stay out there until the night came, until her mum got worried. That would make Kitty be nicer to her. Eleanor took her brother's binoculars from his bedside table, picked up her notebook from her room, went to the kitchen for sliced bread and a banana to snack on, and by the time she reached the front door her chin ached from holding her lips too tight, from holding herself together.

When she reached the park near the bushland a few streets away, she stuck her notebook in the waistband of her pants, freed her hands to climb the tree. Sap on palms, a cobweb in hair, a splinter half sticking out of her fingertip: she grinned as she kept climbing to a height where she could make out the television antennas perched on top of houses; alien skeletons. From up there Wintonvale was a doll village: all cut up into square blocks, with front doors painted grey, white, yellow, all the roofs with black tiles that looked like dominoes, the little gardens of white and apricot and purple, cars sleeping in driveways. She squinted, pinpointed her house, thought of her mother inside sleeping. She squinted, pinpointed the hospital, thought of her father inside sleeping. One day when they're not sleeping I'm going to move very far away and never come back. But, you'll miss your parents. She nodded.

She sat in a branch fork, swung her legs in the air, held her notebook and waited for the birds. I could stay like this forever. She kept her eye to the sky, eye to green, called their names out loud as she saw them: eastern rosella, spotted pardalote, crow, tawny frogmouth, swift parrot, wattlebird, magpie, myna. They flew above her, flew to avoid her. They flew, they flew. And that flying made her happy.

Eleanor

Present

THE CAR SPEEDS down the highway at a rate too fast for itself. The shotgun sound of tyre blow-out and the car swerves, wakes her from the daze she is in. She pulls over and gets out, checks the damage to the tyre. There is no salvaging it.

Eleanor opens the boot, rummages for the spare, opens a side compartment for the jack and wrench. She tells Amy over the back seat, 'There's nothing to worry about, sweetheart. I'll fix this in no time.'

Wind chill and sound of crow in the trees makes her shudder. A crow lands on the car, opens its beak, and claws scratch paint, scratch metal, makes strange music. Another lands on the car bonnet and Eleanor nods at the bird.

And, like a crow, she remembers the word *deceit*.

'Amy, animals are very clever at deceiving each other too. Did you know that some female birds can trick a male bird into believing he's raising his own offspring? And the lyrebird is a master mimic. It can copy almost anything, even a telephone ringing! And some spiders smell and behave like ants in order to trap their prey. Did you know zone-tailed hawks have evolved to look like vultures? What do you think you would copy, little one?'

She tells Amy, 'But you should always be wary of people who tell you one thing but do another.' It doesn't mean you can't trust people. But don't be fooled by the things you want to hear, want to see. Not like me.

She leaves the crows to it, takes the jack and crouches on the ground, gets to work. Why did this have to happen now? She thinks about Leon in bedsheets. The wrench against tyre and hands slip trying to unloosen nuts. 'Fucking stupid thing. Just get off!' She takes a deep breath, begins again, as a motor cascades down the road towards her; the grunt of its speed makes her nervous. She moves away from the road, realises a police car is nearing, and she sweats, shakes pins and needles from her arm. They know. They've been sent to find us. She thinks of how easy it would've been to make a call to the police, how easy it would've been for someone to say, 'Eleanor's not in her right mind. She just up and left. Who can say what she'll do?' Easy because Leon had said as much the night before. 'Your problem is that you think too much.' And he pinned her against the kitchen counter, put his hand around her throat. 'You want to know what I did over there?' Them so close together their teeth smashed.

'I think I know.'

'You don't. But I'll show you.'

And then Amy had cried.

Eleanor quiets the night, looks at Amy in the back seat, watches the police car speed right past her, the car engine reverberating through her body.

She changes the tyre but she doesn't get back inside the car. Not just yet. Eleanor tells her daughter, 'Mummy needs to stretch her legs for a minute.'

Rain starts again, drenches Eleanor, makes everything cling tight; a vacuum seal. She keeps her focus ahead, takes in the over-farmed land, the recoveries from a grass fire that would've passed through a year before, new growth teasing out from blackened trunks.

This walking, like being in waves, slows her heart rate, calms her, just like it always did. George had always told Eleanor that a walk would save you from Wintonvale Hospital. 'It'll make you feel better. Maybe you'll realise the things you think in your head aren't so bad.' But George walked all hours and it still hadn't been enough to save him completely.

Any day now Amy would be taking her first steps. She could already pull herself up from the ground. Eleanor couldn't wait for the day when she would have to keep up with her daughter's stride. Eleanor walks on, sees in front of her Amy's gappy smile as she caterpillars along the linoleum floor, grunts then laughs from exertion. What music, what symphony. She sees Amy stand, tight muscles tensing, wobbling into balance, and look around for a destination. The will of a child to go places. Teetering with arms stretched ahead, a type of flying. She sees herself take a polaroid camera out from her bird bag, snap the evolution of her daughter's progress and keep it to herself. Had her parents captured her own first steps? She'd never been shown photographic evidence. Perhaps they were so overjoyed that they could do nothing else but take her all in, commit the moment to memory. But we stop doing this. When a child reaches a certain age we forget about the miracles they continue to perform and instead return to their past, to the time when we were shocked at our ability to love something, someone, so ferociously. A tiger mouth for a heart; eat prey.

The rain falls and she turns towards the car. If I can get to the mountain, if I can just get distance between me and Leon, I'll be able to relax. She shuts the door and the glove box pops open, the hinge mechanism having broken a few days before, and Eleanor reaches to close it, sees the thick black camera strap, an umbilical cord, at the back of the compartment. She pulls and the camera follows, and she takes off the lens cap, looks over her shoulder at her daughter. The world gives us so much to capture, to document. It hurts when she swallows, when she says, 'I need to photograph your beautiful little face, Amy.' She closes her eye, presses the shutter button, presses again. 'We've got to get going to safety, sweetheart.' She starts the car and eases onto the road, the new tyre smoothing black bitumen.

———

The sun in her eyes makes the car veer to the right. She realigns, notices the blue and purple veins pop on top of her hands; this map of hours. She passes swaying heavy-limbed gums and the car dips into a pothole, crunches the wheel. Minutes become accumulated time. Eleanor's body aches from sitting and she rolls her neck right and left, lets those muscles pull for relief. There is a popping noise from her spine, the crack of bones shifting into new positions. This earthquake; the breaking of Gondwana.

The car hammers the road, a crow settles on tree branch, a car passes by, a car passes by, drivers raise an index finger to Eleanor as they make eye contact, that salute of acknowledgement which says, *We are on this road together*. When she was younger she had asked George why drivers did that. He had smiled. 'It's good to acknowledge a fellow traveller.' Kindness. She had reminded herself to do it ever since. And so cars pass and up go fingers and every now and then a man nods his head, a woman nods her head, Eleanor nods her head and they travel away from each other. The car hammers the road and she notices a roadside memorial: a large white cross dressed in a dead floral wreath, the name SIMON tattooed in thick black text. Simon, how long did it take for the ones at home to realise you weren't coming back to them? Did you see what was coming towards you? Eleanor scans the area as they pass: no trace of a big tree that could have been a crash site, no trace of anything that could have broken Simon's speed. She imagines Simon exiting his car through the windshield, that horrific first flight, and as he headed for the road he called for his mother because it was the only thing he could think to do before landing without her hearing him, without her being able to rush to his side for the last time. We always call for our mothers.

The idea of it makes her tear up, gives her that sickening churn in her stomach. Acid in the throat. She winds the window down, spits herself out of the car, does it again and again. Inside Eleanor is a hurt. I don't feel right. Close your eyes, and she does, shuts them tight. Behind her is engine noise, the sound motors make when pushing into white static, the way Leon's car sounded when he returned home late at night, revving in the driveway to wake her, to warn her that he was coming inside. She looks over her shoulder towards the noise and there: a burgundy car, a broad-shouldered silhouette in the driver's seat. She accelerates, and the Belmont hurtles down the highway, and the burgundy car recedes.

They speed past broken barbed-wire fences, past flocks of sheep with docked tails, pass underneath a black tornado of starlings. Eleanor leans forwards, tries to get a better look, and it's as if half the sky is falling, peeling back clouds to reveal the universe underneath. To be up there with them, free.

'Look, Amy! Look! That's called a murmuration. It's like they're reading each other's minds. Wouldn't it be great to know what they're thinking?'

When she was with George, they'd pulled over by the side of the road to watch starlings play. George smiled, told her, 'One day, when we were getting the aircraft ready, we saw thousands of starlings dancing in a field. We stopped just to watch them. It was beautiful.'

'Then what happened?'

He shrugged his shoulders. 'They went on their way and we went up in the sky.'

Starlings in the sky, her daughter in the back seat. She says, 'Look what's out there! Can you see the road? Can you see the trees? Can you see the way the wind sways the grass? Can you see the car coming towards us? Where do you think they might be going?'

Travel past speed limit signs, signs warning of high-rising tides in flood conditions, of dairy animals walking from one paddock to another, past a collapse of houses long forgotten by their owners, rubble-mound of stone and timber and tin. The lives that were once lived inside: where have they gone?

The car swerves along the shape of the long loop of the road. Eleanor's body tilts as she mirrors the curve of the road. Outside the car: bay and blue roan horses gallop in a paddock, a man sweat-jogs along the highway, and Eleanor's body remembers the work it had done thirteen months earlier, pushing Amy out, feels the pull in her groin, the heat of it. She pushed and it was as if barbed wire was being dragged through her body, scraping across what was once a virgin landscape. She pushed and she felt the most alive she'd ever been. It made her want to die. When Amy finally pulsed out Eleanor felt the excess blood, all the red that had been built to keep a life in place, rush out from between her legs and onto the bed; evidence that her body was now taking a breath. Eleanor inhales, exhales, tries to calm her mind, to keep her focus on the road, but she is getting tired, is exhausted even by the memory of labour. She winds down the window, hopes the cold air will carry the pain away.

The past year with Amy has been a blur: in the beginning she mourned the time before she arrived, marvelled at how Amy's bones were like phantoms under skin, still forming. Weeks went by and Eleanor woke up one morning feeling like she was slipping, that she lived on the perimeter of heartbreak. But she still didn't feel the big love that her new motherhood friends talked about. 'It's just so natural, isn't it?' Justine had said. Eleanor didn't know what natural was. Maybe she was dead inside. Maybe she had become Kitty.

She follows the bends and from the back of the car there is a thunk sound of something sliding against the panelling. The black box. The muscles in her legs tighten, her mouth floods with bile; she swallows it down.

Another bend: the box slides again.

Eleanor tells Amy, 'Your father deceived people. He deceived me.'

———

Ahead is a roadside rest area and Eleanor merges into the left lane, bounces in her seat as the car hits the unpaved entrance. She parks the Belmont under a tree, tells Amy, 'Sweetheart, if Mummy doesn't rest for a bit now we will be in a world of trouble,' turns off the ignition, stretches her arms above her head, welcomes the cracking sounds her spine makes. She looks around: a Mack truck at the far end of the rest area, a smattering of station wagons and sedans filled with families and singles eating, sleeping. Having people around makes things feel a little safer.

Her breasts ache and she needs to feed Amy but she also needs to get out of the car, needs to walk. She leans over the driver's seat and tugs the baby blanket over her daughter, remembers how much Amy loves playing games of tuck and untuck the blanket, how it makes her laugh, and she thinks of all the times they've played, how it never seems to get old for Amy. 'Okay, bub, I have to go and clear my head.'

She locks the car door. There: hundreds of corellas flying tree to tree, of crickets, the backbeat of frogs drum in her ears. She closes in on the big trees, her feet crunching gravel and broken twigs, and her sounds grow louder, in the way of all trespassers. The noise she makes is overwhelming, to the point her ears pop, her head throbs. She takes another walking track, and even though she doesn't want to stray too far from the car, it's the only thing she can do to give herself respite. Eleanor walks faster, feels blood pump through sore and tired legs. Above her, a kookaburra hops across branches before diving into the native grasses to pull out a worm. She stops to watch closely, doesn't notice that she's centimetres away from a bull-ant nest until they take to her, eat at her, a sustenance. We are only gases, sodium, atoms, electricity. We are only life. 'Bloody hell.' She jumps clear of the nest, shakes her leg, brushes her hand against her leg to shake a few off. No matter how many times she walks in nature she forgets about this danger.

The wall of sound around her, a symphony of birds and insects. I wish I'd brought my sound equipment to capture this. A quick thought of normalcy. She shakes it away, thinks of her father, what it took for him to find normalcy. There'd been times in her childhood when he would take off, leaving a note on her bedside table to let her know where he was going but forgetting to tell anyone else. Lost inside himself. Kitty often told her it was best to let him wander. Would tell her, 'If you put too much pressure on him he'll leave, and then where will we be?' And so Eleanor let him be alone, chose her moments to speak to her dad carefully. Once she asked him where he'd gone and he simply said, 'Away from the noise.' The quiet house she grew up in; it hadn't made sense.

'What kind of noise?' She imagined small pockets of fairies, a warble of magpies, too many trumpets and drums in a hall, a thousand thunderclaps.

'Oh, just loud grown-up ones.'

She wanted to ask if that meant war but her mother said she should never mention it. 'Like machines and planes and guns and stuff?'

He nodded. 'War can be very hard. People get hurt.' As if he himself had never been and this was second-hand opinion.

She looked at him. 'You mean like your face?'

'There are different ways of hurting, Eleanor.'

She wishes George was here now. She wants him to tell her that although she is hurting everything will be alright. She wants him to tell her she will eventually get what she needs.

She heads back to the car, sees a family has made a fire in a small steel bin, are toasting bread over flames. A woman with platinum blonde hair and blue eyeshadow smiles and nods at Eleanor as she walks by and Eleanor nods back. 'Nice walk?'

'Yes. It's good to have a break from driving.'

'Where you going?' The woman looks behind Eleanor, searches the cars as if trying to figure out which one belongs to her.

'The blue mountain. I'm taking my daughter for the first time.' Eleanor blows into her palms, tries to warm herself.

The woman taps her face. 'That blue Belmont yours?'

Has something gone wrong in my absence? 'Yes.'

'You left your child in the car?'

Eleanor's breath catches at the idea that Amy might've cried out, might've hit her head against the car window looking for her. 'Yes. I didn't want her getting cold. And she was asleep . . .'

'I would never do that.' The accusation of bad parenting hangs between them. The woman is a good few years older than Eleanor. To be scolded like that. Mothers everywhere. Eleanor hangs her head and the woman tells Eleanor, 'You've got no idea what sort of people are out in the world lurking and being up to no good.'

Eleanor imagines her husband. He is the sort of people. 'I was just so tired. I wasn't thinking.' All the ways she justifies herself, tries to make others think well of her. Half of her wants to argue back, to tell this woman to leave her alone, that she has no idea what's happening in her life right now. The other half is here taking it, considers all the ways to be a better mother.

'If you wanted . . .' The woman isn't letting it go.

'Stop!' Eleanor yells. 'I haven't left my child.'

The woman holds her hands up in protest, says nothing, and so Eleanor walks around to the back of the car, opens the door and climbs over the back seat to unbuckle her daughter. Her breasts leak. She hears herself tell Amy, 'I'm sorry. I'm sorry,' knowing the woman is watching her, and Eleanor lifts her jumper, nestles herself inside Amy's mouth, starts squeezing her nipple to regulate the first flow. The relief that comes. She looks out the window, catches the woman's eye. She begins humming to Amy, rocks them both calm and tender, imagines Amy smiling underneath her jumper. The woman looks away, goes back to toasting bread.

Milk overflows and she wipes her daughter's mouth and swaddles Amy in extra blankets to keep her from the bittering cold, strokes the back of her daughter's neck, kisses her forehead over and over and over again. She tells Amy, 'It's almost over. We will be there soon,' tries to swallow the tears lodged in the back of her throat.

Kitty
1946

KITTY IN THE house, turned-up music, 'I Only Have Eyes For You' on the record player, sang along, prepared for the Friday night dinner and card game. Their turn to host. She lit the oven, started preheating for her baked treats. George was in the lounge room on the sofa, tapping his foot along to the music, staring at the wall, his shoulders raised to his ears. The way he positioned himself, hiding in plain sight. Her stomach, rusted metal; the pain that comes from trying to absorb the past. Badger was in the backyard, kicking a ball, kicking grass, kicking his own shins like the enemy. The boy would hurt himself if he wasn't careful. Why was his father never with him?

'George.' She tried to sing him to her. The record played out, skip-skip-*skissshh* of vinyl under the needle, made the sound of all things ending. She'd heard this sound inside herself before.

Badger called out, and through the window she could see his ball stuck in a tree. '*Mummy!* Come now!'

'George!' Kitty couldn't get out of the mess of uncooked dough on her hands. Over on the sofa: George tapped his foot along to the sound of nothing, eyed the wall. Of all the days to be like this. Nothing ever goes to her plan.

The ball stuck in a tree, her hands in the dough.

'George.' She moved from the kitchen bench to the opening between the living room and kitchen. He faced her then, head anchored to the side, his mouth slightly open like a storefront dummy. He is a breathing husk; no ability to connect thoughts and action together. He was never there when she needed him. George, you're nothing, she thought. She felt shame looking at him. How dare he make her feel this way. How dare he make her wish they'd never married, that they'd never met, that he'd never come back from the war. Mourning would be easier.

'George.'

She stood in front of him and he curved a look towards her, his face half-tight, his good eye registering. 'What's wrong?'

'Didn't you hear the music end? Can't you hear your son calling for you?' She wanted him to feel defective. Dough dried to her skin. She knew he was going to embarrass her in front of their friends. In front of Charlie. Tonight she'd once again have to pour effort into their show of make-believe that everything was perfect.

But the way he looked at her: happy to see her standing there, as if he hadn't expected Kitty at all, as if he'd expected her to have left by now.

She wanted to slap him, claw at his head until he was once more the man she knew he was capable of being. Not this pathetic person in front of her. Pathetic is the woman who stays, she thought. But leaving would mean admitting defeat, admitting that she was unable to fix him.

So Kitty made herself smaller. Put on a marriage show. Plied her mouth into a smile, said, 'Go help Badger. When you've done that, change the record. When you've done that, set the table.' Single orders for a simple life. She noticed the patches of hair on his chin. 'And then go shave.' Kitty wanted to cry. Good. Let him see what he does to me. All this pretending that everything is alright, that I am strong. She wanted to add, 'And then treat me like a person, a wife. Treat me as if we have intellectual conversations, as if we reminisce about our good old days, as if we have inside jokes, as if we build hopes and dreams together, as if we are equals in this relationship.' But she didn't, and he didn't respond, and Kitty felt her blood boil.

'Why can't you be normal for once? Fucking say something, George!'

Finally he said, 'I'm sorry.' Nothing more. The sound of the record spinning; dead music. Kitty leaned into her husband, spat at his mouth, watched the way it slid down his chin. He stood up, went to the backyard.

———

A portrait of marriage games:

The table was set. Lilac linen tablecloth, starched, lace doily under a fruit-and-floral centrepiece: red banksia surrounded by a moat of stone fruit; apricot, plum, peach. Kitty placed a bread plate, white napkin and knife at each seat, whisky glasses out; booze for hounds. The house had been scrubbed and vacuumed and Kitty had wondered what else she could remove from the space. Me: I think I should remove me. Nothing felt clean. She removed the honey, orange and yoghurt cake from the oven, sat it to cool, and when George emerged from the bathroom he was a trail of Blenheim Bouquet, the smell an invitation for Kitty to go to him. She inspected his fingers, under his nails, pleased to see that he'd used the nailbrush. Stop it, Kitty. Stop treating him like a child. But patterns are formed between two people and set in stone.

He smiled at her in his old way, made Kitty want to kiss him, tell him she loved him like this. That for a moment the earlier part of their day together had been erased. Instead, she reached out and straightened his collar, took in the smell of him until she'd had enough, and said, 'Try not to drip anything on yourself tonight. You look too nice.' She hoped she'd smiled when she said it and George grunted, nodded and stepped into the lounge room, waited by the front door to call that it was open. This man who knew his place in this home.

After setting the table, Kitty went to check on Badger in his room. 'Remember what I said? Tonight you have to stay in bed even if the adults are too loud and wake you up.'

Badger sighed, 'I know, I know,' and Kitty cradled his chin and kissed his forehead. 'I'll come in to check on you later.' She wanted to stay in the boy-smell of his room, to never leave and go back to the adults. Kitty stroked Badger's hand. 'Okay, boy-boy. Time to sleep.'

'But I want to stay up and see people come in.'

'You're not allowed to.' Kitty held his hand, felt the sweat between them.

'What if I need the toilet?' This way he pushed and pushed.

'Then you can go straight there and back. You can't come and see us. Mummy will be busy.' She gripped tighter. Badger tried to tug his hand away but she wouldn't let him. He'd been doing this lately: pulling away. He looked like George in that moment, George from hours before. Let him go, Kitty. But she couldn't help it, let herself squeeze her son's hand so tight his bones moved towards each other, the way they do after a fracture: mended but never completely right. She stared at him, his mouth opened to speak, to argue, but he didn't make a sound, just wore the face of a confused child, and then it happened: Badger relaxed into her.

'I'll do what you say. I'll stay where I are.'

Kitty smiled, said, 'Good boy.' She knew it was impossible for him to slip from her. Not like his father. What we learn from a mistake: try not to repeat the past. If I hold on to Badger it'll be like George never went away to war.

The lounge room collected voices and she heard Charlie speak to her husband in good-neighbour tones, heard George laugh along with her lover. Listen to them, without me.

Badger tugged at her wrist. 'I said a kiss goodnight!'

She kissed her boy, turned out his light, and left him for her men.

———

The couples came together: hugged, shook hands, kissed cheeks, department store scents heavy on collar and wrist. They took up their places by the dining table, segregated themselves into smaller friendships. Maudie and Joan, Kitty and Diane, Charlie and Barry and Dom, George and Bert. Single Bert. Always the tag-along, always a bore. Kitty hadn't wanted him there, because it would mean uneven numbers, but George and the other men insisted. This way of them; like keeping him around as a talisman to ward off their own potential wife-abandonment curse. The women laughed, the married men held their shoulders straight-tight like forts while Bert slumped his. This house full of chemistry; made it hard to concentrate. While busy with the last of the meal preparation Kitty tried to listen through the noise, heard, 'Mate, the day they close that warehouse down the better. If that roof caves in, those blokes are fucked.'

In the other ear Kitty heard, 'That would've been a few years ago now. She was a sweet little thing.'

Kitty heard Joan say, 'They tell you what happened to Marv? Bloody hanged himself in the garage.'

In Wintonvale word gets around and word carries meaning. She glanced over at Charlie and she thought about their word, how they'd promised never to let their nights find the day. What would people think if they found out? Charlie flicked Kitty a look over Barry's shoulder and suddenly she was all heat. She was sure George could smell the smoke rise from her and so she came out of the kitchen, pulled Diane along to the other women, towards a distraction.

'Poor Jaclyn. Imagine having to tell the children,' Maudie said.

'At least he didn't do it out in public. Can you imagine? God, we'd have to avoid that whole area for months,' Joan said quietly and they all nodded.

Diane said, 'I thought Marv was doing so well. Jaclyn never said anything was wrong.' These whispers through teeth. Kitty heard her own screams loud in the middle of her head, knew she'd rather die than let her friends discover what was inside her.

'I think we never know what someone is thinking and maybe it's for the best,' she heard herself say, wondered if she believed it.

'Kitty.' It was George, that timbre in his voice. Something like authority, 'Kitty, I'm going to pour more drinks now.'

'Sure.' Did he want her to applaud him for being able to play host?

The women were dressed in primary colours. Diane wore ruby red. Maudie wore cornflower blue. Joan wore corn yellow. Kitty wore blood red. It was a whole thing to be able to blend lives, make perfect fits from new colour schemes. Kitty told everyone to sit at the table. 'Help yourselves.' Maudie cut into a plum, made a mouth-sized wound that fit tight in her mouth. Kitty watched Maudie's lips take the plum away and she couldn't help but think—

'George, how's my mum's clock coming along?' Maudie slipped another slice of plum on her tongue.

George nodded, as if being given an answer, and said, 'Tell your mother it's almost keeping perfect time.' He nodded again.

Maudie put the knife down, clapped her hands together. 'George! She'll be so pleased. I knew you'd be able to do it.'

Did she? What did she see in George that Kitty didn't? Kitty wanted to shove her friend's face into the carpet. The way she treated him, those claps for a tiny boy. But George absorbed it, soaked up the glow. Watching other women's praise, her heart felt like it didn't quite fit into her body. Was Maudie flirting with George? Maybe she could take him away, solve all their problems.

Kitty cut into her fruit, said, 'You can't have him, Maudie. He belongs to me.' The sweetness she could summon. Kitty winked at George and he blushed; his knee hit the underbelly of the table. A glass jumped, some small cannon fodder, and the men called, 'Taxi!', banged palms on the table.

Maudie said, 'There goes Georgie's magic leg again.' Their laughter forced George to lower his eyes, but it went straight to Kitty's head, made her temples ache. She wanted it to end, was already bored of entertaining. She looked around the table at the faces she had seen week after week for years. She couldn't make sense of them. There was something not quite real about them, as if they'd been torn out of a magazine, or cut into small pieces and taped back together like a jigsaw made of bone.

She felt the women stare at her and so she smiled. What's the use of a face if not to put on a show?

———

After dinner they drank and drank. The card decks came out and they played their hands and Kitty folded immediately in the first game. She sipped her drink, her breasts tight underneath her dress. The body and its night memory. Any other night I would be in Badger's room feeding him by now. She still liked to nurse her four-year-old; still close like infancy, still his mother's boy. George thought it was unnecessary, didn't understand it. He never understood anything about her. The weight of milk made her feel as she were about to spill. And what if she did? Who among them would come lick her up? She shook her head, eyes moved over the table, over the small mess being made, over the way elbows folded onto tabletop, over the smiles and wrinkles in the corners of eyes, over George's concentration, his bottom tooth hitching slightly onto his top lip, over Charlie running fingers along Diane's neck, the way they lengthened down her skin. Kitty bit her lip. I taught him that. I taught him how to pleasure his wife. He should be touching me. Diane sat upright, a string from her head to ceiling, like she was being controlled, closed her eyes and parted her lips, showed her too-white teeth.

She'd believed Charlie a few weeks ago when he told her that he'd stopped sleeping with Diane. 'I only want you, Kitty.' His need had given her so much joy. But she could see the lessons she'd taught him played out in front of her, in her home, as if his hands were her hands on his wife, as though her hands were ghosts around Diane's neck. Kitty felt as if she were all around the room, as if she was the one pulling responses from women without even trying. Like a god, I am everywhere, and right now I am stroking her skin, I am making her smile because I convinced her husband that intimacy is a trick of the light. I am between her legs. It is my tongue licking her wide open, my lips gently sucking her clitoris.

Diane smiled at her. 'What are you up to, Kitty-cat?'

Kitty sipped her drink. 'Just thinking how wonderful it is we can all be together. As always.'

They drink to clear the air, to purge stale lungs, to reaffirm friendships. They set up for a second game, take a break from strategy.

'Kitty, may it please you to fetch me another drink?' Maudie dangled her glass in the air and Kitty ignored her. George told Charlie about the new red-and-silver Kelvinator fridge they'd bought, 'Cooler than cold,' and they laughed at the word play and George said, 'Do you want the old one? Be good to have a beer fridge in the garage.'

'It would be good! Why go inside the house when everything you need is in a shed?' Charlie said.

'Well, you should take it. Otherwise I told Badger he could have it for his cubby near the bush to play shops. I just have to fix the handle so it doesn't stick.'

'Men and their sheds! I just don't get it,' Joan said.

Her husband Barry said, 'Use your brain, Joan. We'd lose our bloody minds if we had to be around our wives all the time,' and gurgled a laugh.

'You're assuming you had one to lose to begin with.'

The sound of them all pretending. Kitty closed her eyes. She was tired of playing. And yet, she liked that they always came for her.

'Alright!' George called out. 'Ready to play?'

Around the table they went. Drinks were filled, refilled. Kitty compared herself to the other women, delighted in the fact she was drawing the attention of the men, could feel their eyes feast on her, gobble her long neck, her delicate pearl choker, the red of her lips, no hair out of place. I am their dream. Kitty snaked her body as she lay her cards on the table, moved her hands around the glass, reached for more stone fruit. Let them see how I move my body. Let Charlie see me. She nibbled at her own fingers, licked juices. She glanced at Charlie but he wouldn't meet her eye.

'You got yourself a woman and a half here, George,' Barry said.

Kitty beamed, tapped Maudie on her oven-burnt knuckles. 'Hear that, Maudie? I might have stolen half of myself from you!' And she laughed while Maudie sank lips onto her glass.

George looked up from his hand of cards, adjusted his prosthetic glasses a little, his way to compose himself, to buy time. 'Yes.' Offhanded, disconnected. 'She sure is a woman and a half.'

The way he said it: like she was nothing. Kitty blushed. Is this what he thinks? He can't even go along with the idea that I'd be worth something to someone.

The night went on and Maudie lit her cigarette, Diane lit her cigarette, Joan lit, Kitty lit, and they swallowed down their old fashioneds while the men swirled gin. Charlie paid too much attention to Diane and Kitty guided her leg under the table towards Charlie's leather shoe, purred against him until he sucked in his cheeks. He licked his lips and Kitty flashed over to George. 'Your move,' she said. He mumbled, asked for another card.

'No point taking another card, mate. Aren't winning anyway.' Bert tipped his chair back, laughed himself too loud, laughed himself stupid. God, Kitty couldn't stand him. No wonder Bert's wife left him.

Joan rolled her eyes at Bert, spoke in whisky tones when she said, 'Why don't you have another drink, Bert?' The crook of her eyebrow; elbow angled. Bert stopped swinging on his chair, planted all four chair legs back onto the carpet.

More chatter and cards were dealt, and everything suddenly became too loud for Kitty. Maudie's voice became Charlie's voice became George's became Joanie's became a clock became the record spinning became the wind outside became Badger turning in his sleep became Kitty standing from her chair became Kitty asking, 'Who needs another drink?' All one big noise.

'Kitty,' Maudie said, 'why don't you tell us one of your terrific stories from the hospital. Something salacious!'

'Oh, I don't know.'

Kitty felt sleepy now.

'Kitty, tell us the horse story!' Joan said to Bert, 'Have you heard the horse story? Kitty, tell the horse story – tell him about Country Kettle.'

She was being called on to perform. Kitty knew she was smiling, but it was the last thing she wanted to do. She'd told the story so many times, though, she could sleepwalk through it.

Bert parted his mouth to the side. 'I'd love to hear a horse story from the fuckin' crazy house.'

Maudie and Kitty sucked air through their teeth. George dealt the cards, counting under his breath, before saying mildly, 'I go to that fuckin' crazy house.'

Silence then until Kitty added, 'It's because of the war.'

Bert said, 'Ah, shit, mate – sorry,' took another sip. Kitty thought of how his lips would leave a foul mark around the rim, how long it would take to clean it.

'I was enlisted,' Charlie said. 'Did I ever tell you?'

'But then he had terrible ailments in basic training,' Diane added.

'I've always liked to think that I was there in spirit.'

'If he could've gone, he absolutely would've sacrificed it all.'

Kitty wished they would shut up. Sacrifice. They had no idea what that was. Kitty looked at George, his dull face, and she thought of all the men she'd ever nursed. She snapped the words, 'Isn't it great you have spirit, then?' and Maudie chuckled into her drink.

'George, ready to deal?' Charlie turned to him, wrapped his arm around Diane's chair.

'Yes, yes.' George slid the cards across the table and Kitty forgot about telling the story.

'So, about the horse!' Bert slammed his palm on the table.

George cleared his throat. 'Why don't I just tell you one of mine then, eh?'

What story could he possibly tell? Some weeks he barely said a word.

'By all means, mate!' Bert slobbered on the rim of his glass.

George was animated, told them about how he'd been a navigator, how one night they'd flown so close to the enemy in another plane they were able to give each other a thumbs-up just to make sure it wasn't a dream. 'I'll never forget the night I saw men in flames,' he said. 'One plane got blasted and they caught fire. And the men just shrank in size. Right in their seats. Like little pieces of plastic.'

The horror, so matter-of-fact.

'What an adventure!' Bert said.

What kind of adventure was burning flesh? Kitty thought. No one other than Bert spoke. It was as if they were seeing George for the first time. It felt as if she had been living with a stranger. I've had a child with him and yet he's refused to speak about his experience, refused even to talk about therapy at the hospital, and now here he was, drunk, giving away his stories like party favours to a ridiculous man no one wanted around. Kitty stared at the tabletop, at the way her friends fixed at their collarbones. She knew that trick: it was hers.

Something like jealousy, like fury, struck her fingers and she tapped them on the table, a signal to George that they'd had enough of his war and his services were no longer required. He paid no notice, kept talking, kept up his laughter, kept up the fantasy that he was always like this, that no harm had ever befallen him. A mushroom farmer, her father would've said. His lack of trust in her. The way it stung. He's kept me in the dark about this side of him by never revealing more than he had to. Kitty tightened her jaw and immediately her head throbbed.

She was almost at the end of another drink when she noticed Badger standing at the door of the dining room. 'Why is everything so loud?'

Joan plunged her hands together. 'Oh, isn't he darling!'

All nodded, all laughed.

Kitty looked at her son. He'd broken her rules. The males in her life never took her seriously. What did they say about boys being like their fathers? It was quite the thing. George turned his shoulder at an angle that exposed a small underside of his prosthetic, just enough so that she could see the man underneath. She couldn't bear to look at him like this.

'Badger!' George joyous.

'I was asleep but now I'm not!' This magic trick.

'Come sit with us, boy-boy.'

Kitty couldn't understand why George didn't send him away. 'Guess I'll put him back.' She stood too quickly, was a-topple in her shoes as she seesawed into Badger, scooped him up, rested him on her hip, her dress tight against her. Soon he would be too big to fit her body so easily. Badger's mouth landed on the meat of her shoulder, and as they walked down the hallway Badger patted his sticky-sleep hands on her back. She heard her company laugh and assumed it was at her expense. She spoke low into his ear. 'What have I told you about leaving your bed?'

'I wanted to see you! And it was loud.'

'You can see me tomorrow.' The irritation that came from having the sole responsibility of putting their child to sleep made Kitty semi-throw Badger into bed. She dragged bedsheets over him, made him laugh.

'Quiet.'

'It's funny when you get like a cuckoo train.'

'What?'

'Steamy and noisy!'

Kitty smiled, kissed his forehead. 'You're lucky I'm not a truck.'

'What do trucks do?' Badger close to giggling.

Kitty leaned into him, pinched his nose. 'Beep beep.' She released him, the small squash of nostril slowly inflated. Badger lunged at her, kissed her lips, and he was wet and salty. She tasted blood, realised it was on her tongue and she swallowed it down, unable to recall when she'd bitten herself. It was so easy to forget how hurt happened in this house.

'I love you, Mummy.'

'I love you too, Badger.'

She lay on the bed beside him and he touched her breast. 'Milk?'

Kitty unzipped her dress, pulled it down just enough, and she gave herself to her son. The only good thing was being with him. She heard George laugh from the lounge room. I want him gone. Tears came then but she didn't wipe them away. Her son drank from her and she imagined a new life away from Wintonvale: she and Badger by the seaside, she and Badger holding hands looking for a four-leaf clover. No more unpredictability, no more pretending. She gently stroked Badger's hair, decided that ending her marriage was the right thing to do. 'Soon,' she whispered. 'I could do it soon.' Saying it out loud, how light she felt.

Eleanor

1966

IT WAS EARLY morning and the toilet was blocked again, half-filled with diluted urine, bobbing shit and wadded toilet paper. She'd have to hold on. Cracks in the wall, a spider web of earth movement, of foundations leaning the house towards collapse. This shared house, full of the ghosts of landlords who refused to look after their property. If it weren't for the cheap rent they'd move. Eleanor closed the bathroom door behind her, collected her backpack and camera, and when she came down the stairs Susan was in the kitchen heating baked beans, making toast.

'Toilet's blocked again.'

'I know.'

'We should let Ruth discover it this time. She'll freak out.'

They laughed and toast popped and Eleanor took a slice, buttered it. 'Hey,' Susan said and Eleanor took a bite, crunched it in front of her face.

Coffee boiled on the stovetop. 'Are you coming to the show tonight?' Susan asked.

'Of course we are! I'm coming straight from work.'

'Thank God. Last night was just awful. Some guy in the audience started throwing ripped pieces of paper and matchsticks onto the stage and told us to burn in hell.'

'Jesus. I hope someone kicked him out.'

Susan turned off the flame under the beans. 'It may come as a shock to you, but apparently some people don't appreciate art.'

Eleanor put her arm around her friend's shoulders. 'Well, I do, and I will be there, and I'll give anyone who tries to disrupt you a punch in the face.'

'Ha! You couldn't hurt anyone if you tried.'

'Maybe tonight's the night!' Eleanor kissed Susan's cheek, grabbed her backpack. 'I'm off. Tell Ruth I hope she enjoys dealing with our shit today.'

She headed out the rotted-wood back door of their faded canary-yellow house and out the back gate. Light fog levitated like ghosts above the bluestone laneway and she passed an abandoned double mattress, its metal springs coiled out through orange-brown sweat-stained coverings, passed a lost espadrille, a beer bottle, a headless Barbie. A collection of forgotten lives.

Out on the nature strip: a decomposing myna bird. Always remember the dead, Eleanor, and she crouched beside the bird, aimed the camera, took a shot. The myna bones, bleached and feathered. She stretched the bird, careful not to break its wing span, marvelled at the beauty of something grown from egg to death. She tilted its semi-bald head so she could look properly into the casket of skull to take a better shot, took note of how the weather had formed patterns of decomposition to expose the space where heart and lung once sat. In the feast of nature the heart is the first to go. Eat that nectar, the sweet centre of the body.

Eleanor hung the camera around her neck, stood, brushed crumbled leaves and footpath debris from her pants. 'Good grief. Why did you do that?' A voice behind her.

Eleanor turned to see a woman in her sixties, a dark green velvet pillbox hat, white gloves, rouged cheeks, holding her handbag tight to her chest as she peered down at the bird. Her face pinched into peaks of disgust. The woman looked from Eleanor to the bird, attempting to work out what was happening here, whether Eleanor was responsible for this bird's grounding.

'I normally don't do this.' Yes, you do. Even in Melbourne, away from her mother, she was downplaying her expertise, her passions even.

'It's rather ghastly, isn't it?' The woman stared at the bird and a bike rider sweltered past in a three-piece suit.

'I just took the photo on a whim.'

The woman tsked. 'Why are young people so obsessed with death?'

That's not what this is. The judgement of a stranger made her want to run. 'It's not like I killed it. I just found it!'

'But it's horribly morbid.'

'Well, I guess we all have our hobbies.' Eleanor laughed, hoped her attempt at humour would bring a smile to the woman's face.

It didn't. The woman huffed off and Eleanor walked on towards the cemetery, to the tree she climbed every day before class, before work. It was next to the boundary fence, next to the row of buried nuns who awaited their future order of sisters.

Eleanor climbed the tree; the low-hanging branches made it easier to heave herself up. She sat on a limb, dangled her feet like she was still a girl, imagined her body being pulled towards the ground under the pavement, being stretched as far as she would go. A tram bell dinged and she lifted the camera to her face, pointed it at the ground, waited for the daily bird parade. All the quiet: came a pigeon, came a sparrow, came a crow fattening feathers, came a magpie hulking for fights. She took photos of the birds, set camera angles to capture only the tops of heads, of bodies, a bird's-eye view of birds. She held her breath as she watched them eat, listened to all the ways a beak can sound against concrete, the small tapping of the world, of knocking to open up and be let in to the places that are closed. All things want to be let in. Eleanor had been taking photos since she started uni: always this tree, always this angle. If you repeat an action enough will you get a different result? If she were being honest, she simply liked being above the ground, liked the idea she could see slightly further than she could an hour before.

A crow walked under her feet, cawed, lifted a leg. The sound of the shutter made the crow look up and they made eye contact.

A smile spread across Eleanor's face and she took another shot, focused on crow beak, the way dirt bullied the tip of it, as if trying to silence its song.

Watching over birds was the life she wanted. To be in that tree above flight: the only time her circular thoughts ceased.

Eleanor put the camera away, stared out over terrace roofs, a rolling sea of thick soot and leaf-jammed gutters, of people too busy to worry about what the neighbours thought of the appearance of their homes. She was far from Wintonvale. Now came the strides of office workers, of construction site workers, bodies with restless thoughts: early-morning people beginning their day. She checked her watch; thirty minutes until her first class, hours before her shift at work started. She climbed down the tree, tried not to frighten the crow below.

———

Four hours into her shift at the pizza restaurant, her toes were numb. Eleanor leaned against a table with an uneven leg, tipped it to steady by wedging folded paper serviettes underneath, stretched out her feet, which cramped in her too-tight black buckled shoes. The last couple seated in her section held hands, rubbed their cheeks together; all the ways to kiss a face without kissing lips. Eleanor rolled her eyes, rolled her ankles, rolled her shoulders to ease the stiffness from her joints. She could smell the dried yeast and cooked ham on her work shirt, could smell the sweat that came with this job, the way standing for hours curdled moisture in her shoes, a dampness that never dried, not even overnight.

Eleanor approached the couple's table. 'How's everything? Would you like any dessert?'

The woman said, 'Ooh, I fancy something chocolatey.'

The man shook his head. 'We've had enough,' he told Eleanor. 'We'll have the bill.'

Eleanor turned to the woman. 'Are you sure I can't get you anything? I could wrap something up for you to take away.' The woman went to answer, stopped herself. Go on, say what you want. The woman shook her head, her mouth downcast from the loss of delight. 'I'd better not. We'll just get the bill.'

'I'll be right back.' Eleanor left them. She heard footsteps up the stairs leading up to the restaurant, saw Ruth appear, hands on hips.

'So, there's the traitor,' Ruth said. She stuck her finger up at Eleanor, mouthed, 'Fuck you,' and they laughed.

'Have fun with the toilet?'

'I waited all day for that plumber only for him to tell me he has to come back again tomorrow. It looks like a pipe is in serious need of repair. If we have to shower in our own filth I'm going to scream.'

Eleanor chuckled. 'At least you did your housemate duty.'

Ruth looked around. 'Are you nearly done? I wanna get a drink before the show.'

'I just have to look after this happy couple and then I'm done.'

Ruth took a seat at a cleaned table, drummed her fingers on the laminate, raised her eyebrows. 'Ugh, that guy is in my social science class. He's an absolute pig.'

'Can you please not say that so loud in my workplace? I have to go over there.'

She held her hands up in mock protest. 'Well, I'm merely stating facts.'

Eleanor turned her back to Ruth, took the bill to the table. Behind her, she heard Ruth oink.

———

They walked arm in arm to the small theatre, the way they'd walked together since they were young.

'Shit, I almost forgot – Kitty called.'

Eleanor gritted her teeth. Her mother had called almost every day since she moved to the city. 'What did she say?'

'Nothing much. She sounded a bit down. I think she was hoping you'd be home to cheer her up.'

At nineteen, it was still Eleanor's job to make her mother feel better. 'Nothing will do that.'

They made their way across the north courtyard and she noticed a tall young man walking towards the theatre. John. She elbowed Ruth. 'Look who it is.'

Ruth had slept with John a few weeks before, was keen for more until Eleanor had told her that he was a conservative philosophy student she'd met at a tree-planting session on campus.

'So?' Ruth said.

'So he stands for everything we hate.'

'Yeah, but he was really good in bed.'

This version of Ruth. Eleanor hated that it angered her.

'You're not going to do it again, are you?'

'Maybe.'

John opened the door to the theatre, turned to see if anyone was behind him, and when he saw Eleanor and Ruth he kept the door open with his shoulder. He wore a fob watch tucked into a vest pocket. Eleanor laughed. 'What a wanker.'

'Stop it. Not now.'

He waved to Ruth and she smiled politely. 'John! What are you doing here?'

'I fancied some entertainment.'

Eleanor couldn't stand it. Ruth let go of Eleanor, entered the foyer with John, and in that moment her friend reminded her of Kitty, the way she could change to suit her weather. Eleanor wasn't proud of herself but she wanted to punish Ruth for forgetting who she was, for wearing masks. She wondered how much of Wintonvale had followed her here.

Ruth having disappeared with John, Eleanor went to the small makeshift bar, ordered a glass of house white.

Around her, people wore pretence and black, laughed and slapped each other's shoulders. The way they hugged, like coaxing the night from each other, had all the intimacy of shadows. She wanted to touch them all, to be that close to a stranger, beg them to show her what they were thinking and feeling. I just want to know that we're not alone in this world, she thought. But the urge left and as she sipped wine she was joined by her classmate Andrea. They talked about what would come next.

'My dream is to research overseas,' Eleanor said. 'There aren't enough opportunities in Australia.'

'That's what we all want,' Andrea said. 'My parents baulk at the idea that I'd leave them, though. They still see me as a child.'

Eleanor nodded, sighed. 'My mother would see it as a slight against her.'

'Who knows? Maybe when we're fifty we'll feel free to actually live our lives without feeling guilty.'

The foyer lights flickered and an usher appeared at the theatre door, small torch in hand. 'Show starts in two minutes.'

'I hope this play is as terrible as I've heard it is.' Andrea swilled the rest of her wine, handed her tumbler to the bar staff.

'Actually, one of my best friends is in this play.'

'Oh, shit. I'm sorry.'

'Don't be. Let's just hope tonight is a better performance.'

Ruth walked over, hooked her arm through Eleanor's. 'Ready to have a good laugh?'

'Ruth!'

'What? Tell me a quasi-musical about Anne Boleyn's time in the Tower of London isn't funny.'

'That's not what this is about, is it?' Andrea was confused.

'It may as well be.'

Eleanor elbowed Ruth in the ribs. 'You're a total shit sometimes.'

They laughed as they filed into the theatre, took their seats.

The house lights faded and the stage glowed under a red spot-light. The seats were so close together Eleanor could feel the breath of strangers on the back of her neck.

Susan walked onto the stage, black cape covering her black leotard, called out, 'Come forth, you women of death!' and a lone violin played out from behind the curtain. Eleanor caught Ruth's eye, smiled, remembering when they were all in the school play together, aged thirteen, how they thrashed feathers across the stage. And then how she looked out into the audience and saw her parents. The shock of seeing them. Remembered how afterwards Ruth and Susan had hugged Eleanor, told her, 'You were *so* great,' how safe they made her feel.

Eleanor put her hand on Ruth's leg, whispered, 'It's so bad.'

'It really is.'

She looked at their friend on stage, felt the love they had for her. All three of them in their new lives. The play continued and she hoped none of this would ever end.

———

The phone rang the next morning, ritualistic. She looked at her watch, eleven o'clock, knew who it would be. She imagined Kitty's fingers in the loops of the telephone cord, straight back, raised chin. All those years of seeing her mother take calls, that mother business.

Eleanor held the receiver tightly in her hand. 'Hello?'

'Finally it's you, not one of the girls. I have been feeling terrible lately, Eleanor. Your father isn't well and you know what stress that puts me under. Did I tell you I've lost three pounds this past week because of it?'

No need for politeness. Kitty was past the stage of pretending phone calls were to make conversation. They didn't even need to have anything in common, just as long as Eleanor remained a presence in Kitty's life.

Eleanor sighed, placed the receiver on her shoulder and her mother's voice sang the song of neighbourhood gossip. 'Anyway, you know Shirley told me that Maureen down the street had a gentleman caller. Not even a year has passed since Fred died . . .' *Squark squark squark.*

'Oh, ah-huh, ah-huh, oh, right.' Eleanor well trained.

Mother's bird voice. Some families would cage a thing like you, Eleanor wants to say. She wants to say a lot of things. 'Mum, did you ever think—'

'Now the reason I've called is to ask you to consider moving home for a while to help me with George.' Her mother was serious for once.

'Mum, I've got uni and work and—'

'I ask for so little from you.'

'How can I possibly do it?' The idea of going home. Her stomach churned. I studied so hard to be able to leave.

'You can use our car.'

'I'd be travelling an hour and a half each way almost every day.'

'Eleanor, please.' The rise in Kitty's voice, the edge of tears. 'I'm begging you. It'll only be for a little while.'

What was a few weeks? The obedience of her heart. She heard Ruth in the bathroom shout out, 'God! Not again!' And Eleanor heard herself tell her mother, 'I'll be there in a few days.'

Kitty

1947

MID-MORNING AND GEORGE had gone to his shed to wind back time. In the lounge room Kitty and Badger danced pirouettes to 'I Only Have Eyes For You', danced until Kitty was dizzy, and she told him, 'Mummy has to sit for a minute.'

Badger threw his arms around her and yelled into her stomach, 'Why are you making our mummy sick?'

Kitty laughed. 'It's not the baby's fault. I'm just not good with spinning.'

Badger smiled up at her. 'How many years till it's out?'

'Three more months, silly goose.'

'Will it look like me?'

'Maybe.'

'What if it looks like a puppy?'

'Well, you'll have to throw the pup-bub sticks and teach them how to fetch.'

Badger guffawed and Kitty tried to catch her breath, tried to catch the reality of life changing in ways she hadn't anticipated. But another child would help to balance everything out. The momentary euphoria made it easier to stay with George.

After the dizziness passed, Kitty and Badger left the house for the park. Her son held her hand as they walked down the driveway, matched each other's steps, led each other towards good times. Past plaster lion-mounted gates, along streets lined with white roses and purple-bulbed agapanthus, Kitty waited for the chorus of mothers to stream out of fresh-painted houses and admire her treasured son. And they did.

'Isn't he getting to be so big?' A pinched cheek.

Badger shook it off, frowned.

'Oh, Kitty, you must be so proud of him. Doesn't he look just like George?'

In a certain light.

'Where are you off to today, big boy?'

'I'm going to the park with my mummy.'

And they were in awe. 'Oh, Kitty. Isn't he just precious?!'

He was. Oh, he was.

She liked that they spoke about him like this, revelled in her ability to grow such a wonderful child right under their noses. This was all her doing, all her triumph, producing gold under extreme circumstances. Nobody can mother like I can.

'Are you excited about being a big brother?'

Badger nodded. 'I'm going to teach it how to climb trees and jump puddles and hide really well and make mud cakes and fly really high!'

Every house they walked past, a hand waved from a window and Kitty was delighted at how much awe could be derived from Badger, rugged up in scarf and wool, a beanie on his head. She was weightless.

The park was empty when they arrived. 'All of this is yours, Badger.' Claim the world for your own.

'Yahooo!' He broke from her, ran to the swings, landed on the flat edge with his stomach, made himself fly. Badger pushed, pushed, pushed, went higher, shouted like he was the only one alive. And Kitty thought: maybe he is. Maybe everything has been blown up and we are the only ones to have survived. That wouldn't be so bad. For his to be the last face I saw.

She went over to the swing, bent down and steadied herself on the ground, tried not to think of the dirt on her skirt. 'Badger, look at me,' and he did and his face turned pink, too much smile and puff, and she felt like she would explode.

'Catch me! Catch me!' Badger threw a hand out in front of her, danced fingers.

'You'll fall if I do. How about you slow down and I'll catch you then?'

Badger limped to a stop, heavy breath. 'Being a plane is hard work, Mummy.' He got off the swing, ran to her, and there was snot on her cheek when he hugged her. The wet and cold of him.

She kissed him. I could swallow you all up. And there they were, eye to eye, trying to see inside each other.

Time passed, the playground filled. Badger on the slide, the flying fox, seesaw and eventually back to the swings, cheeks red from too much running, too much winter sun, too much, too much. Kitty concentrated on his brown eyes as she pushed him back, forth, back, forth.

'Higher! Higher!'

Kitty pushed into the entirety of him and her stomach muscles clenched, arms heavied; all that effort to launch a child into flight. Badger was small chuckles, was wibble cheeks, was giggling, was thunder. He threw his head back, looked to the sky, made eye contact with the plane flying overhead.

Other children screamed and threw balls to each other, played knuckles, marbles. One put a marble in her mouth, spat it out when her mother rushed over with, 'What have I told you about choking?' The girl laughed, happy knowing she could bend her mother like a doll.

Kick went Badger's legs, hands tight around the swing's chain, eyes still to sky, as if he didn't feel Kitty's hands push into his back, didn't hear her loud exhale. But this. Happiness.

Badger swung and then Badger spoke: I'm bigger than the trees, I'm bigger than air, I'm bigger than that man, I'm bigger than that cloud, I'm bigger than the roofs of the shops, bigger than the car, bigger than numbers, bigger than the sky. Push me higher, Mummy. Higher! I'm going to shoot myself all the way all the way up to the moon very soon. I'm going to live up there and I'm going to see all of you. Would you like that, Mummy? I know! I could grow the biggest anyone has ever been and I could even take other people with me to the moon! Mummy, has anyone been to the moon? Do people live there already? How far is it? Is it next-week far away?

Little Badger. He stared into that open air and Kitty didn't answer her son, let him talk himself into a dream. Her hands full of him, that compartmentalised anatomy of a child: back, arms, neck, jumper, beanie.

———

Before children stir in beds, before adults question where life has taken them, Kitty left Charlie's house through the side gate and door, hoped that midnight walkers didn't find her on her way home. Shoes in hand, careful not to make the gravel sound, her dress rubbing against bare nipples. Her dress hurt, was too tight across her stomach, was too much. Everything is too much. I should be home. And she walked the street back towards her marriage and the air was quiet and the baby kicked. Things will change soon. And the air was quiet and somewhere a night bird sounded out, 'Mummy, Mummy,' and air went still.

Lights lit neighbourhood homes and Kitty passed through her front gate, startled that nobody slept in complete darkness anymore. Who are they staying up for?

Inside the house: no sound of George or Badger turning in sleep, and she placed her shoes by the front door, went to the bookcase, reached for Eleanor Dark's *The Little Company*, this novel that had taken her too long to read, placed it face down on the sofa and propped a cushion against the arm of the lounge chair. These ways to make a space appear used, to cover her tracks.

Her dress had become even tighter sitting in the house. She unzipped it, folded it down to her stomach, noticed her nipples held on to the memory of Charlie's quick tongue flick; the size he'd made her. Everything bigger. Was this the size of guilt? She refused to feel it.

She checked the clock on the sideboard – 2 am – then took the nightgown she'd tucked behind the sofa and slipped it on, carried the dress to the laundry and continued down the hall, past Badger's room and into the bed next to a sleeping George. Her body cold, she slipped an arm through his, kissed him between shoulder blades. This is something nice, she thought. Something nice for George.

Then a whisper. 'You're back.' He said it as if in a dream.

'I couldn't sleep.'

'I know.' Like he could read her mind. What did he know exactly? Surely he couldn't know about Charlie? How could he? George never seemed to notice anything she did.

And so she said, 'I got so cold reading out there.' Hoped he would accept her version of the night.

Body against body. What can another tell you about your own? She rested against him, hoped he would feel the leftovers of her lover. Two men in the bed and the little one said. I want him to feel someone else's hand on me, all the ways I've been touched and wanted. George's breath quickened and for a moment Kitty thought he would say, 'I know. And I want you gone.' But all that came was his heavy breath.

When you want to hurt a person you love, what sound should you make? She wanted to say, 'Things would've been easier if you had never come back, George.' But then there would be no Badger, there would be no waiting for the next person to appear. So she said nothing and the night circled them. She thought of Badger in his bed, curled into himself, a thumb pressed against the back of his teeth, as he was when he first arrived, like his sibling would eventually be. Them together. Soon life would be better. And maybe then I will be truly whole.

She pressed harder into her husband, kissed across shoulder blades again. This act to prevent him from ever knowing. George flinched and the baby's movement gave her reflux and she swallowed acid.

'George? What's wrong?'

He rolled over, let his desire for her knead into her skin, thumbs and index fingers gently pinched across acres of her body. The sensation of him made her yelp. He kissed her lips then neck, collarbone then shoulder, climbed between her legs to kiss her stomach, her hips.

'Tell me about the book you're reading.' He said it so softly she wasn't sure who he was asking. He licked her wrists and forearm, tongue marking the territory back towards her throat.

'I don't remember.' I can't even remember my name right now.

Kitty scratched at his back, liked the idea of him under her nails. If only it was always like this. The gold days I'd have.

George seemed to be everywhere in the dark and then she felt his mouth over her breast, his tongue flick over nipple, and milk spilled and he licked her all up, moaned into her, and the baby kicked and Kitty felt alive.

———

Those gut-instinct times. Shadows crept across the hallway and Kitty went to the bathroom, the third time in a few short hours, tried to remind herself that the body prepares you for the routine of sleepless nights when the baby comes. Always urinating. She sat on the toilet, ankles cold, but nothing came. She wiped, took note of the colour of herself on the toilet paper, the things that come from you when you're preparing life, and she detoured to Badger's room to check on him. She slowly opened the door. The night-light was on, the bed empty. 'Badger.' Quiet as she goes. Kitty looked under the bed, saw his stuffed toy dog but did not see her boy. To the cupboards and he wasn't there. Kitty stretched her aching back and the baby kicked. 'Badger?' Louder then. She went back into the house, flicked light switches, and from one room to the next called, 'Badger! Badger, where are you? Alfred, answer me!' Kitty searched room then room, waited for a giggle, a click of tongue, of anything, but nothing came and she dry-retched. Badger is still in the house. He has to be. He's always so good at hiding. But the body knows and she dry-retched again and the cold crushed against her skin and she ran into the backyard, called her son's name until she didn't recognise her own voice. George at the back door, no prosthetic. She was shocked at how small he looked, his body now just a thin membrane. 'Kitty, what's wrong?'

'I can't find Badger. He's not in his room.'

'He's hiding. We'll find him.' He tried to sound warm but it infuriated her.

'You're not listening to me! He's not anywhere.' She rushed the stairs back into the house and called for Badger again. When you don't hear your favourite music you wonder if you've lost your hearing. She screamed her son's name out the front door, thought she heard him laugh from the top of a tree and she looked up, saw birds instead. How was it possible for a child to be swallowed by the night? Her breasts ached and she thought about the way night had swallowed her, thought about her walk home. The sound of a mummy call. Kitty heaved onto the front verandah and screamed. 'George!'

When he stood by her side, when he put his hand in the middle of her back, she said, 'I think I heard him. Something terrible has happened.'

'When did you hear him?'

To say would be to give herself away. But she wanted her son. 'Last night I went walking.' She didn't want to make eye contact with her husband.

'And then?'

She screamed, 'I don't know! But I heard a voice out there somewhere.'

Kitty heard something inside George rattle and he said, 'Oh, Jesus,' and he said, 'The cubby,' and he ran into the street calling for their son. He ran and he ran.

———

She didn't remember the neighbours coming for her, didn't remember being taken inside the house, being given a blanket. What she remembered was the siren wail of her husband coming from the street, the death screams of the neighbourhood. When she looked towards the door she saw George carrying Badger in his arms, his body limp in days-old pyjamas. She noticed Badger was wearing only one slipper. 'Where's the other one?' The way she fell out of herself. She stood and rushed to her husband and she touched their child; the density of cold skin carries truth.

Someone said, 'Fucking Christ.' Someone said, 'Let's go now.'

Kitty looked at George. This man who wasn't wearing his face; how far she could see inside him now. Kitty stared at Badger, one eye open, his small hand clutching his blankie. 'What?' It's all she could think to say.

'He was hiding in the old fridge.'

George cradled their boy. George kissed their boy. Then George placed him on the lounge room floor. Badger; like sleep.

'Kitty . . .'

'That fucking fridge. I told you . . .'

Why finish a sentence when speaking doesn't make sense? Kitty's knees gave way and she crawled to her son, took his hand and ran it over her face. She screamed. George threw himself beside her. 'I don't know what to do, Kitty.'

No one tells you how small death is. Their son in the middle of the room. Their son who had kept them together. No one tells you how to parent a dead child. Kitty tucked the blanket she'd had around her shoulders over Badger's body to make him warm, began mouth-to-mouth-resuscitation, and the house was filled with the sound of a mother breathing into her son. His little body unresponsive. George pulled Kitty off Badger and she slapped him across the cheek before sinking into his body. 'I don't want to move him.'

He nodded. 'So we won't.'

George and Kitty lay on the floor next to Badger, draped arms across their child, across each other, and they stared into one another and the baby kicked inside. This baby should die in return for Badger. All these things she thought. She shook her head and hummed 'I Only Have Eyes For You' into her son's ear and it was like they were dancing together. She held on to Badger and George said, 'Kitty, we need to get up.'

She wanted him dead too. 'Don't tell me what to do.' Hummed into her son and so they stayed like that: no speaking, no moving, only eye contact. Kitty felt nothing.

When the night finally came George said, 'I love you.'

'I love you.' She was shocked at how easily she could say it.

But she knew, they knew. This was the end. No amount of love can save a marriage that no longer exists. They fell asleep with their children between them.

———

On the morning Badger was taken to the hospital for his autopsy Kitty bathed her son. She tried to lift his body from the floor but her arms weren't strong enough, didn't know how to cradle the dead, and she asked George to help her carry him into the bathroom and gently lower him into the tub. When George was gone she nursed Badger's head in the crook of her elbow so that it wouldn't slip under the water. She created suds on a washcloth, barely scrubbed it over his skin, over his long fingers, over thighs, over the thin layer of hair that was beginning to cover his little legs, over his freckled nose, over his abdomen that still had the bruise from the day he fell from his bicycle and landed on the bitumen in a belly flop, over his feet, his toes, the last two that had begun to curl over into an angle because of his flat feet. Over, over, over.

The water was still: there was no splashing, no pushing off from the bottom of the bath to make a tidal wave, no bath toys diving in and out, no singing out of tune, no demanding that she make the bath water warmer.

She took his weight, this thing she was used to doing, and doesn't remember him being this heavy on her hip. This is the weight of death, Kitty. She dripped water onto his body, worried for a moment it might be too cold. She turned the hot water tap on, warmed the bath, and as she did she thought she saw something in Badger's eye, wiped her finger over his eyelash, and his eye opened, as it always did when she'd sneak into his room at night to watch him sleep.

'Mummy,' he'd say. 'I see you.'

Then she heard it in the bathroom: *Mummy, I see you.* And she wiped her finger over his eyelash again, leaned in and said, 'I see you.'

After she finished washing him, Kitty called out to George to help her lift him out of the bath and lay him on the towels she'd spread over the floor.

'You can leave now.'

George did as he was told, closed the bathroom door behind him.

The two of them together. She wrapped a towel over the top of Badger's body and patted him dry, kept her eyes on him in order to store him forever in her memory. There on his face: something beyond the quiet of sleep. She leaned over the top of her boy and kissed his lips, imagined him complaining about sloppy-kiss-kisses.

Kitty asked him, 'How am I meant to go on without you?' The two of them together. She held his hand and told him, 'I know you must be scared. But I'm here. Mummy's here.'

She sat on the pastel green-and-pink-tiled floor and cradled him, held his hand tighter, didn't want to let it go. The child inside her somersaulted and she heard herself say, 'I want you to meet your sibling.' I am meant to be a mother of two.

She can't imagine not parenting him, not saying his name every day. No, 'Badger clean your room.' No,

'Badger is playing with Robert across the road.'

'Badger, would you like a glass of milk?'

'Badger, where are you hiding this time?'

'I love you, Badger.'

'I'll bring Badger along. He'd love a visit.'

A tongue gets used to certain formations. She didn't want to lose hers. Kitty looked at her son, knew he had to stay.

When they finally took Badger to his room to dress him Kitty told George that she wanted their son cremated. 'I don't want all that dirt on him.'

George nodded, kept nodding. 'Yes, alright.' Then he said, 'We could take him to the blue mountain. He loved it up there.'

'No,' Kitty yelled then quietened. 'I want him here. Why do you want to get rid of him so quickly? He should stay with us. He's a little boy.'

'Kitty . . .'

'No. It's not time. I will tell you when it is time.'

George, chastened, nodded and nodded, and they looked at Badger resting on his bed and they stayed like that until they heard the knock on the front door that would take him away.

———

Kitty and George went to their bedroom and lay on the bed. They rolled onto sides, looked into each other. What was to be said? George opened his mouth but Kitty shook her head, didn't want to hear his voice. They held hands, did not move, did not speak, waited for darkness to arrive. In the morning they were still holding hands. She waited to hear Badger's movements. Then she remembered. Everything inside her felt as if it were falling. She unhooked her hand from George, pushed him away, rolled over and went back to sleep.

———

There was Wintonvale, early morning: covered in paint, fences in new whites, front doors dressed in new-season colours, bottle green, baby blue, lavender. Stacked paint cans under verandahs, ladders leaning against sides of houses, raked leaves. At the corner of Joynt Street insects buzzed in a green bush, made it look thick and waxed, the plant's white and yellow flowers heavy with an animal-milk stench. Delivered newspapers from earlier in the morning were wet across lawns. There was the morning and there, in houses, bodies were restless, lay in lover's arms, had nightmares, woke to the realisation they were broken. There was Kitty and there was the day she'd decided that she could no longer have her son in the house being like his father: nothing.

Kitty had been in bed for weeks, body sore and overtired, Badger's urn permanently arm's length from her bed. She couldn't reconcile Badger in his new form, couldn't reconcile how her heart still managed to keep him alive, had convinced her that she heard him playing in his room at night, hiding under his bed, growing weeks and months older. He was still waiting to be a big brother. All these promises she had made him. And now.

The baby kicked as it turned, made Kitty shock-gasp, and she was surprised that she remained pregnant, that apparently she was still expected to deliver this new child into the world.

I've forgotten how. But, Kitty, your body hasn't, and the baby surged in the valley underneath her lungs, the way Badger had, and for a moment she couldn't breathe, the way it had been ever since he . . . She stopped the thought. *I need to remind myself how to mother a baby. I need my mother. I need.*

She had needed her mother weeks before, too. When he had died, when friends and the parade of neighbours had come to their house for condolences, Kitty found herself in conversations she knew nobody wanted to have. The way they wouldn't meet her eye, the way they spoke to her as she stood beyond herself in the corner of the room.

'How are you going, Kitty?'

'How are you going in the house, Kitty?'

'Are you hungry, Kitty?'

'Is there anything I can do for you, Kitty? Anything at all?'

Sounding her name as if trying to summon her back to life. *I don't want to hear myself again.*

These were questions to stop silence moving in. Sympathy is a home-cooked meal and the smell of it permeated the house; the nausea of it. 'Excuse me,' Kitty said. Her voice was not her own. 'I need to open the windows.'

'Oh, yes, fresh air is good. Good idea.' Everything always ended in *good* because it meant there would be no more discussion.

Later, when there were only a few people left behind, Joan and Maudie stacked the dishes, began to remove evidence that a group of people had gathered for a dead child. Kitty helped them clean, afraid that if she stopped and sat down she would never get up again, would never want to do anything again, would want to remove her pregnant stomach from her body.

'You look so tired, Kitty. Why don't you rest.'

She wanted to say, Ask me what it feels like to wash your child's cold body that was once so warm. She wanted to say, Ask me what it feels like to open the door to your faceless husband holding your boy's lifeless body, the way his eyes had already turned milky and dim. She wanted to say, Ask me, ask me, ask me, but instead she said, 'No. I want to do this. I need to stay in a routine.'

One of Badger's friends, Ben-Bob, tugged her skirt, slipped his hand in hers. She noticed the smudge of blue watercolour stain on his fingers, that business of colouring to stay out of adult eyesight. He looked at her, her stomach, and Kitty said, 'Where's your mother?'

He squeezed her hand. 'I hope your baby doesn't die.'

The rise inside her body; that flooding. She'd forgotten others could see it. They were expecting that when it emerged from her it would bring a smile to her face, turn her attention away from grief. She wanted to slap the child. She wanted to hold him.

Those nearby heard and his mother rushed over, placed a hand over Ben-Bob's mouth. 'Oh my goodness. I am so very sorry, Kitty.' Turned to the boy. 'We do not say things like that.'

She was right. We do not say things like that. Kitty wanted him to say something else, to tell her things that she didn't know as an adult, didn't want to know as an adult. All the things they didn't say. She searched for George, found him sitting at the table talking quietly to friends he'd made at the hospital. One of them patted George on the back and he nodded his head and laughed. Kitty seethed. The sound of George laughing when it should be Badger. The sound of George in sympathy. What would he know about loss?

We do not say things like that.

Ben-Bob was taken away and his hand slid out from Kitty's, left her cold, and another boy was gone from her sight.

She returned to her tasks, tried to return glass and plates and tea towels to rightful places, but she couldn't remember where they belonged and it was like she'd never lived in the house before. I need my mother.

———

She was in bed. I need to remember how to mother. She thought of her own. A cry for mother is deeper in adulthood and Kitty bellowed for hers. Calling out for the voice that is as old as you, for the sound that cradled you to sleep. I want my mother. I want her to tell me that these feelings aren't real. In the bedroom dark, body stiff, she pushed herself up onto her elbows and from the other end of the house she heard George drag furniture across the floor, along the places that Badger had pulled toy cars through kitchen routes. Her head trumpeted. What the hell was he doing? Why was he rearranging furniture? Up she went again, this time to sitting, and she leaned forwards, the wide of her stomach pulling towards the floor. Furniture dragged and she noticed the Bible left by Diane on the bedside table, said to the book, 'If I pray to you and you don't get George out of this house you can go to hell.'

Kitty stood. Blood rushed to her head, everything heavy in her body. The unbelievable urge to urinate carried her to the bedroom door and when she opened it, the dragging stopped and George called out, 'Kitty?'

'Why are you here?' She would not placate, would not be nice. My child is in a wooden urn.

'Kitty?'

'*Kitty, Kitty, Kitty.*' Mimicry filled the house. Kitty, don't be like this. But she couldn't stop herself, yelled, 'I'm going to call my mother. I need privacy. Do you think you could actually give me that?'

George and his footsteps; stopped. 'What's happening, Kitty?' The rise in his voice made her nauseous.

I can't hold on to anything, she thought. Her body a weight she couldn't lift, and she said, 'Get out! Get out! Get out!' She hadn't seen him in days, wasn't sure when he'd last slept beside her. Maybe she hadn't let him. She couldn't bear for anyone else to be in the house with her. She heard George take the car keys, walk outside, start the car, drive away.

The baby switched sides, all the pressure, and still in the hallway Kitty began to urinate. She let it come out, her stale warmth, wasn't sure she knew how to stop it. All she wanted was her mother.

Kitty went to the phone, called home, summoned her mother's voice into the receiver. She was looking for that specific feeling she had just before childhood ended, the way her mother's hands were able to knot around the small of her back, tether Kitty to her body. Mother; this island. There would be no sinking, no bottom of the ocean. Only sunshine to warm the blood. The phone rang until it ran out and Kitty hung up the receiver. She screamed, 'Answer me,' kicked her bare feet into the wall, and then she picked up the receiver again, dialled, kept dialling: the compulsion to hear her mother's sounds, the predictability of, 'There now, dear. There now, dear. There now, dear. There now, dear. There now, dear. There now, dear. There now, dear. There now, dear. There now, dear. There now, dear.'

But there was no one home to take her call. The phone whispered back a lost signal and she responded with, 'Mummy?' It was only after she heard banging on the front door, heard a neighbour shout her name and inform her they had made another sausage casserole, that she remembered her mother had died years before.

Eleanor

Present

ELEANOR DRIVES THROUGH rain past small blanched-green shrubs, small shelters for whatever seeks shade under rock. She and George used to stop along roads like this on their way to the mountain, lift shrubs, see what lived underneath. 'You wouldn't believe what you can bring out of hiding,' she tells Amy over her shoulder, 'if you're patient.' Black backs of ant and insect, scorpion claw, meat scraps, fur and feather. The days and weeks of animal dedication to build a home, all the constant micro actions needed to keep living. George would point and say, 'Just because you can't see something doesn't mean it's not happening,' and there they'd be, sometimes on hands and knees, eyes intent on rock as on a microscope, and she'd catch her father smile and so she would too.

Like a good gardener, Eleanor left something of herself and her father, something of their smiles, planted under those rocks for the next explorer to find, something to discover of their little built colony.

Eleanor, eye to rear-view mirror, intent as on a microscope. 'Amy, have I told you repetition in nature happens a lot more than you would think?'

She settles back to concentrating on the road. The stretch ahead of them: broken white lines, distant hills, discarded beer bottle, rotten banana peel, dirty white sneaker, chimney smoke, green paddock, and in the middle of the road a dead-bloated grey kangaroo, all open, red-stained fur. She slows to swerve, thinks of the sound death would've made, that puh-chunk of force into warm softness, and she says, 'Shit, there might be a joey. We need to check.'

Eleanor stops the car, leaves it running, opens the driver door and heads to the roo, looks for the sag of her young. Smashed teeth, curled paws, broken leg, exploded stomach, intestines severed by a car tyre: the devastation of a body torn apart. There is no possibility that a joey would survive this particular death of its mother. Eleanor kneels on bitumen, leans into the roo. And it's there: the smell of it, the pulp of fat maggots. Death occurred at least a day ago. Eleanor puts her hand across her nose, her ears fill with car hum. A crow flies above. How many hours since she'd been standing over Leon as he lay in their bed, waiting to see if he'd wake?

Eleanor leans into the roo. And she is relieved there is no joey within the butchered skin.

———

Rain comes. Eleanor overtakes the slow chug of a caravan convoy, witnesses siblings committing acts of aggression against each other on back seats: arm punch, nose pinch, ear pull. Wide paddocks lined with electricity poles; strange ghost gums. A single red leather boot heel side to ditch and, next to that, a bored-looking police officer highway patrol car, lights flashing as threat. Further down the road a woman is standing by the open hood of her broken-down car. I can't stop but I can't leave her stranded in the wet.

Eleanor pulls over, walks to the woman, notices her child sitting in the front seat playing driver.

The woman turns to Eleanor, eyes red and puffy, and says, 'This bloody car!'

'Have you been out here long?' Eleanor hears the little girl mutter *zoom-zoom, zoom-zoom*, smiles. The first smile since last night.

'About an hour? I knew this would happen.'

'I could take a look for you?' Eleanor says this knowing she can't fix it. This instinct to offer help when nothing practical can come of it. So she offers something she can provide. 'If you hop in and turn over the engine I can see whether you need a jump start or not.'

The woman brightens. 'Are you sure?'

Eleanor nods.

The woman goes to her child. 'Come on, sweetheart. This nice lady is going to help us.'

The child quick-flicks her fingernails across her teeth; castanets. The sing-sing ebb and flow of this girl reminds Eleanor of herself at the same age, how her parents begged her to be quiet for at least two minutes; the impossible task of disengaging from your thoughts. She imagines Amy at this age.

Rain thickens and Eleanor stands by the car, a spanner from the boot of the Belmont in her hand. The woman turns the car key, makes the engine click like a cicada until it gives out. George had shown her what to do in these situations, how to operate machines like bodies. Eleanor hits the spanner against starter motor, against battery brackets, gently tugs at visible hoses to see what gives. She says, 'Try now,' and the woman turns the key, brings cicadas again. Nothing.

'Come inside the car,' the woman says. 'This rain is terrible.'

Eleanor sits in the passenger seat of her car. The little girl is in the back seat now.

After introductions, Jean, Maggie and Eleanor talk of long road travel. 'My daughter is in the Belmont.' Eleanor points.

'Do you want to get her?' Jean asks.

The rain harder on car roof. 'Oh, it'll be okay.'

The woman hits her hands against the steering wheel. 'What am I meant to do now in this weather?'

'Would you like a lift somewhere?'

Jean taps her fingernails against leather. 'Thanks, but I'll see if a tow truck comes. Some guy stopped just before you did and said he would send help from the next town. Maybe a miracle will happen!'

Eleanor nodded. 'Yeah, maybe.'

'How long have you been on the road?'

How much to divulge? 'Just a few hours. I thought a change of scenery would do us both a world of good.'

Jean nods, sounds approval. Maggie dangles a toy in front of Eleanor's face. 'I call this one Goblin-poo-bum-head.'

Eleanor catches Jean smile, says, 'I bet she keeps you on your toes.'

'God, she drives me utterly insane some days. I threaten to leave her.'

To hear a stranger be so upfront. 'Really?'

Jean turns to Maggie. 'What do I say to you when I've had enough?'

Maggie lays Goblin-poo-bum-head on her lap. 'You say, "That's it! I'm leaving you out for the trolls," and that you'll tell them exactly how to eat me.'

'Correct. I think you'd taste pretty good with some barbecue sauce.'

Maggie cackles, the delight of a child knowing exactly where they stand with their parent, and she goes back to her toys.

'I'd never have been able to talk like that with my mother,' Eleanor says.

'Me either. Shame, really.'

They sit, wait for rain to ease, and Eleanor glances at the Belmont, ever watchful, and they talk recent events: Jean's new appointment at a high school, the disappointment of being stuck with a mechanic who can never seem to pinpoint the problem. 'If it means I have to become one just to get the job done properly, I'll do it. I'm so bloody sick of it!'

Eleanor likes Jean. It has been too long since she'd enjoyed the company of a woman similar to her.

'. . . of course, the only choice I had was to divorce. What about you?'

Eleanor had tuned out, can't find her place back in the conversation. 'I'm sorry?'

'Are you doing this on your own too?'

'Sort of. My husband . . . her father was in Vietnam.'

'Oh, I'm sorry. Did he not make it back?'

Eleanor grits teeth. 'He came back.'

'Ah, I see. Are you separated?'

'Yes. Almost. Something like that.' The idea of reuniting; a tightening in her chest.

Jean asks Maggie if she needs something to eat, hands over a red apple.

'I don't want that.'

'Just eat it.' Rising heat, Jean sighs. 'Sorry about that. It's been a long couple of days.'

A long couple of days. She thinks of the box in the back of the car, of him standing over her. Have Jean's days been similar?

'Are you on a holiday? Eleanor asks.

Jean stretched her neck. 'My mum's dying. We're trying to get to her before she goes but the bloody car keeps breaking down. It's been a nightmare.'

Eleanor considers how far she would travel to see Kitty before she died. A crunch of apple and Maggie says, 'Can we see your baby?'

Eleanor looks at Maggie and her stomach twinges, makes her nauseous.

'Are you okay?' Jean's mouth shapes concern, puts a hand on her shoulder.

Eleanor gives way to crying. 'My husband and I had a fight. I . . .'

'Did he hurt you?'

'What do you mean?' The years swarm. She knows exactly what Jean meant. And so Eleanor nods, lets her body speak.

'God, I'm sorry. Do you need help?'

If Jean keeps asking I'll have to talk about it. I just want to get out of the car, get to the mountain. Eleanor doesn't respond and the car goes quiet. Maggie kicks her feet against the rear passenger door, says, 'Mum, mum, mum, mum, mum,' the way boredom takes over a body, moves it like a puppet. The noise of this child makes Eleanor's head thump. Maggie becomes a high-pitched siren and Eleanor leans over the seat and yells at the girl to be quiet. 'Sit down and shut up!' The way she's falling apart.

'Eleanor, you may be stressed but that doesn't give you the right to speak to my child like that.'

'I'm sorry.' She turns to Maggie. 'I shouldn't have yelled at you. It was wrong.'

'Okay!' Maggie says.

'I need to get back to Amy but I don't want to just leave you both here. Are you sure I can't drive you somewhere?'

Jean stares at Eleanor, doesn't answer straightaway, and eventually she nods, says, 'I guess you could.' Reluctant.

An uneasy silence. How far could they go like this? The idea makes Eleanor shudder.

A horn blare from the road announces the arrival of a tow truck.

Eleanor breathes out, says, 'Oh, thank God,' realises how it sounds and corrects herself with, 'I really should go back to Amy.'

Jean doesn't say anything.

The idea that someone would be mad at her. 'I'm really sorry, Jean. I don't know what came over me.'

She is on her way back to the Belmont when Jean sticks her head out the driver's window. 'Eleanor, don't go back. Trust me when I say it's never worth it.'

She nods and she nods, wishes Jean well, and Maggie presses her face against the back window of the car and watches as she and Amy drive away.

The way Jean had spoken to her. It had been so long since Eleanor had felt able to speak to another woman like this and she'd ruined it.

Kitty

1947

KITTY DECIDED TO be a good mother and take her son out into the world. She needed to get back into the practice for when the baby arrived, she reasoned.

She hoped, too, that if she took him out the other women would confirm that the past months hadn't all been in her head, that he had died, that she wasn't going crazy and stuck in a nightmare. She wanted women to tell her that what she was feeling was normal, that they too would want to spend time with their child. He had been taken so quickly that she hadn't had a chance to say goodbye to him.

'I'm not ready. I want him around,' she told George when he suggested they let him go.

'Do you think that is the best thing to do?' he said. She did think it best.

Kitty wrapped Badger in a muslin sling and tied him to her body. Her fingers froze when she went outside and she worried about what the weather would do to the urn, to Badger. Do trees feel the cold? Kitty held Badger tight against her chest, a reflex to warm and protect, and she pulled her red coat over him, buttoned herself up. The two of them together. The baby kicked and she took it as a sign that life begot life, that Badger was calling to the new child. How could she separate the siblings now?

Neighbours were out in their gardens, were out tending the fronts of their houses: so and so was raking leaves off the grass, while so and so climbed up and down the ladder taking measurements for new gutters. One so and so, Mr Roundtree, looked at her, and she realised she hadn't seen him since the day of the incident. He stopped midway down his ladder, said, 'You're out today! It's nice to see you.'

She nodded.

'How's George?'

Ask him yourself. 'He's fine. Everything is fine.'

Mr Roundtree pointed to Kitty's chest. 'You . . .'

How do you show something nobody wants to see? She nodded, unbuttoned her coat. 'I just wanted to.'

He smiled at her, looked as if he would say something, then changed his mind, carried on up the ladder.

Kitty patted Badger gently as they walked Wintonvale's streets and she pointed out familiar landmarks of the town, her tongue remembering old roles. She walked Badger to the children's section of the cemetery. 'I kept you from here. Sweet boy.' They passed old gravestones eaten by lime and white, years of weather. Family ground filled with elderly children. Kitty held Badger tight to her chest. To her left: two sisters, two brothers bunked atop each other, ages twelve, twenty-five, sixty-six, eighty-nine. Birth dates, death dates; collected years. 'Look, Badger,' she said, stopped herself. How to explain the phenomenon to her son? How to explain the earth had been opened and closed until there were no more siblings, no one else to make use of the ground? If she were a different woman she would say, 'The land stitched itself up and healed. Just as it should.' But she is not a different woman and there is no healing and there is no, and no, and no. Instead she looked for comfort, thought of what the twelve-year-old might've said the very last time her new home was opened: *Come. Let us pretend we are still children, let's do all that bedtime cuddling again. Do you remember the dreams we had? All those wishes? Let us breathe secrets into one another like we used to; mouth to ear. Oh, brother. Oh, sister. I've been waiting for you to come back to me.*

To have a sibling, a playmate. Kitty kissed Badger's urn, continued on.

Eventually she saw Maudie ferrying groceries from the shops to her car.

'Kitty!' Her friend came to her, placed an arm around her shoulders, her smell of syrup, plum and sandalwood, of oakmoss and patchouli coaxing her close. 'Kitty, you've come out. I thought I might have to pop by and see you today but you've come out!'

Kitty hated the way Maudie spoke to her; it made her feel sick to the stomach. She recognised her own language and tone, the type she used when speaking to the men at the hospital, to George. This was the wording you used when you were frightened of the other, when you didn't want someone to become upset and cause a scene.

'I wanted to go for a walk.' She forced herself to smile.

'Well, that's wonderful. But you should've called me. I would've taken you so you wouldn't be alone.'

Kitty batted at her coat, the soft bounce tap of soothing a small child.

Maudie followed Kitty's hand and said, 'Is the baby giving you trouble?'

'It's Badger.' The unexpectedness of her admission. She surprised herself, unbuttoned her coat, like undressing for a lover, revealed her secret to Maudie.

Maudie saw the sling, the top of the urn peeking over, dropped her smile, said, 'Does George know where you are?'

'I have no idea.'

'Are you alright?'

There was a peculiar look on Maudie's face and she put her hand to Kitty's forehead. It was the first time in weeks Kitty had let someone touch her.

'Why wouldn't I be?' My son died. Why were people still asking these questions? What answer did they want from her? Then Kitty said, 'I didn't know what to do with him, Maudie.'

Her friend frowned. 'Kitty . . .'

'I thought if I went outside with my child I'd remember how. I'm still his mother, Maudie.'

'Yes, of course you are.'

She stared at the urn and Kitty said, 'Please touch it. Please touch him.' She wanted to be sure that what she held in her arms was real.

For the longest time Maudie didn't move. And then she reached out a hand and touched the top of Badger's urn.

It was just like when she had first brought him home after giving birth. Kitty cried from happiness and Maudie kissed her cheek. 'Oh, your boy is beautiful, Kitty!' And Badger was alive again.

Maudie drove Kitty and Badger home and she said, 'As long as this is doing you good, Kitty.'

Later, while she rolled lamb and rosemary rissoles between her hands, she said to George, 'They march the men down the street to remember the dead. Why can't I do the same? It's just until the baby comes.'

She sat Badger at the dining table, told George to come join them for dinner, and he took his place at the head of the table. Families change and this one had changed again. They both stared at Badger. 'It's just until the baby comes,' Kitty said again. They ate their meal in silence.

―――――

A crystal vase of pink carnations, three metal mixing bowls, a set of scales, a block of butter; these kitchen trophies next to her son on the kitchen counter.

'Badger, the secret to baking is good butter at the right weight.' She knived the golden delicious into equal portions, placed one in each bowl. 'Do you remember I showed you how to cream the butter when I made you your birthday cake last year? Well, we're going to do that again but this time we'll use dark brown sugar.' She spooned sugar over butter, smiled at her son. 'I'm hungry just thinking about it!'

The record player was spinning and she hummed. Together, they filled the house still. She measured flour, measured baking powder, and her body measured the first stretch of skin pulling her into pain, that old way of preparing the body to push. Kitty put the wooden spoon in the mixing bowl, clenched her legs and buttocks together to stop the great expulsion. It was happening too early. George wasn't there, had taken off the day before to go on a long walk, took with him binoculars, no map, a small smile. She thought bitterly that George had looked genuinely excited to be apart from her. Perhaps they had both been excited.

And now this.

The arrival of children is the departure from yourself. Another contraction made her heat, made her leave the kitchen, made her forget to take Badger with her. She paced the hallway and thought of calling for help but to do so would be to admit that things were about to change again.

Kitty rocked back and forth on her heels, breathed deeply, tried to slow everything down, all the things her body knew how to do, and she paced, noticed how odd everything seemed to be, like she was in another woman's house. Who is the person who owns these heirloom vases in a display case, who wraps the end of sofa arms in lace doilies, who leaves small bowls of sugared almonds out knowing no one will eat them, who has set the mantel clock thirty minutes fast so she can be done with the day sooner? Who is the woman? Was I like this when Badger was coming?

She paced, felt a warmth spread between her legs, and when she looked, blood crawled like milk down her thighs, made every inch of her skin too warm, convinced her she was on fire.

Kitty went to the bedroom, stood in front of the mirror, undressed, placed a hand over her pubic hair before touching between her legs to get a measure of herself. Fingers pushed inside; a dilation. She caught her reflection. Kitty hadn't looked at her body like this in a long time; she recognised nothing. Who am I becoming? She made eye contact with herself, moved closer to the mirror, pressed against it as hard as she could. I look tired. I look sad. The next contraction came and she maintained her focus. It was the closest she'd ever been to herself. It hurt. She didn't know how much more she could take. There'd been a certain solace in pregnancy, living halfway between what was and what was to come. Another contraction and her hands slapped the mirror, she cried out. The confrontation of seeing yourself. She said, 'Is this who I am?' Accept yourself, Kitty. But she shook her head, knew the impossibility of the task, refused it. She walked to the cupboard, pulled out towels and linens, and went to the bathroom.

Kitty stood by the bathtub, her body regressing to a phase it once knew. It is true what they say: you never forget. Her stomach; Richter scale. Skin pulsed and pulled to make way for new ground and it hurt, like fuck it hurt, the electrical current of her body wanting to explode. She ran her hand over her stomach and under her feet the pink and pale green bathroom tiles were the temperature of Badger's skin that day and she vomited on them, all the liquid she had filled herself up with that morning. Nothing ever tastes better the second time around and into the bathtub she went, squatted and spread her legs, held on to the faucet for support.

Came the contractions, came the blood down her legs; it is true what they say: sacrifice is what is needed.

She needed to urinate, to shit, and so she did, all that pressure on the body to produce something. It was on her feet, her ankles. She turned the water on, tried to wash away the mess. The sound of water falling onto porcelain made her shake. This is not meant to be happening. I don't want this to happen.

Then Kitty buckled, onto hands and knees as another explosion took over. The water lapped at her skin and she called out, 'George,' called his name over and over, knowing he would not hear her. If only I could leave my body now, run to find him. Then none of this would be happening to me.

It wasn't time to push but the pressure was great. She took a breath, another, and the baby's movement was a thrash and kick, pounding so hard to get out. Kitty cried out, a sound of herself she hadn't heard before. She hadn't made this sound when she had Badger. This one was beyond, a collision of known substances, of everything that had gone before, against everything she knew to be true. Force is always pain. Whoever was inside wanted to cut right through her, make light through the dark. Kitty sat herself upright in the bath, widened her legs, the pressure of herself splitting like an atom: motherhood before and after Badger. To go through this again. She couldn't.

The next contraction came and time passed and time pushed her closer to pushing, pushing, pushing. Everything tender, everything stretched and burned. Her body shook from shock and outside the bathroom window the sunset was becoming blue, was becoming closer to the night. I don't want to do this alone in the dark.

Another contraction and this time her body pushed without resistance and out came a guttural sound, something like dread, something like relief.

Here she knew: the body measures the weight of life and death equally. To hold one you must be able to hold the other. Kitty, there are reasons we can't see what grows inside us: to see what we are capable of is too much. The faucet was cold but she held on. Out came the acid-sweet smell that was inside her. Why won't someone come and make this stop. Why won't someone come and take me away. Why couldn't this child have died inside her. She called out for her son. But what came was the kick of a daughter. She held tight to the faucet.

What was she going to tell this child about the life that existed before? The contractions then and she screamed, 'Badger,' until the walls received her as an echo, demanded she listen to her own pain. Kitty refused.

Blood is milk, that life force, and it came out of her and Kitty pushed, she pushed, she pushed, she pushed. Giving birth to two children. She called for her son over and over and over and she pushed and pushed and pushed, put both hands between her legs, felt top of a crown, a head, a shoulder, looked down at a small face, the blood covering her hands. Kitty pulled at the baby, guided her towards the world. The weight of this child. Kitty couldn't find the energy to keep herself going. But the blue hour was almost finished and the darkness was coming and she pushed again for the last time.

There was only silence when her daughter was finally out. To go through all that and not hear a sound. She couldn't bear it. 'Breathe. Please breathe.' This automatic begging. Kitty heard herself whisper it, couldn't bring herself to finish the sentence. 'Please.' Her daughter stared at her and Kitty forced all the air she had in her lungs out onto the baby and the baby screamed for her life and Kitty cried out and they screamed together into the beginning of the night and Kitty was a mother again.

Kitty

1948

WEEKS BECAME MONTHS. Kitty took to sitting outside with her son on the red love seat while her daughter slept, took to playing with the jasmine vine, crushed small white petals between fingers, that narcotic smell which comes from heat and purpose. Look at me here being all pulled together. Kitty watched over the street, watched neighbour after neighbour after neighbour walk by, wave suburban politeness, drop their gaze. These people she knows going about their lives who now seem like strangers. These people who do not ask her about her life, not in the way they used to. Why don't they ask me what it's like to lose then gain a child, ask how when you hold one you mourn the other, how when you give love it feels like a betrayal?

Why not ask me whether or not I have considered killing the newborn because having her around is too painful?

Kitty rocked in the love seat, told herself to smile wide, show the neighbours that she's fine now, that she is back to normal.

She cut a look towards Charlie's house. Three months since. He barely says anything when they pass each other but she's got a thing or two to say. The first: Fuck me. Fuck me like you used to, like I know you still want to. The second: I need you to hold me so I can feel something other than myself.

On the love seat she smoked her cigarette, rubbed her still-half-round stomach, enjoyed the feel of the semi-flat surface just above the pubic bone where a head rested, followed gravity. She rubbed. Children always leave their mark. The only people who had asked her anything of substance lately were children.

A few days before Kitty had been in the front garden pretending to check her roses when one of Badger's friends, Joshua, stopped at the front gate. He wiped his nose on the back of his hand, looked at it before licking. 'Hi,' Joshua said, waved two fingers; rabbit ears.

'Hello.'

He looked behind her. 'Where's your baby?'

'She's inside resting.' She's always inside resting.

'Oh.' He wiped his nose again.

'Do you need a hanky?' Her hand automatically to her skirt pocket, a holster.

'No.'

It was the easiest conversation she'd had in months. 'What are you doing now?'

'I just escaped from the hugest volcano you've ever, ever seen! All this lava came spilling out and it just burned all the concrete and houses in its way. Did you know lava is really hot? Did you know that if you touched it, it would kill you to actual death?' Eyes lit up, were wider than wide, made Kitty smile.

'I didn't know that!'

'It's really, really true.'

'I believe you.' Kitty went to soft palm his cheeks, pulled back.

'I also have chocolate in my pocket.' Joshua pulled out a wrapped Freddo frog from his back pocket and showed it to Kitty. She lost count of all the Freddo wrappers she'd found hidden in Badger's room. She touched it.

'Can I have it?' She knew she shouldn't ask a child for sweetness.

'Okay.' He gave it to her, with a look of disappointment. Kitty unwrapped it, held the Freddo to her nose, that sugar milk, bit off the frog's head. The chocolate melted on her tongue and she cried.

Joshua stepped towards her, was quiet. Eventually he said, 'Do you miss Badger?'

'Yes.' But he never went away. He is still here. She expected the question to sting but it didn't. It felt good to be asked, to know that she wasn't the only one thinking about him.

'I do too. He told me I could have one of his toys and he was going to get it for me the next time we played but then he died.' The little friend stared up at her. 'Am I allowed to say he died? Mum said not to say it to you.'

The way he had to crane his neck to see her, scrunch his eyes to keep the sun out. It made her laugh and she kept on laughing, kept on laughing until she cried again.

'Sorry, Mrs Turner.'

She swooped down to hug him. 'It's really okay.' His little heart against her, his sweaty skin. Almost as if Badger had crawled out of the urn and walked down the path to her. 'Which toy did he promise you?'

'The green tin robot.' A child never forgets promises made.

'You can have it.' His reward for braving the things adults hadn't been able to.

Joshua smiled. 'Badger is a fun friend. And you've got that baby now!'

It took Kitty a week to hand over the toy. She wasn't sure she should be parting with anything. But then.

Months became months and on the love seat she heard the baby cry, reminded herself that it's expected she go to her. She inhaled cigarette smoke, patted Badger, the knock-knock of wood. 'Your sister is a crier.' All the ways she had thought about stopping her from crying. The baby cried and Kitty stubbed her cigarette in the ashtray, swung the love seat before getting out and taking Badger with her.

In her daughter's room, the baby was hysterical and Kitty covered her ears. She didn't remember Badger being this bad. She stared at the baby, watched her redden and purple. 'You're lucky I haven't hurt you yet.'

Where did these thoughts come from? She wondered if others had them too but she was too afraid to ask for fear she'd be the only one, that they would take her away to hospital, or worse: they would take Badger away. Kitty closed her eyes, took a deep breath, looked back at the baby. Who have I become? Kitty reached into the cot, lifted the child out and offered her breast. The baby greedy for it.

'Shhh, Eleanor,' Kitty said. 'Shhhh all the way back to sleep.' To Badger she said, 'I'm trying to get used to saying her name. It's going to take time.'

Eleanor

1969

KITTY HAD PROMISED her that the family meal this week would be life-changing. 'But what if I don't want my life to change?' Even she knew she was lying though.

'Don't be so contrary, Eleanor. We're having a special guest for dinner and I want you to look nice.'

'Don't I always?' Eleanor pressed her fingers into her gum to stop her teeth from throbbing. It was happening a lot lately. It happened when she spoke to Kitty.

'Quite frankly, no.'

She pressed her gums again, thought she could detect a smile in Kitty's voice but she couldn't be certain; her mother was never what she seemed. Eleanor gritted her teeth. 'Fine. I'll see you soon.'

Twenty-two years old and still doing as she was told. Eleanor hung up the phone, dressed for her family.

Later, she parked her Belmont on her parents' street, checked herself in the rear-view mirror, her frosted-pink lipstick, the way her brown hair feathered across her eyebrows, how at times like this she looked so much like Kitty. Spitting image, the Wintonvale women had told her. Please don't let this be true.

Eleanor picked up her handbag and a shoebox from the front seat, hit her forehead on the lapis hanging from the mirror. 'Every bloody time.' She should get rid of it, but Kitty had given it to her as a graduation present.

'I just thought you'd like the colour. Apparently it wards off evil.' So matter-of-fact. Eleanor couldn't recall her believing in such things.

Eleanor stopped the lapis from its pendulum rhythm then through the windscreen noticed a tall, wide-stanced figure at the foot of the driveway. She looked properly: a too-smooth cupid-lipped face above broad shoulders, a muscled chest. Leon Fleischmann. She'd had an ill-advised crush on him for a split second in their final year of school. He went to Sydney to study medicine and she never thought of him again.

She shook her head, got out of the car. 'Please don't tell me you're the life-changing meal.'

'I could be.'

He was slightly more charming than she'd remembered.

Eleanor shut the car door. 'It's not going to happen.' She tried not to look at his body, all the ways his clothes pulled tight.

'It might.'

'It's not.'

'We'll see.' He smiled at her, pointed to the shoebox. 'Present for me?'

'It's for my dad.' She held out the box, an offering to curiosity.

Leon reached for it and their hands collided, his the touch of the sun.

When he opened the lid he said, 'What the hell is this?'

The way he said it made her body seize, heat across her face and through her limbs. She wanted to rip the box from him. Eleanor had found the dead crow two days before, had been fascinated by the way both halluces were missing, the left wing only half formed. 'Dad and I study them together from time to time. It's really not that strange.'

Leon handed the box back, muttered, 'I guess the apple doesn't fall far from the tree.'

This knock on her family's past. Was he referring to Kitty or George? 'What did you say?'

'Nothing. I'm sorry. I was trying to be funny. It didn't work, did it?'

'Not in the slightest.' She dreaded the night ahead, was reminded why she'd never pursued anything with him. And yet. That thing about him was still there.

'Can we forget it was said?'

'It depends on how life-changing this meal is.'

Kitty opened the front door, arms wide for receiving. Eleanor noticed her mother's tight red dress, the one she used to wear when Eleanor was young, the one she wore to leave an impression. 'Darling! You're here.'

She came to the kerb and Eleanor could smell the thicket of aldehyde and buttermilk, of blanketed rose and iris. Kitty smiled at Leon, said, 'How wonderful you're here! I hope you two have been catching up already?' She clapped her hands together, quick-darted her eyes to the shoebox and raised her eyebrows at her daughter. 'I thought that seeing as Leon is home for the next while it would be lovely to have two young people enjoy each other's company.'

Leon edged closer to Kitty and hugged her. 'I'm humbled you invited me for dinner, Mrs Turner. Dad is happy I'm out and about and talking to a woman.' He laughed, winked, and Eleanor shut her eyes, chided herself for never seeing things coming until they were there.

'Darling, did he tell you he's at the barracks?'

'No, he did not.' She looked at Leon. 'So that's why you're back? You support the war, do you?'

'Eleanor! Don't be aggressive,' Kitty scolded.

Eleanor buttoned herself down, obedient daughter.

'It's okay, Mrs Turner. I don't mind.'

Eleanor would never have picked this son of a doctor to leave his comfortable life. 'I honestly hope for your sake you're not drafted to Vietnam.'

Kitty frowned. 'Yes, well. War is a terrible thing. Sometimes necessary.'

How could this come from the mouth of a woman who spent a lifetime with George?

'I just think it's the right thing to do. Makes me feel useful.'

'I don't agree with you. I doubt my father would either.'

Kitty tugged at Eleanor's arm. 'Okay, that's enough of all this. We can agree to disagree and pretend this conversation never happened! I have made a wonderful meal for us all. Lucky we're having this outside and not inside.'

Kitty ushered them up the path to the house.

Inside, George sat on the sofa, smiled at his daughter, gave her the thumbs-up at the shoebox, nodded at Leon. Leon crossed the room to shake George's hand, and Kitty clapped her own hands together, made the music of charm. 'Isn't this a fun thing!'

Leon turned a beam to Eleanor. She tried not to look at his body, tried not to think about touching him, the things he had said outside, tried not to think how much she liked seeing her mother happy, seeing her father relax with a stranger. Maybe life could change.

———

It was easy to be with him. A month later they decided to go to Freyport to set the boundaries of possible new love. At least that's how Eleanor saw it. 'Show me what your PhD will be,' he'd said. 'I want to know everything about you.' To be seen by someone: not even her own mother had asked her to express herself like this.

'Only if you show me everything about you.'

There they stood on the forest cut, overlooked the ocean, followed deep waves to the point of the horizon: the blue sea meeting blue sky; a new hemisphere. They trekked, his eyes to treetops, hers to ground. Every now and then he pointed his camera at Eleanor, told her to smile, and she did. 'I like your teeth. I like the way your tongue runs over them.' The camera shutter: click, click, click. She tried not to laugh at his camping outfit as he strained to move: black jeans, black biker boots, black leather jacket so overused you could see the grey underskin of the animal it had come from. 'Are you sure you're comfortable in that?'

Leon waved his hand at her. 'You're not the boss of me.' A grin.

They went further into the forest and he filled the tree canopy with, 'Wow, would you look at that! Wow, would you look at that! This is all just extraordinary!'

She opened her mouth to tell him all the ways he made her happy, but nothing came out, was too scared that if she revealed all now it would be too much and he would leave. I just want him to stay. Sounds of cicada thrumming in thickets of trees grew louder and they went further into the bush: rainbow lorikeet, small wallaby nibbling on grey-brown fur, damp smell of old-growth forest.

They walked over and through neon and bottle greens; colour that once existed beneath the earth was no longer hidden. The joy of seeing it made Eleanor's stomach fizz, made her want to shout glory. She could smell Leon in the wind, the musk of sweat and dried sun, of the way she used to smell after being trapped in her dark house when Kitty had her migraines and she couldn't go outside. She'd walk as fast as she could around the lounge room, pretend she was running a quiet marathon, try not to wake her mother. That heart race, the staleness. Finally when she couldn't take it anymore, she'd go outside into the sun. Everything new.

The happiness she'd feel at being alive. That was what she could smell on the wind: a type of shared existence. Leon smelled like home. She wanted to share a life with him, inside him.

Leon stopped. 'What's that bird?'

She squinted before looking into her binoculars, smiled. 'It's a shining bronze cuckoo. I haven't seen one in ages.'

The cuckoo landed on a branch, beaked its wing. 'You know what they do? They lay their eggs in a host nest so that another bird will look after them. And then, when the cuckoo hatches, it ejects the host's offspring from the nest.'

'Sounds pretty cruel.'

Eleanor shook her head. 'They do it so the parent cuckoo is free to go off and do something else. Lay more eggs if they want. It's genius.'

'So you'd be okay if someone expected you to raise their offspring while they went off and did something else?'

Eleanor lowered her binoculars and smiled. She liked that the realities of the natural world made humans question existence. She liked that when it came to this she knew more than he did and he wasn't afraid to ask. 'Humans do it all the time, except usually it's the men who go off and do something else and they don't seem to have a problem with it.'

Leon laughed, scared the cuckoo away. 'Touché.'

'You know what? I like that I know more about this than you ever will.'

'Is that right?'

'Yes.'

'Would you like it if I knew things you didn't?'

She raised her eyebrows. 'It would depend what they were. Do you contain mysteries I should know about, Leon?'

The way he looked at her; calculating the sum of anticipation. 'I might have some.'

Is one that you already love me? She couldn't help herself and so she said, 'How do you feel about me?'

'You'll find out.' He winked at her and they continued on through the trees.

Eleanor took in the way his body stalked over the tree roots, his sure-footedness, as if nothing had ever broken his stride before. To be like that. Her father had taught her that paying attention to where you stepped helped you to understand where you had come from, but there was Leon moving forwards. There was Leon looking into the world. A man so different to the one she'd grown up with. And here she was behind him.

Eleanor took strides the length of giants to catch him, and when they were side by side, she heard his breath fire from his throat. This is the sound of living.

'Leon.' His name was a reflex. There wasn't anything to add so she grinned at him.

He turned, returned her smile. 'What?'

'I honestly don't remember if I was going to say anything else.'

'I have that effect on people.' He was electric when his hand touched hers, made Eleanor feel as if she had been set alight and stripped of flesh then bone then dust. In that moment she wanted him to consume her until she no longer existed. This must be what people talk about when they talk about falling in love: wanting someone to show you all the ways you could exist even when you're nothing.

Eleanor kissed him, liked the way her tongue wore him like a suit, tailor-made just for her. Passion wasn't a game she'd ever seen her parents play together. There was a part of her that felt satisfied in knowing that she was better than Kitty at something. But she couldn't help it. Her mother made her compete with her brother all the time. Why not compete with her for a change?

Leon pulled back, said, 'Save that energy for later. I want you to do something for me.'

'What is it? Is it a good thing?'

'I hope so!'

They walked on and time passed. She watched the back of his neck sweat and she wanted to lean in, lick him clean, taste what he was made of. These things he made her feel.

Leon stopped suddenly and turned to her. 'I was going to wait but I can't help myself.'

He closed in on her, put his mouth over hers; moss growing over rock.

'I think you're magnificent,' he told her. 'I need to have you.'

Her breath stuck in her throat, the hurt from a seismic shift of the heart welcomed. 'I . . . yes. Me too.' Feelings couldn't form into words.

'I'm ready to share one of my mysteries now. Do you trust me?'

She nodded.

'Do you want to play a game?'

She nodded.

'Close your eyes.'

She did as she was told, heard Leon unzip his jeans, let them drop to the ground. He grabbed her right hand, tugged at her index finger and licked it. 'I want you to put yourself inside me.'

Eleanor opened one eye, saw her finger go back inside his mouth, saw his face was soft. She would never have imagined he would ask her to do this. 'I said close your eyes.' And she did, traced her finger over his stomach, over hip, over arse. His breath was quick and she matched him and then she slid her finger inside. He was warmer than she expected.

Eleanor heard a bird trill overhead, heard a wallaby jump across the leaf litter to her right. He probably doesn't want to know more about birds on this trip. A shame.

Leon moaned, said, 'Now a second one.'

She did as she was told and she liked it. She nuzzled into his neck, licked him; this scientific method of discovering human matter. She reached down with her left hand to his crotch, thinking that soon this would be the destination, but he said, 'That's not the mystery, Eleanor.'

She stopped. 'What's going to happen?'

'Now a third.'

Eleanor hesitated. 'I think this is too much for me.'

Leon kissed her before he whispered, 'Don't you trust me? I trust you. I need you to feel the same.'

He was so warm, they were so close. She liked the way he sounded in her ear; a remedy. People and their needs, people and love.

Eleanor knew all about them. Despite herself she did what he wanted, felt him flinch before accepting her again. I didn't know I had this in me. She counted to ten to calm herself, heard her voice slip out numbers. He yelled out, frightened her, and she pulled away from him. Leon grabbed her hand. 'It's okay. Close your eyes.'

Before she could tell him that she'd had enough, the fingers that were inside him were then inside his mouth scraping against teeth, scraping towards the back of his throat. They held eye contact and for a moment he was pure animal. The way he enjoyed his own taste disgusted her. Don't judge him. You mustn't judge. He trusts you and you want him to love you.

Leon held her still in his mouth, let out a moan, and she felt him wet against her leg. He pulled her fingers from his mouth, kissed her, said, 'You're magnificent. I've never asked someone to do that before.'

She considered him. She'd never experienced anything like it, was confused by how something that had at first felt exciting quickly turned to something she wasn't sure she'd want to do again. 'I've never been asked to do that, either. Tell me, what's the mystery?'

He smiled and she took it to mean love. 'Please don't be mad. But the mystery was to see if I could make you go along with it. And it turns out, I could.' He had predicted her before she could predict herself. 'And you've made me very happy, Eleanor. I know now I've found someone I can be myself around.'

She nodded, understood. All those years of hiding inside herself because she couldn't always make others happy. But she could make him happy, let him be himself; he'd already proved it. All around: flame-red floral, neon green moss on rock, thick tree canopy, the blue sky. Everything new. Leon new. Eleanor glanced at her hand, at her uncut fingernails. 'I'm worried that I might have hurt you. Inside, I mean. Did I hurt you?'

'Not in the slightest. You could never hurt me.'

This good thing to hear made some of it feel better.

Later that night, in the tent, they held each other and he said, 'I'm so glad I'm here with you.'

'Me too.'

'Your mum will be pleased we spent this time together.'

The idea of telling Kitty what they had done. Eleanor laughed and then he did too. Night animals skittered away from the sound their two voices made in unison.

'And to think I thought you were very boring.'

'I'm many things, Eleanor. You'll see.' He kissed her and he kissed her.

Kitty

1952

IN THE KITCHEN Kitty searched Eleanor's hair for lice and Eleanor looked at photos of her brother at the zoo, taken the year he died. 'When can we go?'

'One day soon.' Kitty knew the chance of her breaking a promise was high. But what if this time I didn't? She searched her daughter's hair as she had done for Badger, told herself that the act of mothering one child was the same as mothering another. Kitty, this doesn't mean you're close. She shook her head. I've given Eleanor a full and happy life. Often she'd find a louse egg yet to hatch, wonder which part of the life cycle she had found. What part of the cycle am I in with my children? She tweezered fingers together, crushed the egg, started again.

'I'm not itchy,' Eleanor said, just as her brother had. 'I don't have critters!'

'Shhhh.' She brushed her daughter's hand away. Mother knows best. There was always something to be found.

George was sitting at the dining table, said, 'Kitty, I don't think she has lice.'

Kitty stared at him. What would he know? He'd never painstakingly preened a child's hair before, never had to feel the way fingers ached from boredom. Her body tightened, the beginnings of a headache. Maybe when the night comes I can see Charlie and he'll take all this pain away.

'Not one day – Mummy, you said we could go today!' Eleanor wriggled out from Kitty's hold, pointed at the calendar, the giant red ring around Saturday.

When am I? Kitty had been doing this a lot.

'Right,' she said. 'Right.' Why couldn't George have reminded her about today?

The promise of animals, that kingdom of fur and feather. George said, 'We should tell Eleanor how zoos acquire wild animals so she knows how delicate you need to be when introducing live creatures to a new environment. Not everything goes to plan . . .' He went back to the newspaper.

'And what good would knowing that do? Do you know how they got there?' Her neck itched and she scratched, kept scratching. Why try to explain a reality to a child if you yourself don't know it?

George pointed at the paper. 'Well, how about that: one of the baby tamarins died. Its mother killed it.'

Things mothers do. 'George, Eleanor is sitting right here. You'll upset her.'

'I'm not upset, Mummy.'

'Animals die, Kitty.' Both of them speaking at the same time. There are too many voices.

Kitty said, 'Not like this.'

'Like how?' Eleanor said.

George put the paper down. 'Sometimes we forget just how wild animals are.'

'Ooooh.' Eleanor rubbed her hands together and Kitty pulled at her daughter's hair, that way of bringing someone back into line.

'George, that's enough. She doesn't need to know about animals mauling each other like savage beasts just so they can eat . . .'

George raised his eyebrows. 'She eats meat all the time.'

How this man annoyed her. 'That's different.'

'How? Meat is meat!'

'You don't eat zoo animals, George.'

They smiled at each other, the smallest of curves on mouths that used to enjoy the taste of each other, used to enjoy the tease that came at the end of a petty argument, and the conversation ended the way they always did: before they had to speak about their life together. The truth was Kitty didn't want to know about the baby monkey dying. Why couldn't a zookeeper have intervened?

Eleanor stood up from the chair, nudged her head on George's shoulder and he kissed her forehead, whiskered his fingers under her chin then along her neck, made Eleanor jump and hoot. A memory of Badger and George playing this way the day they took him to the zoo. Kitty watched her husband and daughter, how easily they seemed to fit together, so comfortable with each other. I only want her to smile like that at me. Both her children were able to draw something out of George she never could, as if they were pulling light from him into their hearts.

'Daddy, when we go to the zoo can we see the giraffes?'

'Of course we can,' Kitty interjected, taking control. 'Badger loves the giraffes.'

George dropped his head. 'Kitty, stop.'

'Stop what?' She was up for an argument if it gave her more of his attention.

'You know.' He wouldn't look at her.

They were quiet for a time and from outside telephones called to one another. 'This thing with Badger. It's enough. He's not meant to be going anywhere except the blue mountain.' The hushed venom. He'd never spoken to her like this. Since when does he tell me what to do when it comes to my son?

'Can we go to the blue mountain instead of the zoo?' Eleanor jumped.

'No.' Kitty stamped her foot hard against the linoleum. I can be a child too.

George stood. 'Kitty, don't do this.'

'Why can't we?' Eleanor and her whine. I could slap her.

'Today was meant to be a family outing to the zoo, and now you're suggesting we do something we haven't fully discussed or prepared for. How dare you!'

Eleanor went to Badger on the counter, placed a comforting hand on the side of the urn.

'Kitty . . .' But he didn't have it in him to finish. He never does.

'Why are you doing this to me?'

'He was my son too, Kitty.' George looked away. 'I'm going to go to the shed.'

He left her there, left her with those feelings, like she was sinking. She never got the best of him.

Eleanor came to her, held her hand. 'I could be the zoo if you like?'

Eyes to daughter, to a toothless smile. 'What?'

'If we can't go, we could pretend we're there without Dad.'

'How?'

Eleanor slipped from Kitty, squatted, gorilla hands to her chest, grunted, made Kitty laugh despite herself. Her daughter's eyes, like the sun rising in a hidden valley. For a moment Kitty felt full but then Eleanor animaled her way down the hall into her room and the feeling was gone. I need more.

———

That night, when the owls were out, when Charlie came with a torch and she met him by the back gate, when she led him inside George's shed, when the tick of clocks made white noise, when she said, 'I really don't care what you do to me tonight,' when Charlie told her to lift her dress and open her legs, when he stuck a finger inside her, the rough skin of his outdoor life chafing her, hurting her, when he bent down, licked her clitoris, and he let out a small moan, Kitty noticed a hole in the shed roof, how it opened to the night and let moonlight silver the space around them. It made her feel like she was in a dream. She clawed her nails into Charlie's thick hair, pushed his face harder between her legs, couldn't help but notice George's tools lined along the bench in order of length, assorted mechanical clock gears and pendulums laid out and cleaned, his green, holey woollen cardigan that she gifted him in 1941 slumped over his work chair. On top of a shelf drilled into the wall was a camera and next to it three small photo frames holding black-and-white photographs. The first showed Badger clinging to the railings at the zoo and pointing to an elephant, Kitty behind him, her hand resting on the small of his back so he didn't fall. Next was Eleanor squatting by a tree trunk and watching over two birds that may have been parrots as they pecked seed from ground. The smile on her face, the way she cupped her chin in her hands as she balanced on her small ankles. This sight she'd never seen. He must've taken it on the mountain when I wasn't there, she thought. Third was a photo of three men standing in front of a war plane, shirtless, laughing, arms around each other's shoulders, cigarettes hanging from youthful mouths. It had never occurred to her that there would've been joy between men while everything seemed to disintegrate around them. She felt Charlie as he concentrated on pleasure (hers, his, she wasn't sure), but she couldn't take her eyes away from the glimpse of how George interpreted the world. How I wish I could be in his world. But, Kitty, you are here now fucking your neighbour in your husband's shed. All too late now. She shook her head, tried not to cry, heard herself say, 'We should be together, Charlie.'

Charlie pulled away, looked up at her, wiped his mouth. 'Isn't what we do right now great?' Charlie kissed her, went back on his knees, went back between her legs, but she was numb, was falling out of her body. What use is greatness when you can't feel?

Eleanor

1970

THE HOUSE ELEANOR and Leon moved into at the edge of Wintonvale had mould; green and black puffs grew like ivy along the walls in the second bedroom, spread across the windows, the cupboards, the roof. The carpets were damp, and encouraged the spread of the mould to other areas of the house. 'This house will kill us,' Eleanor said. 'I knew we should never have moved in.'

'On the plus side, we own a house!'

'At what cost, Leon?' She exaggerated her role of exasperated partner.

Leon looked at her, shook his head, grinned. 'I'm sure it can be easily fixed.'

'We can't stay here.'

'Where would we go? Your mother's?'

Eleanor laughed. 'You'll be sorry.'

'Maybe she won't be so bad.'

'It'll be bad, Leon! Believe me.'

She called her parents and they came over so Leon could ask George for a man's opinion. 'You'll need a builder for this,' George told them. 'No telling what is happening under the foundations.'

'See, I told you!'

Kitty said, 'Well, I think it would be splendid if the two of you came to stay with us for a few days while all this gets fixed.'

It was the end of the discussion and the return of her childhood.

On the second day after they moved in Kitty suggested she and Eleanor bake a cake. 'Let's do a family favourite for Leon.'

'Sounds wonderful, Kitty,' Leon said.

'Yeah, sounds great.' Eleanor hated herself for sounding too cheery.

Leon sat with George in the lounge room, playing cards, and Kitty touched Eleanor's elbow, said, 'Thank you for saying yes.'

Eleanor wondered whether this was a true thing from her mother or if it was a performance. Eleanor, here is your mother as you wanted her. Take it. And she did.

Out it all came, the preparation, the instruments, the method, the ingredients, and Kitty cracked an egg.

Soon a record played, filled the house.

It had been such a long time since she and Kitty had been anywhere near this type of formation.

'Who taught you to bake?' Eleanor asked.

'My mother, of course. We used to bake together all day Saturday so we could share food after church the next day.'

The mother/daughter tradition hadn't extended to Eleanor. Maybe I'm the end of the line.

'Can I ask you something?'

'Sure. What do you want to know?' Kitty folded flour in on itself.

'Did you ever consider becoming something other than a nurse? Maybe you could sell your cakes now?'

Kitty eyed her daughter. 'Sell them? Why would I want to do that? It's just a thing I do.'

'Mum, you're really good at it.' And she meant it. 'You never thought of starting your own business?'

Kitty added cocoa powder, added regret. 'I suppose I could've. But it's too late for all that now.'

Her mother supervised as Eleanor measured ingredients and mixed the batter. 'What am I doing wrong?' Eleanor asked.

'Why do you think you're doing something wrong?'

'Because of your face!' Eleanor dipped her finger into the bowl, tasted the batter, then slid the bowl across the countertop to her mother. 'Something's off. It tastes strange.'

Kitty dipped her finger, sucked it like a child would. She had once told Eleanor that when she was young she used to eat so much of the batter that there was almost nothing left to bake. Eleanor loved this story, loved her mother's greed. Proof she wasn't always the woman I grew up with.

'It seems perfectly fine to me,' Kitty said.

Eleanor tasted it again. 'It's bitter! Try it.'

Eleanor slid the bowl, Kitty slid the bowl: they laughed, kept laughing, and Eleanor didn't want to have to bake the batter they'd made. Can't we just eat it raw like this?

'That's enough, now,' Kitty said. 'Into the oven we go.'

In went the cake, in went Kitty to the men in the next room. Eleanor headed for her bedroom, stopped at Badger's on the way and opened the door. 'Lucky you're not here,' she said. 'You'd have to deal with her too.' She tried to push down the lump in her throat that had formed.

———

Late that afternoon, Eleanor took her camera and her sound recording equipment, resumed her old habit of documenting all the hidden things in Wintonvale. Like documenting myself. She walked to the train track, stepping over empty longnecks, a beaten-up old boot, past the shuttered homes, past the bushland towards the large manmade pond near the outskirts of town. These routes she had taken her entire life; her body a compass. She found a clearing by the reeds, set up her equipment between two trees, hung the camera around her neck, sprawled in the grass. Frog murmur, kookaburra laugh; sound waves to clear her mind. All by herself. She grinned. Eleanor watched a family of wood ducks swim across the pond, the float of feathers hypnotic, and she lay on her back, stared at clouds, their shapes of lost animal kingdoms. Eyes became heavy, and the frogs drummed, and there was peace, there was sleep.

It was dark by the time she returned to the house, entered her childhood bedroom. Leon was half-naked on her bed, reading a book. 'Where were you?'

'Walking around the pond. I set up some recorders so I—'

'We agreed you wouldn't go out like that.' He smiled, said it monotoned, a different meaning.

'You agreed,' she said, attempted laughter.

'A lot of weird men walk out there.' Air sucked through his teeth, sound of his displeasure, this noise she heard more and more lately. He stared at her before looking down at his chest and arms, flexed his muscles.

'It's not that bad,' she said, took her coat off and hung it on the chair by the window.

'I don't like it. What if something happened?'

'It's fine! Nothing happened.'

Leon summoned her. The way he held his body, the way his eyes narrowed. A dull ache across her abdomen; a worry. All communication through body language. We talk in animal language: fur to fur, skin to skin, sonar. 'Are you angry?' she asked.

'Why would you say that?'

'Because it feels like you are.'

'Always reading into something, Eleanor. You think too much.' His top lip pulled down, that sneer he couldn't control.

And she went to him, stood by the bedhead. 'I'm sorry I upset you, Leon.' The way words fall out of mouths; like walking off an edge, the way you do when you stand too close to a mountain ledge. This feeling that came when she did as she was told.

He smelled of pine needles, of dirt-covered tree roots after rain. She closed her eyes. Where had he been? He grabbed her hand. 'How sorry are you?' He tried to tease, pulled on her fingers one by one.

'Very,' she said and he sat up, knocked the book from the bed, shoved his hand under her shirt and his skin on her skin was like fire.

He lowered his voice. 'Should we play the sorry game?' He bit her earlobe before snaking his tongue inside her ear.

'My parents are just outside.'

'So?' He slipped his fingers inside her and she closed her eyes, I am not here, and she heard Kitty's voice in her ear, 'Sometimes you let them be happy no matter what.'

She kissed him, the way she does when this happens, and he said, 'I love you, Eleanor,' and she nodded.

Leon ate at her ear, her teeth, her lip, made his way down her neck, collarbone, mouthed her breast, teethed on skin around her hip, ate, ate. Eleanor shifted away from him and he pulled her back in, growled into her; wrestling bodies that could be mistaken for passion.

Eleanor said, 'My parents . . .'

'You think too much, Eleanor,' and he lowered over her stomach, down to her groin. 'I want to see inside you.' He took her underwear off, and she felt his fingernails deep inside her vagina, his nose on her, his pointed tongue inside, and when he came up for air he said into her body, 'This is my cunt.'

He'd never said this to her before. She tried to pull her knees together and she widened her eyes, stared at the ceiling, thought of the way birds come into the world understanding that although it comes at a high price, seasonal movement is the only way to survive. Eleanor thought of her own migration. If I get up will I fly so far away that I become lost in clouds and never return? She heard Kitty in the hallway.

'This feels so good, Eleanor.' He breathed heavy, a beast. It was too much. 'I want to take a photo of you, just like this, to capture the moment.' He pulled away from her, pulled the camera onto the bed.

'Leon . . .' Fly away, fly away.

He kissed her mouth. 'Shhh. You'll spoil it.' And the camera lens was hard against her inner thigh, and the shutter clicked like window shades slamming shut, and he breathed into her skin and his heat made her stomach churn. This humiliation.

Kitty called, 'Dinner's ready,' and Leon pushed himself up, smiled at Eleanor. 'I almost forgot where we were for a moment.' The sweetness in his voice, like nothing had happened. She didn't forget. Eleanor knew where they were.

———

Eleanor couldn't sleep, aching from folding in on herself, and at dawn was in the kitchen with the fridge open, hands on the milk, when George walked into the room, the shuffle of his slippers on linoleum like a whisper before he said, 'You still greet the day this early, do you?'

'I didn't mean to wake you,' she said.

He waved his hand. 'I hear everything.'

'Would you like me to make you something, Dad?'

'What are you having?'

Eleanor looked back into the fridge: eggs, fruit, dish of sausages and mashed potato, cheese, butter, orange juice. 'Nothing appeals.' And she closed the fridge door.

They stood in the dark for a time, George's breathing rumbled like the ocean, and for a moment it felt as if they were back in a small boat under the stars on a fishing trip when she was younger, and her body swayed and the floor was water and her body floated with the tides.

The fridge hummed and then her father began to weep.

'What's wrong?' she asked.

A long wheeze from his throat. 'The house is full.'

'I guess it must be a bit strange.'

'I'm sorry.'

'Let it all out, Dad.'

The thunder sound of him made her shiver. Eleanor said, 'Should we go for a walk?'

'That would be good.'

They left the house as they were, before the others woke up.

They walked together, matched strides. Eleanor turned her head towards her father every so often, waited for him to say something, anything, to finish a sentence, a train of thought.

'Do you think you'll have children, Eleanor?' He said it like he already knew the answer.

'I don't know.'

'I can understand that.'

'Why are you asking?' They never spoke like this. Not lately.

'I just wanted to know what your plans are for yourself.'

She slung her arm around him. 'I'll let you know, Dad.'

'Leon told me he'd like to have children with you.'

'Did he? When?'

'Last night after dinner.'

She tried to imagine these two men mapping out a future without her. 'To be honest with you, the idea frightens me.' Who would I become?

George looked to the sky, looked to the treetops moving in the wind. 'You'd find your own way.'

'I'm sure Mum would have a few things to say.'

George grinned, then was sad. 'She's not always right, Eleanor.'

This was an act of treason. They stopped at the edge of the section of bushland where Badger was found.

'Dad, what's going on?' The idea of something affecting her being beyond her control.

'One day I'm not going to be here, but I don't want you to feel bad about it.'

Her head hammered. 'Are you dying?'

George shook his head. 'I've just been thinking about what's next.'

She never understood her father, the way he would barely voice an opinion and then a day would come when all he did was talk. I wish he'd said more when I was a child. 'What *is* next, Dad?'

'I've always thought I'd finish at the mountain.' He turned to her, brushed hair out of her eye. The idea of him not being there anymore. She didn't know what to say. She hugged her father. 'Thanks for telling me.'

'Don't tell your mother.'

'Okay.'

'She'll try to make you stop me. And I don't want you to have to do that. I want to go there and fly off the mountain face and feel weightless.'

They walked further into the bush, entered the space where the cubby had been, sat under a tall ghost gum, didn't speak to each other. A crow sounded out above them, a magpie pulled grass seed from dirt, and there was a humming and for a moment Eleanor felt the earth's vibrational pull underneath her. The way the world keeps turning.

She could sense George staring at her. 'What?'

'It's important for me to tell you something. One thing I've learned in my life is that children work their own magic.' George paused. 'He was a lovely boy, Eleanor. And you were a joy.' Her father's memory; pulling rabbits from hats. The years he must've held on to this.

He nodded at her and he said nothing else and he cried and the tree was hard against their backs and the morning warmed them and she sat with her father until he had nothing more to let go of.

———

Kitty had made breakfast, had set the table for four, had three different types of eggs to choose from: hard-boiled, fried, scrambled. Leon was at the dining table, coffee in hand, newspaper spread across his lap, was rosy-cheeked, was back to the way she was used to seeing him.

Kitty opened her arms. 'There you both are!'

Leon put the paper away. 'We wondered where you went to.'

'We sure did.' Kitty pulled chairs out for them to sit.

'We were walking,' George said.

'Anywhere nice?' Leon sipped coffee.

'Not especially.' Eleanor didn't see the point of elaborating the movement of nature to her mother and boyfriend.

'George, I bet you're used to waking up early. Probably still have that military clock going.'

George nodded. 'I guess so.'

'I know that's why I'm always up early.'

'You look like you just woke up,' George said.

Leon forced a chuckle.

'Isn't he a kidder? George, you're such a kidder.' This peace-keeping mother.

'Dad, he's allowed to sleep in once.' Eleanor didn't want the morning to dismantle.

'Personally, I don't think it matters what time we get up. The fact is we got up! What matters is I made us eggs.' Kitty removed her apron, kept her smile, and made the conversation go away, made it easier for them all to exist in a moment together.

Eleanor sat next to Leon and he kissed her hand, told her, 'You look lovely this morning,' made her blush.

'My, my! You've got a keeper there. George, isn't he a keeper?'

Today he was. 'I do.' All the different ways to feel about someone.

'Let's eat!' Kitty served eggs, served orange juice, and they talked about venturing to Eleanor and Leon's house to check on the mould work, talked about how they should play a game of bridge later. 'That's what Saturdays are for, aren't they?' Kitty said, and they all agreed.

Leon cleared his throat. 'I also have plans for today.' He stood up from the table, folded his napkin and put it on his chair. 'It's clear there's every chance I'll be going to Vietnam, and that's given me a lot to think about.'

Eleanor shot eyes to her father. The way he stared at Leon, like he'd heard this before.

'I've been thinking that I couldn't imagine not coming back to happiness, and Eleanor makes me happy.'

Kitty clapped her hands. 'Oh, Eleanor. This is very charming. George! Isn't this charming?' This enthusiasm for love, contagious, seemed to lift her mother into another sphere.

'Eleanor?'

She knew the next lines, knew what her answer could bring. 'Leon.' She frowned.

'Don't overthink it. Let's get married.'

'Oh my! This is wonderful.' Kitty turned to Eleanor. 'You're getting married, Eleanor!' Kitty sprang from her chair, went to her daughter and held her. There were all the years of withheld mother love coming towards her.

'This is what it feels like.' It slipped out of Eleanor but no one seemed to hear it.

Kitty

1957

IT WAS THE morning of another hospital stay for George, another morning when household living had become too much for him. He was disappearing again, cried at the sound of slammed doors. These signs that things would be bad again soon.

She told him, 'Your night terrors are worse than they've ever been.'

She told him, 'I found you sleepwalking in the kitchen again.'

He said, 'But I don't remember a thing.'

'Of course you don't.'

She knew she should be ashamed of herself for exaggerating the reality, but having George around, the way he could never seem to lift himself out of war: she was so tired. 'It'll be better when you come back home,' she said. It'll be better when I have had a break from all this. And he agreed. He always agreed with her now. She called their doctor and things were arranged.

They buttoned up beside each other on the bed, hands expert in quick change. George and his small grunts as he covered himself in a white shirt and grey jumper, the effort from everything, and she wondered how it was possible that they still slept side by side, still went on without intimate touch, still made-believe this was a functioning marriage.

'Socks on.' It was no longer a question; she steered him towards life. George did what he was told and their knees touched, an old language, and she looked at his long feet, the way his heels had thickened; dried morchella.

What would it be to place a hand on his stooping back, rub him into comfort? She went to do it but rescinded. Her husband's feet disappeared into wool, and he said, 'I'm about right, I think.' He nodded and she nodded and she said, 'Your bag's already packed. I've even packed you a book.'

'Of course.'

Kitty, look at your husband, this man whom you had once insisted on loving. And she did, barely recognised the curvature of his face, this stranger she'd known almost her whole life. Kitty smiled at him, the smile she uses to signal bon voyage, sweet see-you-later.

George reached for her, grabbed her hand; reacting without thinking. He hadn't done this since the night Badger . . .

Her body magnetised towards him and he to her, and like something they used to be, they kissed. He in her mouth; too warm, too much. And then they were in the time before they had ruined each other. She hated him for it. It could have been like this. Now I just want you gone. Despite herself she kissed him back, tried to summon a version of George into the room right next to Badger sitting on the dressing table. But he didn't come.

'What if I never see you again?' he whispered. The words landed on her earlobe and she wasn't sure if they were meant for her. George held on to Kitty and he said, louder, 'I'm scared I'll never hold you again. Please can we keep holding each other.' After all the years she'd wanted to know what her husband was thinking, it was finally there in the room. She didn't know what to do with it. But now. If I hold him tighter what else will he tell me?

She did what he asked, his heart close to hers. She'd forgotten his blood rhythm and their bodies swayed, that old dance, and there they were: the night they met. This is what it had been. If only they could go back to that and stay perfect. But without moving forwards there wouldn't have been children, wouldn't have been experience.

George held her, mumbled into her shoulder, and for the first time it felt like a real possibility that this was the end and he would never return. She let him go.

'Kitty.' He filled the air with her name. A word he'd said so many times. How different its sound now.

The embrace done, George took the bag she had packed and Kitty said, 'Make sure you tell Eleanor you will see her again.' He nodded and left.

After a time, Kitty made her way to the lounge room, where George and Eleanor sat quietly on the sofa, side by side. To be like that. How was it enough for them both? George's arm slung over Eleanor's bony shoulders; Badger's binoculars hanging from her neck. 'What are you doing?' Kitty said.

'Birdwatching,' George replied.

'Something just moved in the treetop!' Eleanor pointed to the far corner of the room, where the plastic maidenhair fern hung from the ceiling.

Kitty loved and hated that they could imagine something beyond what was in front of them. She looked at George, his dumb smile. How easy it was to be the good parent when you were never here, when you were given the mental space to come up with new worlds while the other parent was busy keeping this one together. I could do that, Kitty thought. I could make something from nothing. 'George, we will have to go soon.'

No movement from the sofa. Eleanor turned to her father, stuck a finger in her mouth and pulled it out like a plum, made a pop sound, made George guffaw. Even before the war Kitty had never been able to do that. She wanted to say, 'You have no idea how hard I've had to work to get this man to a position for you to enjoy him.' She wanted to say, 'Know your place, girl.'

She wanted to. But Kitty laughed along, remembered the role she had to play, and three tunes filled the house like three before.

George hugged Eleanor. 'Make sure you're good for Mum.' And he pulled a small piece of folded paper from his trouser pocket, slipped it into Eleanor's hand. The way they passed notes to each other, little secrets between children. I'll never know what they say to each other.

Eleanor nodded and side-eyed Kitty. Was this a test?

'She always is, aren't you, darling?' This act Kitty performed. Only a few more hours until it could be dropped. Kitty said, 'Can't keep them waiting, George.'

A regimented husband stands at attention no matter how he feels. 'I'll be back, of course.' He kissed Eleanor on top of her head as she looked down, her face scrunching in on itself. She should pull herself together, Kitty thought. Her looking like that. Like she doesn't want to be around me.

Kitty clutched her handbag, its soft calf leather like Lux soap flakes against skin, walked past Eleanor and pulsed her free hand under her daughter's chin, lifted it up: there was the glass-eyed look of drama. 'Don't make this difficult, Eleanor. It's not fair on your father.'

That crumpled face. George was by the door, saw it all, said nothing. That'd be right, she thought. I enforce a reality while—

'Can I go see Ruth?'

'Why?'

'I want to play.'

Kitty, with her child's face still in her hand: jaw clenched, milk and adult teeth grinding against each other like work. If Eleanor kept that up she'd have no bite to her. Kitty closed her eyes, took a deep breath in. 'No. You have chores to do.' Kitty, why can't you be nicer to her? And so she said, 'Alright then.'

Her daughter smiled, quick-kissed the inside of Kitty's palm. That feeling of her: would it ever come again? Do it again, Eleanor. Kiss me like that again. But like all moments it vanished, and Kitty wiped her palm on her dress and went over to George, pushed him out the front door.

All that good that was in the room was left behind.

––––––

George buckled his knees, buckled into himself while Kitty turned the key in the ignition, and he cried like a lamb. If he lets it all out, will it be better? Kitty patted his knee, hospital sympathy, and George said, 'I'm sorry,' and the car accelerated out of the driveway with such force that both of them started.

'Can we drive around?'

Kitty checked the petrol gauge: half empty. 'What for?'

George held her hand, held her thigh, began to rub his thumb along her dress, then underneath it, along her skin, his uncut nail nicking at her edges, taking small pieces of her with him.

'George.'

'I'm sorry.' He kept going and he cried. And he cried. And he cried. Something about the way he gnawed at her skin, that way of trying to uncover her. What was he keeping from her? George kept at her and Kitty slapped his hands away, slapped his face, slapped him over and over. He removed himself from her and she heard herself say, 'Why couldn't you have left me alone?' Why couldn't you have died? And if he had, what would be left? To have lost a son, a husband. To be one of two left over, two women in the house. She realised she had already begun to age her daughter out of her life: she'd fast-forwarded the rest of Eleanor's childhood, skipped puberty, had already made her an adult, a peer, someone to be wary of, someone to compete with for the attention of the world. Hold on to your child for as long as you can, Kitty. But to do this she'd have to hold on to George for a little longer. 'Do you still want me to drive you around?'

'No,' he said. 'This is enough.'

She drove him to the hospital but something didn't feel right. She didn't feel like herself.

———

Outside the car as she drove home: women walked with newborns, elderly couples held each other's elbows strolling down paths, and a small grey dog ran out onto the road a few metres ahead of her. Kitty slammed on the brakes but her tyres couldn't find traction and she collided with the dog. The noise the car made when it jolted made her wince and the engine stalled. Why couldn't people prevent things from running away from them? Now she'd hit an animal, a thing someone might grieve. Now I have to get out and check the damage done. It wasn't her fault. Kitty held tight to the steering wheel and she cried, banged her palms on the wheel until they ached, until the car horn sounded. She couldn't recall seeing a collar on the dog and without a collar there's no one waiting. Why did this have to happen today? Kitty looked at herself in the rear-view mirror – red eyes, red mouth – composed herself.

She looked for witnesses, saw none. She started the car and drove home to her daughter without looking back.

———

When she entered the house, Kitty could hear Eleanor speaking from deep inside her bedroom. She had done as she was first instructed, stayed home where she belonged. Kitty clutched her heart, closed in on Eleanor, stood at her door, saw her cross-legged on her pink-and-green bedspread counting out feathers. Next to her was a doll and a hairbrush, a journal and pen, and next to them, on a small chair, sat Badger. Eleanor said to her brother, 'How high do you think we could go when we fly away from here?'

Here was proof her children conspired against her. I knew it; I knew they wanted to leave me. Kitty would have to invent ways to stop them. But she couldn't take her eyes off Eleanor's fingers, the length of them; a dexterity that only comes when you play with secrets. Kitty wanted them for herself. Eleanor held up each feather to Badger. 'This one is from the mountain. Dad said you already had one. And this one is from the backyard. This one is from the park. This one's from the school gate. Mum hates this one.'

Kitty hadn't stopped to listen to her daughter before. Not like this. Her daughter laughed and Kitty failed to see what could set off a ten-year-old into happiness. What else does Eleanor do when I'm not looking?

———

After dinner, after dishes were stacked by the sink, Kitty folded Eleanor into her arms, felt her daughter shrink against her chest with something like terror. And she said, 'Why not get the hairbrush from your room and bring it here.'

Eleanor nodded into Kitty's breasts and ran towards the olive branch from her mother. The quick steps made Kitty smile, and Eleanor returned with a gap-toothed grin, brush in hand, and her nightie half tucked into her underwear, signs that Eleanor had had to crawl under her bed to find her brush, didn't want anything to stand in her way of completing a task. Kitty couldn't help but feel a type of love in that moment. Why can't it just be like this forever? These feelings that could exist inside her had never gone away. For so long she had believed that happiness would never come again. What has denial given me? Kitty teared up and Eleanor turned her back on her mother, sat at the foot of the lounge chair, curled her hands around Kitty's ankles. Kitty slowly stroked the brush through her daughter's long hair, the sound of bristles against a scalp, the one that she would kiss in the early days but had stopped so soon afterwards. Eleanor, I'm sorry. But she didn't say it out loud and instead brushed through the knots while Eleanor ran her sentences together. 'And then I was this massive peacock in a really tiny tree, almost like Godzilla but a bird instead, and all these people were throwing rocks at me so I flapped my wings to get rid of them. Oh! And the other day when I was coming home from school I saw a dead frog on the footpath and half its guts were squished out and Ruth said it was absolutely disgusting but actually I thought it was really interesting.' The small thoughts of this girl: the revelation of who your child really is.

Eleanor held Kitty's ankles tighter and long strands of hair fell onto the carpet, brushed against her skin like cobwebs. Kitty tried to hold on to this feeling, but she knew all good things are eventually taken from you. Hair fell onto the carpet, like pulling loose threads, the eventual end of things.

After brushing her hair, Kitty took Eleanor by the hand to the bathroom and brushed her daughter's teeth. 'Open wide, Eleanor.'

'I can do it myself.' But she let her mother do it all the same, opened wide her little mouth, let Kitty in. Gums were soft and Kitty placed her hand under Eleanor's chin so that she could get at the hard-to-reach places. Skin was soft and Kitty placed her fingers on Eleanor's neck. A child's pulse is faster than you think. All that life they have to catch up on. Kitty tickled Eleanor, small gentle swipes along her neck, and Eleanor laughed and squirmed, dribbled toothpaste down her chin, down the front of her nightie onto Kitty's flat black shoes, onto the tiles Badger's body had once rested upon. Houses and their histories. Kitty would clean it all up later.

She sat by Eleanor's bed after tucking her in, read to her. Kitty liked the sound of her own voice, her nightingale song. See, God? I am being good. I am a good mother. I have always been good to her. When Kitty had finished reading Eleanor slid her hand into her mother's and said, 'That was nice, wasn't it?'

Kitty gripped the small fingers. 'Yes.' Yes and yes and yes.

Eleanor snuggled into the covers until she was just a cheek, a forehead, a set of eyes, and said, 'I know Daddy says he can't help it, and I miss him, but sometimes I'm glad he has to go away. Then it can be just you and me.'

Just the two of them forever. It felt too much too soon. 'You and me and Badger.'

A moment's beat, a mistake realised. 'Oh yeah! Sometimes I forget about that.'

Kitty tried not to let it sting. Eleanor had been brought up beside her brother her entire life and she was already starting to forget him. Part of Kitty wanted to slap Eleanor, to punish that selfishness. But Eleanor closed her eyes, said, 'I love Badger so much,' and Kitty softened. She stroked her daughter into comfort, let her know that things could be alright, and noticed the way her wedding ring spun through Eleanor's brown hair; a harvest.

'I love you, Mummy.' The clarity of a declaration.

Kitty bent down to kiss Eleanor's half-hidden forehead, hoped she was smiling at her daughter brighter than she ever had. Because the words *I love you too* and *You are mine* and *I'm trying so hard* wouldn't form no matter how she tried.

———

Streetlights were lanterns, brought a knock, a moth, to the front door: Charlie.

Kitty had waited for him in the lounge room, wore her tight black dress, had reapplied her lipstick and perfume, had seated herself on the lounge; her bare knees felt unusually tender underneath the velvet, made her chew the inside of her cheek. This knock an intrusion. It sounded again and she worried Eleanor would hear it. She shook her head, shook those thoughts away, and in that moment she realised she didn't want to go to Charlie and instead she wrapped herself in a cardigan, went to the kitchen. Out of the fridge: eggs, milk, butter, apple. Out of the cupboard: flour, sugar, baking soda, vanilla. All onto the counter and another knock at the door, Charlie saying quietly, 'Anyone home?' Kitty brought out the ceramic mixing bowls and went about making Eleanor her favourite cake.

Preheat the oven, beat butter and sugar. The body understands how a project can be used to heal itself. She thought of George, how he would be wrapped in his bed linens, book in hand, comfortable enough to take off his prosthesis. And like George, hers came off too. The body remembers how to live. Charlie left, his boots like faded drum beats down the garden path, and Kitty poured the cake batter into tin, put tin into oven, crept into Eleanor's room and sat in the middle of the floor in the dark. Like being inside someone else. Light snores of an exhausted child. They were together, quiet. What would it be like to stay like this, just her, just me?

Kitty left the room, went to her son, still waiting for his mother in the kitchen. He had never looked so small. She picked him up from the bench and told him, 'I just need to see,' went down the dark hallway to her own bedroom and put Badger inside the cupboard among her furs and George's old service uniforms. She felt a chill in the air and from the kitchen the oven bell tolled, told her the cake was done. She shut the cupboard door.

———

Hours later, in her bed with all its memories of family bodies, she had the feeling that she was being pulled down into the mattress, down under the house, where she would sometimes find George on his hands and knees in the dirt. 'Can you smell it?' he'd ask. 'I think there's rotten meat.' Sometimes Eleanor would be under the house with him, dusky pink trousers smeared with dirt as she scouted for her father. And all the times Kitty had said, 'No. I don't smell a thing.'

But there. She could detect the smell of meat and she was being pulled into the mattress. Why not join them, just this once. For the first time since their beginning, she missed George. Missed the heave of his lungs as he slept, listening to his breath, missed having someone between her and Eleanor, between her and the fear that another child would be taken. In that moment she wanted him back. Not to love her, although she might accept that too, but she wanted the body that would shield her from the cannon fire of everything that could come next.

She thought of their wedding vows and reached for George's pillow, put it between her legs, let duck down prick the insides of her thighs, and she rode herself into the place George screamed into, where his nightmares and dreams called to her, begged her to be a good wife. She shoved the pillow as far as it would go and she whimpered, didn't care if Eleanor heard her. Let her see who her mother is when she finally lets go. Everything was warm and she could smell everything that was underground, breathed it in.

For a moment she left her body, the sensation of weightlessness was overwhelming, and when she came back inside herself she ground harder into the pillow, into George, and she thought of him and their daughter and she was happy.

Eleanor

1971

THE CHANGES BEGAN after marriage. Leon tantrumed through the house, stopped picking up after himself, stopped speaking to her. 'What's wrong? Is there something I can do to help you?' Eleanor asked, but he said nothing. Maybe Leon worried about going to Vietnam, worried about coming home like George, so he was already preparing to end the relationship to spare her? These were things that she worried about too.

She didn't like living in a house that resembled the past. She would do anything to make it better. But Leon kept stiff lips and silence. So Eleanor left work early to make Leon his favourite meal of mustard rump steak and scalloped potatoes, layered frosted pink lipstick, layered herself onto herself, the parts of her she knew he loved best. But he hadn't looked at her when he came home, carried his foul mood down the hallway and sat with it at the dining table, cutting away at flesh.

'How was your day?' Set down knife and fork in hand, made efforts to be even more attentive.

Leon chewed and she noticed for the first time that his jaw seemed to be bigger, she'd never noticed that his jaw clicked in and out . . .

Finally he said, 'Why haven't we started a family yet?'

She nearly choked on potato. 'Sorry?'

'I thought we made a promise.'

Had they? Eleanor couldn't recall. 'Leon . . .'

'I work all day and I come home and it's just you and me and I'm accumulating money that's just sitting there and I'm fucking going to go to war and I don't know why you just won't do what we agreed. What the fuck am I working towards?'

'I'm sorry. I'll try and move the research around and we can work out a good time to have a baby . . .'

'You're selfish, Eleanor.' He cut his meat, cut back into silence.

She stood. 'I'm not hungry. I'm going to go to bed.' She left the table, went to bed early, left him there with his silence. Things will be different in the morning.

———

Men can change the patterns of night, hide the moon to trick the eye. The crack of knees woke her. Is it morning already? She opened her eyes, still dark, and found Leon closing in on her.

Something about the way his body sucked air from the room made her freeze and he made a fist of himself, hard like a punch, leaned into her ear, said, 'Let's make a baby,' kissed her cheek, licked the side of her mouth. What is he doing? He rubbed against her hipbone and she closed her eyes, hoped that if she didn't move, was beyond still, he would leave her alone. The sound of his saliva collecting in his throat as he rolled her onto her stomach, his fingers sweeping the length of her, over her arse, spread her wide, and her body went into shock as he arranged her so she could not move. She could not think when he ran his hand underneath her pubic bone, could not move as he stroked her hair, could not move as he pushed her wider, could not move as he seeded a finger inside her vagina, could not move as he pushed her wider and wider and wider and wider, another finger inside, another finger inside and he moved them in and out of her and she couldn't move when he pressed his torso in between her legs, couldn't move when he pushed himself inside her body, and he thrust and he thrust and he made a jackal sound and he thrust and he thrust and he thrust and he pushed her legs wider still and he called out, 'Do you like that?' He thrust and he thrust and he put his hands around her throat and she couldn't move and he thrust and when he ejaculated inside her, when he tightened his hands around her throat, she thought, This is the night I die. When he released his hands she couldn't move and he pulled out of her and he kissed the length of her back and he whispered in her ear, 'Baby, I just gave you the world.'

When he eventually rolled over and went to sleep and she was sure it was safe to finally move, she slipped quietly from the bed to the bathroom and took a shower. The ache between her legs; blood, swelling, pain. The hot water stung needle point as it hit her face but she couldn't think of how to move out of its range. The things he had said; what world does a man like that create?

———

Leon was still beside her in the morning, his foot nubbed against her calf, hard toes into tight muscle. He was snoring lightly, the sound of peaceful sleep, the sound she knew so well. The sight of him made her throat ache and she remembered how he'd grabbed her, hands metal and cold, a collar tightening, stealing her breath. He didn't want you to get away, Eleanor, and she blinked to nod, blinked to see if it would make it all disappear.

How was this still the same man? How did a stranger crawl into her bed? She swallowed again; her tongue scraped the roof of her mouth. I need water. I need to move. But for the life of her she couldn't seem to lift her body from the bed. I can't do anything anymore. Counted to ten, tried again, imagined her room was filling with the ocean tide and that she needed to leave immediately. The fear of drowning, of suffocation. It was enough to move her.

Eleanor left Leon in bed, fought the habit of a morning kiss, and when she made it to the bathroom, pulled her nightgown above her waist to sit on the toilet, saw latticed red bruises spread across her inner thighs like *Clathrus ruber*. Her knees knocked together, a self-defence to hide evidence, and she let herself go and urine stung and if she let herself be honest she would admit that sex with Leon over the last few months always hurt her in some way. But never like this.

The moon yields to a sun to remind you that all things continue, that nothing stops just because you want it to. Eleanor parted her legs again, took in her bruises, wanted to cry but no tears came. She shook her thoughts away, tried not to think of the pain in her thighs. Before she had sex for the first time, Kitty had told her, 'I'll be able to tell when it's happened. You'll walk differently, you know.'

Eleanor hated the way her mother spoke to her about sex. Everything about it seemed too intimate yet clinical. But there in the bathroom she wondered if her mother would be able to detect what Leon had done during the night. What would my walk give away then? How many strides would it take to understand violence?

The dark smell of her urine made her stomach churn, the memory of the way Leon had smelled the night before: too ripe, too sour. She vomited, and bile burned her throat. Eleanor gritted her teeth, tried to catch herself in her hands so what was inside her wouldn't fall to the floor, but the dull orange and mucus of her hit the tiles, pooled around her legs. The heat of herself; too much like last night. I want my dad. She vomited again. I want him to tell me that my husband made a mistake. 'I know men,' she wanted him to say. 'And he shouldn't do this.'

Eleanor reached for a towel, mopped up the mess on the floor before washing her legs down in the shower.

Leon was leaning against the counter when she went into the kitchen. He smiled at her, drumming his fingers against the side of the bench, bared his teeth, made her jump.

'What's with you?' A light tilt to his voice.

'You scared me.'

Leon smirked. 'Little ol' me? I couldn't scare a thing.' He pointed to the two cups on the counter. 'Made you coffee.'

Eleanor, don't go near him. But her body moved without permission, picked up the cup, and Leon pulled her in, tightened his arm around her into an approximation of a hug. She didn't know where to place her hands, her head. Our bodies don't fit anymore.

'What's wrong?' The way he said it; as though she'd hurt his feelings.

'I don't know.' All things. All things are wrong.

'You're being weird. Didn't you sleep well?'

His question made her flinch. Did he not remember? Eleanor pulled away, met his eye. 'I don't . . .' She couldn't finish.

Leon smoothed his knuckles along the side of her cheek. 'Why were you in the bathroom?'

'I was sick.'

'Did you eat something that didn't agree with you?' He was telling her the answer, was testing her. Not the first time he'd done this. They'd had similar conversations when she'd woken up feeling tired, woken up unable to even recall a dream. Her husband had held her as he always did, told her again and again that she did things in her sleep. 'You need me to take care of you.'

But there in the kitchen, the way he looked at her as if he was seeing through her. Like he was waiting for her to make a mistake.

'Leon—' She stopped, folded her arms across her chest. 'Did something happen last night?'

'What do you mean?'

'I don't know.'

He reached for coffee, sipped. 'There's obviously something going on in your head.' Put the coffee down and grabbed her arm.

'Stop.' Eleanor didn't recognise her own voice.

He held her tighter, bicep bulging, made sure she wouldn't move away from him, and she flinched again. Leon shook his head. 'So, a man can't even go near his wife?'

Eleanor, you're making it worse. She tried to shake thoughts away, tried not to cry. It's already worse. What use would fighting back do? And yet. 'I'm sorry. I don't know what's wrong with me. I got frightened.'

'Of fucking what?' Low-toned. He didn't raise his voice.

Bile in the throat again. Everything inside her wanted to run. 'I don't know.'

They were silent, then Leon said, 'You know what? Lately you make me feel bad about myself.'

Eleanor heard thunder in the ceiling, a wall of sound in her head. 'What do you mean?' The bruises on her thighs pulsed, making it difficult to stand.

Leon moved in on her until their bodies touched. 'Do you like this?' An attempt at a lover's caress.

She did not. 'I don't know what you mean.'

He ran his finger along her jawline. 'Remember how you used to let me touch you? Remember how safe that felt?'

She nodded.

'I just can't see why you're scared of me, Eleanor. Do you think you had a bad dream?'

Her body so used to the patterns of agreement. She nodded, began to cry. This can't be the same man.

———

She lost herself in work: warm in the sun, on firm ground as she set up her equipment, strung microphones in tree branches. Near her two magpies attacked a crow as it pecked into the ground. The crow side-hopped but the magpies grew giant and flared wings, attacked again and again, their black beaks nipped crow wing and top of skull and the crow cawed, tried to hop away. 'Move! Fly away,' she said. This thing she always said when she saw this behaviour. Even crows could predict her response.

Eleanor kneeled, removed her binoculars from her neck, the hanging weight distracting now, uncomfortable over her breasts in a way she hadn't noticed before, and the second magpie rose in the air, one foot, three, five before angling its legs towards the crow, diving at it once more. Cracked wings together so that the pop of feather and bone echoed into tree trunks. On it went, one bird after the other, crack dive, crack dive. For a moment Eleanor thought she heard a magpie laugh. Stop anthropomorphising. But it was so easy to do.

Sun behind cloud and wind whipped eucalypt limbs into a waltz. How was it possible the magpies didn't seem to notice the sun's heat was slowly disappearing? Eleanor jotted, *Look for ways subtle shifts in environment change attacking behaviour – may change behaviour*, stretched forwards to loosen a day of work. The pull of tendon gave relief, did it again, and a plane flew above, made Eleanor smile, mutter, 'Mechanical bird,' and she laughed to herself. This girlhood heart: she never seemed to be able to outgrow it. The birds attacked but she found peace. More and more she preferred this mode of herself: working, being reduced to an observer, reduced to skin absorbing heat, forgetting everything outside of here existed. Safety.

She leaned on her elbows, lowered herself until her chest hit dirt. Her heart drummed slow into the top soil, down into the earth core, into the centre of something bigger than her. That's what I want to do: go deeper and further than I ever have before. Everything became quiet. She closed her eyes, imagined she was in New Caledonia looking for insight into possible theories of crow engineering, those ways of using talon and beak to make a life easier. This is where she wanted to be: away from here, away from the confusion, away from her mother, her husband. Her lips soured at the last. The idea had been calling to her more and more these days, a constant whisper in her ear. And she'd been listening. After she'd made the mistake of telling him that she'd applied interstate and he told her, 'You didn't ask me if that was okay,' she applied for more jobs and grants like a petulant child, told him nothing. The secrets she kept were mounting up.

She checked her watch, all the minutes that took her closer to home time. Nausea flooded her body and she closed her eyes, I don't want to leave here just yet, and she listened to the earth talk, listened to wings crack, the way it made the spinning inside her body stop for a moment; all peace. This is what I want: to live alone.

———

Later, when she was home, she called Ruth. 'Hey, it's me.'

'You haven't called me for weeks.' Ruth clicked her tongue.

'Really?' Were days really slipping by that fast?

'It's becoming a really annoying behaviour.'

'But I just called you about going to see the exhibition.'

'That was in June. And then you never followed up to set the date.'

It was true. 'Why didn't you remind me?'

'Because I'm not your fucking parent and I have better things to do.'

Eleanor hated it when her friend was like this. 'I'm sorry. Please don't be mad.'

Ruth groaned and Eleanor could feel the temperature lower. 'Come on, tell me what's up,' Ruth said.

'I feel like . . . Sometimes when I'm on my own it feels like I'm being shown an advance copy of the next few years, and when I go to read it I can't believe what I'm seeing.'

'What don't you believe?' Ruth yawned.

'Sorry. Am I boring you?'

'I merely yawned! God, you're so sensitive lately. What's going on with you?'

Everything. She still hadn't told Ruth what Leon did to her at night. 'Nothing! I'm just . . . Do you? Do you ever feel that way?'

'Of course I do. I like to think of it as the future self telling you what to do.'

'But what if it's not?'

'Okay, Eleanor, I know you didn't call for philosophy. What is going on? Is it your mum? Is it Leon? Did you suddenly win the lottery and you're mad at yourself because you're about to give it all away? Because if that's the case, I'll take some. I don't mind making you angry.' She cackled.

'No. It's me. I feel wrong. I feel like I'm not doing anything right.'

Eleanor heard Ruth drag a wooden stool across her floor, sigh as she sat. 'What were you just doing?'

'I was working.'

'And how did it make you feel?'

'Normal. There were these two magpies . . .'

'Yeah, yeah, there were birds. I get it. The point is it's the thing you love. Stop telling yourself you do everything wrong.'

Hearing this, like hearing herself out loud. She just needed someone to keep telling her these things. 'I don't want to be here, Ruth.' The blood rush of it.

'What do you mean by that exactly?'

'I don't know. I just feel like I'm sinking through my skin and I don't want to be inside me. I feel like I need to be somewhere else.'

'Where is somewhere else?'

She was silent. Couldn't Ruth just tell her? The room spun, and she saw white spots scroll across her eyes. 'I have to go lie down.'

'Wait. Are you okay? Should I come over?'

'No. I'm just having a moment.' She hung up before Ruth could say anything more.

She stood up, nauseous again, couldn't tell whether it was the phone call, or having to express those feelings out loud, or not being able to distinguish the present from the future. Her temples ached, had for days now, and she thought about time slipping. I used to be so good at placing myself in time, knowing what needed to be done when. How have I been able to lose my sense of life going on? She went to the calendar stuck to the fridge. There was a red dot on the last day she had marked off in May, a calculation of cycles. It was now almost the end of July. Why had she stopped marking? Days had become weeks . . .

Her head throbbed and the nausea came again, this time heavy and with purpose, and she heard her father in her head: the body knows before the mind does. What had Leon done to her? She looked at the calendar again. She couldn't be. She didn't want to be. Not with him like this.

———

Two things happened at once: Leon was sent to war, Eleanor was pushed along the path to motherhood. He was overjoyed when they told her parents. 'I just can't believe I'll be a dad when I come back.'

'We will take the best care of Eleanor, won't we, George? And the baby, of course.'

He wanted sex on the last night they were together and she withstood the last duty she'd have to perform for him for a long while. He kissed her when it was over and said, 'I'm so glad I have you.'

'Me too, Leon.' A lie is a tool for survival.

'I'll be coming back for you. Don't you worry.'

Oh, but she would.

Leon slunk his finger over her hip, tapped bone. How he stared at her bare skin, stared at her face like he could see through her. His way of looking: a butcher bird eyeing raw meat on the pavement. Then he lifted Eleanor's right arm, bent it into uncomfortable degrees above her head on the pillow, tilted her faded-bruised hips towards him before spreading her knees apart. Eleanor could feel cold air creep inside her. He smiled at her and she wanted to disappear. 'You look like a little statue I carved. I love you like this,' he said. He spat into his palm before wiping his wet hand on the inside of her thigh. 'Just shining marble,' he said to himself.

Leon got up from the bed, went to the chest of drawers and pulled out a polaroid camera. 'I want to take you with me so I can see you whenever I want.'

The ways you survive. She didn't move, knew better. Eleanor closed her eyes, felt her husband close in on her, heard the click of a button before photographic paper hissed out of the camera and fell at her feet. When she finally opened her eyes, Leon was shaking the photographs into life with one hand and stroking his penis with the other.

The way he moved: her body should've become an alarm but all she felt was the dull-rock heavy weight of her limbs, the way

214

she wasn't there anymore. 'Will you show anyone those photos?' Body clenched, waiting for his response, and she imagined Leon with other men like him staring at her photos, the way they would play themselves like instruments in hidden rooms; nightmarish chamber music.

'No. All for me,' he whispered before coming onto the floor.

Her body let go, she let go.

Later, Eleanor watched her husband pack his version of her into his duffel bag and then she fell into a deep sleep.

———

Then she was alone in a body she couldn't understand, that no longer felt like her own: what is existing? She made the mistake of calling her mother. 'I can't go through with this.'

Kitty sighed, mistook her daughter's implication. 'You're giving it too much thought. Just let it happen and you'll see it's nothing. Eleanor, this has made me so very happy!'

Kitty came to the house every day after that. 'How are you feeling? You look pale. Why aren't you going outside to get some sun?'

She brought her small camera to document Eleanor's pregnancy. 'Nobody thought of taking photographs of me when I was pregnant.' Kitty was matter-of-fact, that way of letting Eleanor know that she had no choice but to go along with it all. That this was how it was. But her mother like this. Maybe this is how we erase the past. Eleanor offered her mother cups of tea, offered conversations about books, her studies, would ask about long-ago relatives and their children – anything to get Kitty to open up about herself and engage with something other than the impending arrival of a baby. Kitty wanted none of it.

'Motherhood will change you, Eleanor. I can tell you it certainly changed me.'

Changing, becoming a mother. 'I'm not ready. I didn't expect this to happen now. I . . .'

Kitty stroked Eleanor's hair. 'Motherhood will be the greatest thing you've ever achieved.'

Being reduced to a biological function. Eleanor couldn't help but cry.

'Now we'll have something in common. You'll see just how hard it was for me to raise you. But it'll be wonderful.'

Eleanor shook her head and her mother said, 'Just let go.'

After her pep talks, Kitty asked Eleanor to pose for a photo. 'Go side on.' Eleanor would do as she was told. 'Put your hand on your belly.' Eleanor would do as she was told. 'Lift up your dress so I can see how big you're getting.' Eleanor would do as she was told because she couldn't bear the consequence of saying no. The humiliation of keeping her mother happy. And yet. They were so close. Maybe I could learn to get used to this.

Kitty took her photos, circled Eleanor as if she were a specimen, as if she wasn't there. Kitty placed a hand on Eleanor's stomach, absent-mindedly touched her own, breathed deep and slow; animal bonding.

'Make my baby kick.' Kitty had whispered but Eleanor heard it louder than almost anything Kitty had ever said. There it was. The baby had become *my baby*.

Eleanor, let that sink in. 'What did you say?'

Kitty looked at her, smiled. 'Nothing, dear. I said nothing at all.'

———

She would go to the mountain. And it would end. Eleanor got the Belmont ready, didn't tell anyone she was leaving. Off she went, the landscape slowly carved small changes between the arbitrary interstate borders, and the baby was somersault and kick, made Eleanor scream into the windshield. 'I'm losing my mind.'

Eventually she arrived in the mountain town, parked her car in a street bordering the beginning of the trail she and George used to take when they'd go camping together. She locked the car, put the keys in her pocket, put her hand across the small kick in her stomach to settle herself.

Eleanor began to climb the cold mountain. She balled her hands into fists, the only thing she could do to keep them warm. Her hands were red and purple, splotched white, the same colours as the rocks she walked over, and she thought: I am peeling back to nature.

Her legs ached as she climbed higher, underused muscle. She was nauseous, felt bile warm her throat before sinking back down to the pit of her stomach. 'I know what you're thinking. I'm still going to do it,' she said to sky. Eventually she arrived at the first ledge, stepped as close to the edge as she could, unfurled her fist and held on to the safety rail.

There's a feeling that comes when you stand on the edge of a plateau, look down over the plains below, those trees valleyed together; all that endless endlessness. The way the mountain range surrounds the valley, makes everything inside it so small. This beautiful thing. 'Look how it keeps going.' I am small, the world is infinite. The feeling that comes when you stand on the edge: the body wants to jump, as if the future self is impatient, wants to leap out and experience everything for the first time.

Eleanor closed her eyes. 'How am I meant to keep going like this?' She screamed it. Over the months she hadn't been able to get past the fear of turning into her mother, the way women can break women without realising it. What if I can't show love? What if it's not enough? What if I can't show my child who I am? What if I'm never myself again? To become a mother now. Sometimes at night she prayed to a God she didn't believe in. 'Please don't let me wake up in the morning.' And then the sun would eclipse her and she'd cry and somehow the day would continue and when the night came she'd be on her knees again praying for the end.

She pressed her face into the mountain, whispered, 'I don't want to be here anymore.' A kick inside, body jerked, the feeling of her body slamming against rock, the hurt that it would bring, the mess it would make of her, how it would open her up. Like birds flying into windows, like soldiers surging with rifles, like mothers birthing children, like children running into waves, like Icarus flying into the sun; that quick burn.

Open your eyes. And she did, realised her heart was beating, that she'd caught her breath, that she was alive, was surrounded by a million years of things eroding, of gradual change. The baby kicked and she kept walking along the trail, up the mountain.

These tracks; mountain hips, all winter grey and brown. She wound her way around them, and the baby kicked, and Eleanor's lungs tightened from the cold air. She carried herself and her baby through grey and brown and dark red, those muted colours that took a million years to show themselves. It is possible that in a million more years everything on the mountain will be neon, will be brighter than a star, brighter than a planet, will light up the edges of the valley, blind you, let you see with your heart.

Eleanor reached the ledge where she and George and Badger had always gone. She was tired, could no longer go on. Tired from carrying all that weight inside her, from fighting the cold. She sat inside a small cave just off the path, placed hands on the hard rock, ridges that jutted out like pelvic bone, those skeleton shapes. The anatomy of the mountain: like it was waiting to be born.

The rock was shake-bone cold, made her teeth chatter, her lower back twitch, the baby kick. She noted how some of the rock looked like hollowed-out pockets, these little hiding places, imagined all the insects that had crawled in and over them, the webs weaved, the air that had whistled from them. All of it without anyone noticing. This life goes on.

Eleanor touched the cave ridges, like hardened veins; this long life. How many years does it have left to give? How many years do I have left to give?

Damp patches in the cave, the places where water has learned to fall and slowly eat away at hard rock, and Eleanor traced her fingers over them, over the small electric green moss and small fern growing out of rock, put them in her mouth. Even in the damp dark there is still the ability to grow something beautiful, grow life.

A crow cawed in a tree; the baby kicked, mind raced. You are more than this feeling right now, more than the way you see yourself. Trees made music, water trickled inside the cave, and she watched the path in front of her, watched the shape of trees, listened to them howl against the strong wind. This old way of finding herself. In that moment: she found a wholeness, contentment. She didn't once feel like she was somebody else. Maybe this could happen again?

She stood up and took a deep breath. Maybe today isn't the day I fall.

Eleanor

1972

SHE CALLED HER mother in the night, rested her head against the kitchen wall, let the cool, green chartreuse plaster take the sting out of her headache, told Kitty, 'I think I'm losing my mind. I don't know what to do with her when she's like this.' I keep thinking I hear people in the house, I keep seeing things out of the corner of my eye. 'I'm so tired.' Her chest contracted the way it used to when she was a child, a teenager, an adult, now a mother, as if this very moment had been visiting her since birth, warning her of the things to come. Eleanor, one day you'll wake up and realise you're not who you thought you were.

Her chest burned and Kitty exhaled down the phone line. 'You're not equipped to do this on your own.'

She heard Kitty light a cigarette and Eleanor coughed. My mother is telling me I can't mother. 'What are you saying?'

'I'm saying to calm down and I will come by tomorrow.'

Kitty hung up and Eleanor untangled herself from the phone cord, hung up the phone, sat on the kitchen floor and waited for her daughter to cry.

Eleanor hated the way the first two months of Amy's life had been characterised, as if admitting that she hadn't yet bonded with the baby, admitting that she found motherhood overwhelming, made her unusual. When Leon had called after Amy's birth he told her, 'This is the most natural thing in the world for you to do. Why can't you just relax and enjoy it?' Him, speaking to her about the natural order of things: he could go to hell.

Her mother's friends Joan and Maudie came to visit her two days after the birth, brought her pea-and-ham soup. 'How are you feeling, dear?' Joan asked.

'I'm . . . I don't know. Sore. I feel . . .'

They nodded. 'Oh, you'll ache in the beginning. It happens to us all. But gosh, isn't it a blessing?'

Eleanor ached alright. But it was for something in the past, something that wasn't quantifiable.

'Now, your mother has said you need washing done. Where's your laundry basket?'

They took over her life for a week and then . . . nothing. Like using up magic wishes. Eleanor called Ruth to tell her that she needed her to come and get her, come and drag her from this life, but Ruth was never available. 'Nah, call back later. She's not here.

Actually, I haven't seen her for a few days. Mind you, I haven't been home myself . . .'

She hung up the phone. Stop feeling sorry for yourself, Eleanor. And so she went back to her daughter and tried to find blessings.

By the time Amy was three and a half weeks old everything was already so distant. The first time Eleanor had held her after the birth, the small breaths against Eleanor's chest. If I keep going through time and I can't feel it, will anything exist?

Days bled into days and she became terrified because all she wanted to do was retreat to the past, retreat to a time when she didn't have Amy, had never met Leon, had never left the city to return to Wintonvale. Just like mother, just like father. And yet. What if I suffocate my daughter with the past just like they did to me?

She called Ruth again. 'Hello?'

Eleanor's heart smashed at the sound of her friend's voice. 'Ruthie, it's me.'

'What's wrong?'

'I'm a mother.'

'We knew this day would come.' Ruth tried laughter, didn't work.

'I'm not good. I feel like I'm not here. I'm just so tired. Could you please come?' She cried, kept crying.

Ruth sighed. 'Eleanor, I can't. Not at the moment. Mum's sick. She's here in the city with me.'

'Ruth, I had no idea. I'm sorry. Why didn't you tell me?' It was the first time in their lives that Eleanor didn't know something about Ruth. Everything was falling apart.

'I just didn't. Listen, now's not a good time. I'll call you later.' And then she was gone.

Days bled into days and then it was night and she called Kitty and Kitty said, 'I'll come by tomorrow.'

———

The next day Kitty arrived at Eleanor's doorstep bearing a casserole like a trophy in her arms, brought with her the smell of gravy powder, oil-soaked carrots and chicken, of her parents not speaking to one another around the dining table.

'It'll be much simpler to look after you if you just move in with your father and me for a while.'

'Good morning to you too.' Eleanor let her mother in, let her see her T-shirts stained with baby vomit soaking in a bucket in the middle of the kitchen, let her see the stacked plates that still needed to be washed, let her see, let her see. Kitty placed the casserole on the counter, looked around.

Eleanor followed her gaze to the dining table: the field note-books, her father's old camera, the photos she took two years ago of a duck guarding the body of a drowned duckling in a pond. Kitty raised her eyebrows and Eleanor said defensively, 'I'm thinking of submitting one of them to a magazine. I found them the other day when I was cleaning out Amy's bedroom and they were better than I remembered . . .'

'You didn't tell me you were taking photos again.'

'That's because I never stopped.'

'I see.' Kitty turned on her heel, went to the sink and filled a glass of water. 'I don't know who would want to look at a drowned duck but maybe that's art nowadays.' She smiled at her daughter, took a sip. The way Kitty could sting with words.

'I just need to do something that makes me feel like myself.'

Amy gurgled from her room, broke the tension. 'I'll get her,' Kitty said.

'Mum, I'll do it. She won't expect you and it might upset her.'

'Nonsense. I'll go. You relax. Go look at your duck.'

Kitty came back cradling Amy and both were happy and Kitty said, 'See? She likes it. Eleanor, I'll take care of you and the baby. Why don't you come and stay with us? Just for a little while. You shouldn't be alone.' She'd sounded sincere.

Eleanor didn't have the energy to resist her. 'Let me get myself sorted here and we'll come over.'

'Put that casserole in the freezer. You can have it for when you return.'

If she were being honest, a small part of Eleanor wanted to be with Kitty, wanted Amy to be loved by people other than herself. Children cannot survive on the love of their parents alone. Love from the world is just as important. Sometimes love comes with strings, Eleanor. She shook her head, tried to quieten her thoughts. 'Alright.'

———

Eleanor and Amy were greeted by Kitty and George standing together at the front door, a sight so rare that she couldn't remember the last time she'd seen it. She noticed they were holding hands, were dressed for cocktails: George in navy-blue trousers and white shirt, Kitty in a red jumpsuit.

'Jesus Christ,' Eleanor muttered. 'Amy, they've gone all out.' She couldn't help but smile.

'Look at that baby! George, look at that baby!' Kitty cooed from the doorway, pinched George's arm as if trying to wake him from a dream.

When Eleanor approached they spoke with a shared tongue, said, 'Welcome,' opened their arms to her. This is who my parents must've been once.

Holding the baby, Eleanor stepped into their embrace and they stood like that for a moment. It was the closest they'd ever been.

Inside the house was light-dunked: every curtain was opened, every wall sun-bleached. Gone were all the dark corners. Why do I only get to see this now that I've become a mother? 'Thanks again for having us.' She held Amy tight, scared she was going to drop her from shock. Kitty squeezed Amy's cheeks.

'It's good to see you, Eleanor.' George adjusted his collar, was stiff-voiced. Why are they acting as if I'll break if they say something wrong?

'Dad . . .'

'Everything is set up,' Kitty said. A grin, large teeth, gave her the feeling to go to her bedroom. And so she did and found there was no cot. 'Aren't we sleeping here?' She looked at Kitty who was by the bedroom door.

'Wouldn't it be nice if you got to rest without worrying about the baby?' Her whole face rose; a dawn sun.

'What are you talking about?'

George said, 'The cot is in Badger's room.'

So this was the reason for George's strange behaviour.

Her mother never permitted anyone to sleep in that room. The rules were breaking.

'Amy will sleep in there,' Kitty said.

'Mum, I'd like her to be with me. She's not sleeping on her own just yet.'

Kitty pursed her lips. 'I see.' This quiet way of scolding; a humiliation.

Eleanor drew a breath. 'Let me have a look.'

Eleanor carried her child to her brother's room and inside it was moon-bright, silver light bounced off framed child-made drawings, an open window carried the smell of eucalypt and warm pavement, carried street voices, carried a man yelling at his children to 'hurry the fuck up' into the room. There was a cot by Badger's bed, and inside it was one of his baby blankets.

'I washed it,' Kitty assured her.

'Thank you.' What else could she say?

This tomb finally opened so it could swallow a new child. How was it that her mother was willing to open up the past and have someone else make it their own? Was willing to let another child supersede her own, was willing to let Eleanor's baby's smell fill the room, take over what had been preserved until now? Amy's baby noise would wake the dead, would remind the house that life keeps coming. This thing Eleanor had never been able to do: becoming a mother had finally granted her entry into a realm that was once off limits. Now that she had given life she understood what it was to lose it. I resent you so much, Kitty. And yet. Here I am: close to you, close to my brother again, without consequence.

Amy's arms reached above her head, and she yawned, kept her arms raised as if waiting for a turn to ask questions in school. 'You did that a lot,' Kitty said. 'Always putting your arms up, always reaching for something.'

'You've never told me that.'

'Don't be silly. Of course I did. It was your *thing* as a baby.'

It was easy to forget Kitty kept things to herself. So much of this woman I don't know.

George stepped into the bedroom, said, 'Does Amy need to sleep?' and Kitty answered, 'They just got here! She's not allowed to sleep.'

'I really don't want Amy to sleep on her own.'

Kitty touched Eleanor's arm, said, 'I'm sure Eleanor agrees. It's not bedtime.' But Amy yawned before shoving a thumb in her mouth.

'Amy's exhausted. Neither of us have slept well lately.'

Kitty removed her hand. 'I see.' Her voice cold.

'I'll pop her down for a nap later.' Eleanor removed her backbone, put it away in the drawer.

Kitty reached for Amy, took her from her mother's arms and walked out of the room, leaving Eleanor and George behind.

'What's with this?' Eleanor asked, waved her hand around to indicate the room.

'We thought it would be a nice surprise,' George said.

'We?' Eleanor laughed. 'We.' She sat on Badger's bed, this thing she hadn't done in so long, ran her hand over the cot railings, over cold brass. 'I thought you got rid of this.'

'Everything comes back, I s'pose.' George, hands in pockets, tried to hide himself. She heard Kitty from the front of the house – 'Do you love music, Amy?' – and George said, 'I should go now.' He left Eleanor to sit alone in her dead brother's room.

———

Hours filled. She watched George and Kitty parade Amy through the house, show her the backyard, reminisce about past parties, how her uncle and mother would play together in the clover along the fence line.

'Your mum was stung by a bee over there.'

'Eleanor and Badger pitched a tent here to camp in the backyard. Maybe you'll do it too.'

'Your mum used to wee behind the lemon tree over there instead of using the toilet.'

Her life unfolded in front of her daughter, told from the safe distance of a kitchen window. From there the messy emotion of parenting was taken out until the facts remained, as if Kitty had already decided these were the stories to begin a new history. In this version they were the attentive parents of two adventurous children who loved the outdoors so much they couldn't be called inside. Much better than saying, 'I couldn't bear to have Eleanor in the house so I ignored her.'

'You two look very pleased with yourselves,' she said. This couple and their newborn, watching ghosts relive past lives. Kitty slung a too-thin arm around George's broad-acre shoulder; the mismatch of their bodies momentarily locked together made a pattern. Kitty licked her lipsticked teeth clean and George mumbled something to her before they turned to Eleanor, informed her, 'We're taking Amy to meet the neighbours.' She understood then that she was not part of their plans.

Kitty and George slipped down the side of the house. Eleanor waited before following them out onto the street and fell in a few metres behind. Bright sun in windshields made cars slow, made some drivers toot horns in recognition. Some wound down their windows and called out, 'Good morning, grandparents!' George waved, Kitty waved, one hand still firm under the baby, her body remembering a former history, these things that had been done before.

Walking behind her parents, Eleanor felt as if she were trespassing. 'Wait for me,' she called. They didn't look over their shoulders.

Maudie walked by, stopped to admire Amy. 'You look adorable together, Kitty!'

Eleanor caught up, said, 'Hello,' and Maudie placed her hand against her throat, remembered where observations about the child should be directed. 'Oh, Eleanor,' she said. 'She gets more beautiful each day, doesn't she?'

'Yes.' But it's not always a beautiful time.

'Is she latching well now?' These things you ask when you don't know what other conversation to have. This woman I have known my entire life no longer knows how to talk to me.

'She's doing very well, aren't you Amy?' Kitty ever ready. There was nothing her mother didn't know.

Eleanor took a step back. Why speak when your mother speaks for you?

'You always had such a way with children, Kitty.'

'You never forget how to nurture, that's for sure.'

'Wait! Does this mean you won't be coming to the card game tomorrow?'

'We'll definitely be there, won't we, George?'

'Oh, goody!' Maudie clapped. 'Perhaps Eleanor would like to come?'

Kitty said, 'She's got the baby. She can't.'

Maudie touched Eleanor's arm as they passed. 'It really is great to see you out and about, Eleanor.' Words like a reassuring hum.

'What has Mum told you?'

Kitty shot her a look.

'Nothing, dear. It just gets easier, trust that.' Maudie patted her twice more and Kitty and George continued on. Eleanor followed, felt the heaviness of herself between her legs, the blood that still came from the birth, from all that pushing, as if she still had someone inside her. She slowed. Everything felt like it was on fire. Will I ever return to normal?

As they approached the end of Joynt Street, neighbourhood women came out from houses to greet them. Eleanor stopped, looked down at her pants; a small sea of blood rising. Trying to catch up to Kitty was bringing her undone. She called out, 'Mum, stop. I'm bleeding.'

The women turned to face her, said, 'Goodness me.'

Amy began to stir and Kitty bounced her up and down. 'You really should have stayed home, Eleanor. Go home and rest up.' Mother knows best. She couldn't tell if Kitty was disgusted, ashamed or concerned for her.

'I'm fine,' Eleanor said. 'But I think Amy's had enough.'

'You are most certainly not fine.'

One of the women nodded. 'Go home and rest, dear. Let your mother look after the baby.'

'No.' Her breasts leaked and she stepped forwards, took Amy from Kitty. 'I'll manage.' She could feel her exhaustion become rage, tried to swallow it down, didn't want to give them anything more to gossip about.

'Then let your father walk you. George, take Eleanor home.'

He nodded, took Eleanor by the elbow, and they headed back to the house.

'She's so overbearing,' Eleanor complained.

'She's just excited. She's been a bit down lately.'

'What about?'

'She's probably worried about you.' His old noncommittal responses; nothing had changed here.

By the time they reached the house Amy was screaming for sleep, for milk, and the blood throb between Eleanor's legs had spread to her thighs. She went to Badger's room, reclined on his bed and fed Amy. The sensations of a body simultaneously numb and too sensitive to stimuli made her want to leap out of her skin. Was it normal to feel so disconnected? Amy screamed when Eleanor put her in the cot. 'It's okay. You just need sleep.' Amy screamed louder, turned beet-purple from the effort.

George opened the door. 'Do you need help?'

'I just need her to sleep!'

She scooped Amy up again and returned to the bed, rubbed her baby's small back. 'I can't seem to please her.'

Eleanor rocked back and forth and eventually Amy settled and George said, 'You're pleasing her.'

He came further into the room, said, 'Why don't you go nap? I'll make sure she goes to sleep.'

'I don't know.'

'Please? I didn't know what you brought along with you so I put some things on the bed for you if you want to have a bath or . . .'

Eleanor kissed his prosthetic cheek, his thick resinous skin, and she handed him the baby, watched as he cradled her daughter, how he and Amy looked at one another, and then went to her room.

———

That night she dreamed Leon was back from war, was standing over her while she slept, his face fire and ash. He unzipped his jeans, unzipped his skin. That night she dreamed of Kitty and George in the corner of her bedroom, cradling Badger.

Pitch-dark when she woke, blood between her legs and milk spill on her blanket. She switched on the bedside lamp, put her hand between her legs, then checked the bedsheet. A dark red blood smear; if she didn't act quickly the blood would stain permanently and Kitty would never let her hear the end of it. Eleanor got up, took everything to the laundry, filled a sink full of water and put it in to soak. If this keeps up I'll have to go to the hospital.

She went to check on Amy.

Under Badger's door: a crack of soft light. 'Amy?' For a moment she'd wondered if Amy had become an adult in the course of the night, had decided to read a book. She smiled at the absurdity of her sleep-deprived thoughts, took hold of the door handle, stopped. What if Badger was with her? The idea of a boy rising from the dead to keep an eye over his niece was a comfort. Eleanor rubbed her eyes and opened the door.

The night-light was on but the cot was empty. Am I still asleep? Then, out of the corner of her eye: a rocking chair, two humans keeping metronomic time.

Kitty, slowly rocking back and forth, held Eleanor's daughter against her bare skin, against her bare breast; her nightie pulled down to her waist.

Eleanor's heart raced, throat clamped down.

Kitty, low-toned: 'Don't ruin it. You have no idea how good this feels. I just want to believe for a moment that I could be a mother again,' she whispered.

Eleanor squeezed her hands into fists.

Kitty rocked the chair, moved her feet over the rug, that rough sound of skin on wool and Amy startled, eyes opened, and she turned her head to latch on, her tiny fingers slapped her grandmother's breast for milk that wouldn't come.

To see her mother like this: this woman who was incapable of respecting boundaries, incapable of holding back primal wants. When Eleanor had been vulnerable with Kitty, told her that she was struggling to find her footing as a new mother, that she was scared of not being enough for Amy, scared of being too much, that she wasn't happy in her relationship with Leon, that she fantasised about him never coming home from war, that she wanted something bigger than just being a mother, that she was sorry that she couldn't be more for her and George, that she wished Badger was around, that she wished, she wished, she wished, Kitty had patted her on the back, told her to concentrate on the task at hand and it would all work out. Just remember, every generation mothers, Eleanor. You have to learn how to be one. It's not easy, but you'll find your own way.

'Were you planning this the whole time?' Planning to use all my fears against me, to show me once again that I'm deficient?

This constant competition between them.

All those boiled-down feelings Eleanor had been carrying: they were rising. In this moment, she wished her mother dead.

'Put her down.' It was all she could think to say at the betrayal.

And when Kitty didn't respond, Eleanor said, 'Why do you do this?'

'At least you can have other children.' It was an accusation.

Everything she had tried so hard not to manifest because she didn't want to be like Kitty, didn't want resentment and anger to define her. I can tame my dark places. She'd prided herself on it. But now: the dark places were opening. I want to hurt her the way she's hurt me. Kitty had denied Eleanor access to her, had demonstrated that her daughter's love wasn't enough to open her heart, but there she was handing it all to Amy with ease. The best thing you'll ever do is be a mother. These words. The different meaning they were now assuming.

All those boiled-down feelings, the screaming inside:

Fucking stupid arsehole motherfucker. I hate you. I love you. I hate you. I hate that I need you and that you are so needy. I can't stand you. I don't want to see you again. Why couldn't you show me who you really are? Why can't you keep away from me and why wasn't I enough? And I could've turned the world to gold if you let me, and I am still full of the blood that you put inside me and it's the same as Badger's and everything about you makes me hate you so much and your stupid fucking face and your stupid sounds and laugh and cries and you're selfish and you're manipulative and you're abusive and I don't know who you are and why you are able to make me do things I don't want to do and why I am loyal to you and do you know how much I have resented you and why don't you ever respect anything about me and how dare you be so selfish and I am so grateful that you kept going when George couldn't and I wish you'd left the family and what am I going to do when you die and what do I have to do to make you smile and why can't you let me be my own person and why can't you do anything but criticise and why can't you embrace change embrace life embrace growth embrace happiness and who were you before I met you and you fucking fuck and do you know what a lifetime of trying to please you has done to me and do you think Amy will grow up happy and how do you balance fear with love and I wish you were dead and I love you but I don't like you and I can't accept you in my life anymore and I hate that you're so childish and I hate that you can't articulate how you feel about anything and that you don't take personal responsibility for anything and you never remember that your actions hurt and you're always the victim and you gave me life but you told me so often how much you thought about killing me told me how you would have done it and then you say don't hate me, Eleanor, and you've never told me you love me and you're never going to love me and you're never going to love me and you're never going to love me and you're never going to love me.

She took small steps towards her mother. How many times had she sat in darkness and played mothering games? How long had she been planning this whole situation? 'Is this why you wanted me here?' Eleanor said, feeling stupid for believing her mother had wanted to look after her. I never learn my lessons. Venom swelled in Eleanor's cheeks, her tongue. She was ready to bite down and release it. In this moment she felt nothing but betrayal and she could feel herself becoming numb. She didn't want to understand her mother anymore. Those days were over.

All the times she had wished her mother out of her life, Eleanor had never wished for her mother's death. But here it was: bitter-tasting. Just like her mother. Lean into the anger, Eleanor. Lean into the thing that scares you the most about yourself.

Kitty and Eleanor were a tangle of arms when Eleanor tried to lift Amy away. These bodies that once fit inside one another. When Eleanor was inside Kitty she knew her mother better than anyone else: her heartbeat when she was angry, tired, happy, scared. Her heartbeat when she was holding Badger, scooping him up and telling him about the great times he would have with his sibling. She knew her mother's sex, her dreams, the rhythm that came with work, the way she bent and strained and lifted when she helped men off the ground at the hospital. She knew her voice when she asked George if he was okay, if he needed anything, or when she decided she'd had enough of him for the time being. Eleanor shook her head. But now I don't know you at all. This thing between us has to end. I don't want you in my life anymore.

Kitty wouldn't let go, let out a low grunt, a sound Eleanor had never heard before. Eleanor held Amy tighter, tried to peel Kitty's hands from her baby's skin, from her daughter's shoulders and torso. Kitty scratched at Eleanor, drew blood, and when Eleanor turned to stare at her mother, Kitty was vacant, was lost somewhere Eleanor couldn't reach.

Kitty smelled of Avon rose skin lotion and Betadine throat gargle. It made Eleanor's stomach churn. Kitty stopped her rocking, stopped covering herself up, stopped pretending. Kitty opened her mouth wide, then she tilted forwards and bit Eleanor's forearm hard. The shock of it. Kitty breathed on Eleanor, warm night breath. The sheer proximity of her mother was frightening. Eleanor wanted to push her away but couldn't get her body to cooperate.

'Why?' It hissed out of Eleanor.

'You ruin everything! You always ruin everything. You don't know what it's like to be me.' Kitty's voice, as if she herself didn't believe what she was telling Eleanor.

Amy howled and Eleanor stepped back, holding her daughter, putting more distance between them and her own mother. 'You don't come near her anymore. You don't come near me anymore.'

Kitty whimpered.

'I don't love you anymore, Mum.' This thing Eleanor said, meant. This thing she had leaned into. 'As far as I'm concerned, you don't exist.'

The end of them had arrived. Amy bawled and Kitty screamed, fell to the floor, tried to hide under Badger's bed. Good, Eleanor thought. Good, good, good. She went to say it out loud but instead she heard herself scream, Amy scream, until George came running into the room.

———

It was her father who knocked at her door. Days since she had left their house, since she'd spoken to her parents.

'Hi, Dad.'

'I came to see how you are.' He couldn't look her in the eye.

Amy clubbed her hands in front of her, beat the air.

'Things are the way they are.'

He took a step towards her, palms out, the way of white flags, nothing to hide. 'I'm sorry.'

Why wasn't Kitty here doing this? Why couldn't her mother come to her and beg for forgiveness, to ask how she felt?

'I won't stay long. I just wanted to see you.' A soft decay in his voice, that way of something slowly disappearing bone by bone.

'Are you alright?'

He said, 'I'm going to the mountain today.'

Jumping off the mountain face, flying away. This thing he had told her before. She nodded. 'Oh, Dad.' She wondered if she should cry for someone who had gone so often, if it would make a difference to the way she felt about her father. But there would be no coming back, and here he was one last time. Eleanor held her father's hand, her child in the other arm, let herself cry.

'Maybe I should've gone a long time ago.'

'Do you really have to leave?'

'Yes. I don't want to stay with your mother anymore. It's not right.'

'What will you do?'

He smiled at her, half his face lighting up. 'I'll just sit and wait. And then I'll be gone.'

'That sounds peaceful.'

'I'll be able to remember you all up there.' George held her, and there was a thinness, his shallow breaths, his light scent of Imperial Leather soap. 'I love you, Eleanor.'

'I love you too, Dad.'

He placed a small, folded note in her hand, this way they had, and she didn't want to look at it, didn't want to read the last instructions he would ever give her, but she unfolded it, glanced quickly, saw, *Please live*, the only words that stood out from so many. Over George's shoulder two boys rode their bikes down the street, their knees in ripped tracksuit pants, their windblown scruffy hair, canvas backpacks tortoise shells: her dad like this once. And he said, 'You and Amy have each other now.' And then he was gone and she shut the door.

———

She let herself think back to lost months. Throughout her pregnancy she'd felt her body expand beyond what she'd thought was possible. She had been warned by her mother's friends that you were never quite the same after you had a baby, how the body was destroyed. But they didn't tell her about the internal changes that no one saw. She wasn't the same, that was true. She often felt like a predator in her own body, hunting for the last remains of her old life: relics, ancient times. Think of yourself as past. There is a mismatch of the person you could've been and the person you are once you accommodate a life inside you. Like some kind of birth rite that is handed down from one mother to another, it's the inheritance of never being able to fully be yourself again. You are always somebody's someone.

As weeks then months passed, Eleanor spent time outside, spent time talking to and observing birds, observing Amy. She took her notebooks outside with her, recorded the daily movements of her daughter, the different ways a crow moves its head, uses talons to build its own life. Construct a world that helps you thrive. And they began to thrive together, began edging closer to something like real love.

One afternoon Eleanor pushed Amy in the pram through the Wintonvale village shops. She stopped to tie her shoelace and a man in his late forties, balding, a full war-medalled chest, dragging his feet, came up to the pram, looked at Amy, said, 'Baby.'

'Yeah, she's a good one.'

He took a step back, laughed. 'It's funny you have a baby! I had a baby once. But I lost it.' He laughed again, scratched his stomach with his nicotine-stained fingers, repeated, 'I had a baby once.' He straightened his stance and his face tightened.

And she said, 'Okay. Well, I hope you have a nice day,' walked away.

She continued along the footpath and eventually came to the park. Trees arched towards each other, a canopy of brown and green, and Amy watched the world move overhead: trees, clouds, magpies, crows, myna. Every time a bird flew across the sky Amy smiled, kicked her legs under the blankets. My child discovering the world.

A crow flew above and Amy noised out towards it, smiled and smiled, and Eleanor felt herself float up out of her body, land back inside bone, this feeling she'd never encountered before, the warmth of sharing the world with her daughter. For a moment she couldn't breathe and her heart untethered, travelled through her body. This is love. This is what they mean by love. She watched her daughter reach for the sky, reach for her mother, and Eleanor cried, said, 'I love you,' pushed Amy further into the park, into the trees, into the world that waited for her.

Kitty

1960

HER MIND BELIEVED it still belonged to a much younger woman. It was the feeling that she'd disappeared, that she couldn't feel herself inside her body; that feeling which had never gone away. How long had it been there? It was there when she'd had Eleanor, there when she'd lost Badger, there at her wedding, there and there and there. Being lost: this forty-three-year history of searching that had made her body. What would it be like to meet yourself in the middle, find alignment?

The empty bed was a lover in her hand, slipped into her as she fell back into cold sheets. No George. She hadn't noticed he'd left, had stopped noticing anything about him. Then she remembered: goat hunting. He'd gone on a monthly shoot to keep the feral population under control, to keep some of the men under control. The anger they had, endless war days. Better to shoot animals than shoot wives, or themselves. It had been good to send George out hunting. It got him out of the house, away from her.

It was their turn to host the hunting celebration. It was the last thing she wanted to do, but the idea of her neighbours thinking of her as being broken was much worse.

There was a knock on the bedroom door and her daughter asked, 'Would you like a cup of tea?' The sound of her child's voice, the way it lowered to the ground. She recognised herself in her daughter, the part that played the role of love because it was expected. It's what all good women do. She doesn't love me. After all I have done for her, she doesn't love me.

'Yes.' The firm bed prevented Kitty from sinking.

'Okay.' Eleanor half-smiled at her, and for a moment they took each other in.

If Badger were standing in the doorway he'd come to me and tell me he loved me, would know how to make me feel better.

'I'll go get it.' Eleanor left and Kitty got out of bed, slipped into her baby-pink satin dressing-gown, lassoed the belt around her ever-shrinking waist. She took a breath. Get through another day, Kitty. Just get through another day. It had been so hard lately.

The kitchen, two places set: boiled eggs in cups, buttered toast, matching teacups, a vase of flowers from the garden. Eleanor pulled a chair out for Kitty and she looked at the effort of her daughter's morning, said, 'Your father has gone on the goat hunt.' Always the assumption all good things were for George.

'I know. He left a little note for me to say he'd gone and if he wasn't back by evening to send for help.' Eleanor sat at the table, grinned. 'I made sure we have the exact same.'

The exact same. This is for me, for her, for us. Eleanor cut through egg, the steam-white inside; a new pope elected.

Eleanor cut toast in half, dunked the thick slice into egg. 'Go on, Mum. It's really good.'

Kitty did, cut into boiled egg, dipped toast. Yolk on the tongue; a morning coat. Smiled, the way you ought, and out of the corner of her eye Kitty could see Badger resting on the countertop. My children are blessings. A happiness in her chest. Perhaps today will be the start of something much better. It's never too late to begin again.

Sleep knotted in the corner of Eleanor's eye and Kitty stretched towards her, gently wiped it away. 'I got rid of your bad dreams,' she said, rolling the sleep between her fingers. 'All gone now.'

'You haven't said that for ages.'

'Really?' Where was time going?

'Can we work on the costume for the school play today?'

'I've got to get the food ready for this afternoon.'

'Please? I want to wear it.'

What difference would an hour make? 'Okay. Fine. Of course we can.' Said it like she meant it. Being in that moment with Eleanor: nothing before this moment existed. It's never too late to begin again.

Eleanor beamed. 'Ruth split her costume down the side and now her mum has to redo the whole thing!'

'Oh dear. What is she wearing again?'

Eleanor rolled her eyes. 'We've talked about this a hundred times. We're all wild forest birds and there's a wolf and a giant nest . . .'

'That's right: Ruth's the nest.'

Eleanor howled, banged fingers on the table. 'NO! She's the wolf. No one would be able to fit inside a girl-nest.'

Kitty laughed at her ability to still think like a child, how easy it is to make-believe a different reality. She'd been doing it herself for years. She stopped laughing, ate her toast, concentrated on Eleanor. This girl, her girl, suddenly in front of her.

———

Scraps of material scattered around the sewing room. Eleanor squawked black feathers into the air, jumped toe to toe while Kitty dug through the cane sewing basket for elastic. She couldn't recall the last time she'd seen Eleanor play like this. When did I stop paying attention? Over the years she had wondered whether it would be different now if she'd let Badger go. It's never too late to begin again.

'Eleanor, come here.' Waved her over, measured her arm span then measured and remeasured around her chest. An inch difference. Her daughter was developing breasts, developing the years that would eventually see her leave the house. Kitty measured her daughter's hips, was relieved there was no change for now.

She pointed at her chest. 'When did this start?' An accusation of deceit. Eleanor folded her arms across her small breasts, looked like she might cry. 'I don't want to talk about it.'

'Have you started menstruation?'

'I don't want to talk about it. I just want to wear the costume so I can run around in it.'

'But you've changed.' This realisation that her daughter was growing right in front of her and she had missed it. Almost another woman in the house. Kitty imagined the way men would soon look at Eleanor, how they would want to touch her. The thought of her daughter having sex. She's not ready for that; not ready to find out how unfulfilling people can be. Kitty wanted to say, Don't feel pressured to do things you don't want to do, but what came out was, 'You know if you have started it means you can get pregnant now, Eleanor. And when you have sex I'll be able to tell.'

Eleanor hung her head. 'I don't know what that means, Mum.'

'I just meant that when you have sex you'll be different.' Why was she telling Eleanor this? Her own mother had said it to her as a way to scare her into virginity but saying it now didn't make sense.

'I don't want to be different. I just want to stay the same.' Eleanor sounded as if she might cry.

'I just . . . we all change, Eleanor.' But sometimes I, too, wish we didn't.

'Does it hurt?' Eleanor asked.

'What?'

'Bleeding.'

'Everything hurts at first.' And second and third and on and on.

Eleanor lifted her wings and flapped, loosened feathers. 'I don't want to get my period.'

'But if you don't, you won't be able to have a baby.'

'Then I don't want one.'

'Well, then you won't be a woman, Eleanor.' Out she stung, knew she was lying to her daughter. How was all this going so wrong?

Eleanor burst into tears and Kitty wrapped an arm around her shoulders. 'There now, dear. There now, dear.' She breathed into Eleanor's neck, the hint of cotton on skin, the soap of last night, of morning toast, of feather, of her own perfume leaving a trace, of the entire world tracing this skin that once was made inside her. Kitty breathed her in, reminded herself of the first time she'd held Eleanor. 'Please stop growing. Just for a little while.' Kitty wasn't sure if Eleanor heard her because she didn't reply and so Kitty let go of her daughter.

The bird costume came off, and after Kitty had made adjustments she helped Eleanor back into it one black-stockinged leg at a time, pulled the rump of leotard and feathers all the way over hips, over stomach; all the excuses to touch these new parts of her body. Kitty saw the layers of herself in her child. I need to make sure I don't miss another moment of my daughter. I need to make sure she knows she is loved.

When the wings were placed over Eleanor's arms, when the bird mask covered her head, she disappeared and the room became an aviary, and there in her daughter's place a bird: crow-flitting around the room, searching for open windows, for ways to leave, and Kitty could do nothing but stand and marvel at the mechanics of flight.

———

Later, Kitty set about being the perfect hostess, prepared for the neighbourhood get-together to celebrate the return of hunting men and their kill. Eleanor had refused to take her costume off and feathers began to fill the house. The bird mask sat atop her head as she helped herself to the canapés Kitty had made and in went party pies, in went quiche fingers, in went cucumber sandwiches, devilled eggs, in, in, in. 'Keep that up and there'll be nothing left.'

'But I'm starving!' Spoken through a mouthful.

'So will the neighbours be if you keep eating.'

George brought home a small tan-and-ginger goat to string up on the back verandah for future butchering, his watch and hands spackled bright red. She knew he'd already tried to hide the effort it took him to take the goats down.

'How was it?' Her hands in dough.

'Cold. We didn't find too many today.' He was somewhere else.

'Did you kill that one, Dad?' Eleanor crammed another sand-wich in her mouth.

'I had to shoot it.'

'Did it cry?'

'In a way. They always do. It's not particularly nice, but it's the quickest way.'

'Did you cry?' Eleanor bit into shortbread, crumbed chin.

'Not really.'

George, this man who cried all the time. Where did he disappear to so that this version could kill a small goat? She'd often heard the hunting party talk about their kills, how patience was the key. 'After a while, it's just a target that needs to be hit.' Some of the men had nodded. Almost all of them had gone to war. How many targets had they hit there?

'George, don't upset her with these grisly details.'

'I'm not that upset.'

She should be. Children shouldn't know about hunting, what their fathers do. 'Well, I don't like it.'

George, his eyes fixed on the goat on the back porch, its tongue drooping, eyes wide open, nick of blood down the side of its face. 'I have to prepare the goat now, otherwise it'll spoil.'

Kitty sighed, said, 'Make sure you wash your hands after you're done.'

Eleanor said, 'Wait for me,' and Kitty told her, 'No. Stay in here, Eleanor.'

But she was overruled by curiosity and Eleanor followed her father out the back.

Kitty looked out the window, heard George tell their daughter, 'Now I have to open its throat, but it's okay because the goat won't feel anything.'

'Why do you have to?'

'The blood needs to come out or no one can eat the meat, and that would be a shame.'

The knife went into the goat's throat and out came blood and she heard Eleanor say, 'Is it cold?'

'Would you like to touch it?'

Eleanor nodded and Kitty wanted to scream to stop it this instant, to stop talking like this, but George held Eleanor's finger under the rush of animal blood. What kind of father allowed their child to play with death?

'It's a bit warm.' Eleanor pulled her finger away and George wiped the blood on his shirt. 'Are you sure the goat can't feel it, Dad?'

George nodded. 'Trust me. Once you're dead you can't feel a thing.'

Kitty winced. Sometimes I can't feel a thing.

———

The afternoon brought a backyard of guests. Drinks in hands, hands on hips, the circuitry of women's polite laughter collided into worn-out jokes from men. A few cars sailed down the street, children called out to each other from front yards.

'No! *You* get the cricket ball from the yard.'

'But I didn't hit it over the fence.'

'Stop being a baby and go get it.'

'I hate playing with you so much. I'm telling Dad.'

Kitty paraded canapés around the yard, winked neighbourly love. She wanted everyone to remember this day, how special she could make them all feel. No one could say Kitty Turner doesn't know how to put on a show. Lydia from number forty-six sat close to the clothesline, baby Jean on her lap, bounced her high and the baby's mouth gaped. She reached for long black hair, reached for the excess of her mother. Lydia made eye contact with Kitty, said, 'Would you like to hold her?'

'You know I can never say no to babies.'

Kitty held Jean, breathed her in, was overwhelmed by the way her skin still retained the smell of labour blood and warmed breastmilk; this bouquet of lily of the valley. She kissed the baby's head, handed Jean back to Lydia. 'Enjoy her.'

'I can't stand how wonderful she is.' Lydia swamped Jean with love and Kitty turned away, saw Eleanor run in and out of the house, chasing her friends, cawing like a crow; beastly games. The way she moved her body as if she'd never considered it as anything other than the place she lived; a freedom. Eleanor called, 'Don't run inside,' and Kitty was pleased to hear herself in her daughter's mouth.

Toddlers played under the back verandah: Stevie, happy in her nappy, her bare chest, toddling with a cup of juice towards the hanged goat, sat underneath it; a shelter from the lowering sun. She swirled her hands in blood, finger painted her small face, her teeth.

'Ewwww, Stevie's a blood eater!' another child screamed, laughed.

Stevie's mother ran to her, moved her away from the animal.

'Want goat!' Stevie pointed.

'Goat is yucky, Stevie.'

'Goat sad.'

'Goat not sad, sweetie. It's alright.' She looked over the porch railing. 'Kitty? Can we have a towel to wipe away the blood?'

There was always mess to clean up at gatherings. It was a definite downside to it all.

'Eleanor!' Kitty called. 'Go fetch a cleaning cloth from the laundry.' She wouldn't be ruining her towels on spilled animal blood.

Kitty returned her attention to the gathering, spotted George leaning against the fence. He stared over the shoulders of the other men as they joked around and she knew he was somewhere else, always heading somewhere else. She smiled at her husband out of politeness, out of pity, but he seemed to stare past her and so she left him behind.

All the things in the air: music, baby Jean, children's hands dappling the light, an aeroplane, small swarm of street dust, cigarette smoke making haloes around high hair. She thought about how Badger used to crawl around this space, how dirty he'd get, sodden with grass, how she'd wash around it at night because she liked the way dirt smelled on skin, as if him being that close to the ground meant that he was deep-rooted, was proof of life. But gone are those days as these days will be gone.

Something heavy in her throat then. She touched it, felt a lump the size of the past.

'Kitty? You alright?' Joan, drink in hand.

'Just a memory.' The way it came out. This truth, like passing on a fact she had read about in a nursing textbook.

Joan came closer, the smell of riesling on lips. 'Do you want to talk about it?'

Kitty leaned into her friend. 'Isn't it nice to have all these people here?'

They smiled at one another and the moment passed and Kitty went back to playing hostess. She danced from one group to another, took delight in the way they all ate her homemade goodies. She offered devilled eggs to Charlie, pushed her serving tray towards his chest, said, 'Something to fill you up?' The way they looked at each other. A twinge under her dress, between her legs. He studied the tray, took the egg closest to Kitty.

When he said, 'Please.'

When he said, 'What else do you have to eat?'

When he said, 'Can you show me where in the kitchen it is?'

She nodded her head, led him past Diane, past their neighbours, led him through the back door, led him into the kitchen, led him, led him.

Signs that children had been playing in the kitchen: little shoe prints covered the floorboards, dropped black feathers lay across them. For once she didn't mind the mess, was too preoccupied with leading herself to a good time.

She stood at the counter and Charlie came behind her, raised her dress to hip height. Her body flooded with warmth. He whispered, 'You drive me crazy, Kitty.' She cut crusts off cheese sandwiches and he ground his teeth. It occurred to her that one day they would be caught. She hoped they would be. Keeping secrets was tiring. As she was about to tell him what she wanted, Eleanor ran down the hallway towards them. 'Hello, darling!' Kitty swallowed and Charlie stepped away from the counter, took a sandwich, began to eat it. What had she seen? Eleanor stopped, stared at one then the other. 'Where's Dad?'

'Your dad's outside,' Charlie said.

Kitty glared at him, didn't like that he would answer on her behalf. 'Did you want him, darling?'

'No. I just wondered where he was.' Eleanor pulled her crow mask down over her face, waved her crow wing, ran out to the backyard. Kitty pulled her dress down, followed her daughter, leaving Charlie behind.

Outside, Diane motioned to her. 'Come over here, Kitty.'

Kitty obeyed, linked her arm through Diane's.

'We were just talking about the Johnson boys stealing the hospital delivery van,' her friend said.

'Those boys are going to find themselves in jail soon,' Maudie tsked. 'I'd be absolutely mortified if they were my sons.'

'I just want Billy to be reliable, like Charlie,' Diane said.

What kind of desire was this?

The other women nodded and Kitty looked for Eleanor in the yard, heard a child say, 'Can we play with your brother?'

The distance of the sun between cloud and land brought the golden hour, warmed and soothed, made her body feel as if it were stationary, that finally she had nowhere else to be but here.

'Mum! Mum, hurry!'

The sound of her daughter screaming made the sun disappear and form shadows on her skin. Eleanor sounded as if she were in pain. Kitty turned, faced the house.

'Come quick!'

Eleanor again, as if reminding Kitty she was a mother.

Someone said, 'What on earth?'

Kitty ran up the back stairs, ran the black shoes off her feet. Bodies parted and she saw Eleanor's crow body standing by the kitchen table sobbing. Two small children, Stevie and Louise, stood nearby.

'Uh-oh. Oh no,' Stevie said. She pointed at Kitty. 'Uh-oh. Oh no.'

A body is a frequency, feels a current long before it hits. Kitty made a deep-down sound, felt sick.

'Mummy.' Eleanor's bird mask had slipped down her face, was lowered over her mouth.

I'll cover your mouth so you can't breathe, Kitty thought.

'Uh-oh. Oh no.' Stevie again.

Eleanor forked her arms underneath the child's armpits as if removing a hazard, and it was only then that Kitty looked down at the floor, at Badger spilled across it. How was it possible that a body could travel so far? Kitty went to speak but nothing came out.

Badger hid under the table, under stacked chairs, under a small black patent leather shoe, in the lid that had kept him hidden for so many years. I haven't seen him since the funeral. Something hard in the pit of her stomach.

'Mummy.' The high pitch of it. How quickly you can loathe a word.

'Do not call me that!' Kitty said, a knife's edge.

Stevie screamed and Louise bawled and from outside Joan called, 'What on earth is going on in there?'

Kitty looked back down at her son, the grey of him, and she fell into him, the force so hard that bone stuck to bone. She threw her hands onto Badger and it was like holding him for the first time.

To feel the person you love in your hand: Kitty howled, howled again. So difficult to breathe.

Eleanor reached for Badger's urn, began scooping her brother back into the place that had become his body. 'It's okay, Badger, it's okay.'

Eleanor cried and Kitty watched this child, this beast, take her son away, and she razored out, 'Don't you dare touch him.' Kitty slapped Eleanor's hands away, slapped her chest, her face.

'Mummy, stop! It hurts.'

'What did you do to him?' The sound of her hands against her daughter was the strangest music.

'Oh my God, Kitty. Kitty, no.'

Diane threw herself at Kitty, gripped her hands.

Kitty spat in Diane's face, protective mother against predator. 'Get off me.'

'Come on, Kitty. Stop this.' Diane tried to soothe her, calm her, and Eleanor leaned towards her mother. 'Mummy.'

Kitty pushed Eleanor away. 'Stop calling me that,' Kitty said.

Eleanor was panicky. 'Mummy, I didn't do it. Stevie opened him up. I tried to stop her.'

Kitty slapped Eleanor's face. 'You didn't care for your brother.' How could she love Eleanor now?

Diane tried to heave her away from Eleanor, said, 'Kitty, stop hurting her. Let's get you up.'

But Kitty kept at her daughter, scratched at the bird costume, tore into feather and mesh, scratched until she drew blood. 'I knew you would do this! I knew you would ruin everything.'

Eleanor scooped Badger into the urn.

They're going to take my son away. Kitty opened her mouth, poured him onto her tongue, back into her body. Tried to swallow the grit and bone, but she couldn't. Why wouldn't her son fit back inside her?

'Help me!' she screamed. 'Someone help me.' Someone help return my son to me.

She felt Diane prising her hands away from her mouth; the sensation of death stuck between her teeth. She heard George bellow, saw him run to their daughter, cradle Eleanor in his arms, rock her while she sobbed. 'It's okay, sweetheart. It's okay.'

Kitty wiped her mouth, lurched at Eleanor. 'Everything bad is because of you. You've ruined everything.'

Eleanor sobbed, and George pushed Kitty away. 'You don't mean that, Kitty.'

Diane threw her arms around Kitty's body, breastbone against breastbone, and wrestled Kitty to the floor.

Kitty held onto a handful of Badger. 'They're going to take my son away. You need to let me go.'

The sound of a mother howling for her child is the sound of death scorching the earth from the inside; Kitty burned the room, tried again to raise her hand to her mouth but was overpowered by Diane.

'Badger.' Kitty screamed his name, screamed it again and again, and Eleanor screamed along.

Maudie and Joan ran into the room, threw themselves onto Kitty, restrained her. How soft they were, the smell of them: of warmed sea salt, of their hearts crawling out from between their legs, of blood. Kitty closed her eyes. She thrashed herself into her friends, chanted, 'He was mine. He was mine. He was mine. He was mine,' and she heard Diane sob, and then Diane said into her ear, 'Kitty, let him go. You need to let him go,' and she stroked Kitty's forehead, soothed and shushed her, until Kitty finally went limp.

———

Guests gone, a quiet house. In the dark she lay on the bed, listened to George and Eleanor at the front of the house: a sweep of broom, a lighting of stove, a clatter of saucepan; heard life go on without her.

Kitty held on to herself, arms over chest, tried to curl into a ball then stretch as far as her body would allow before her joints popped out of place. Nothing could comfort her, everything an ache. She swallowed, tasted blood from screaming, saw her friends' faces when she closed her eyes, saw their wide mouths, their sharp white teeth, the nightmare of them watching her. What am I going to say when I see them next? And Eleanor. What do I say to my child?

A soft padding down the hall and then the bedroom door opening. She's here. I can feel her before I see her.

Eleanor had changed out of her bird costume into pyjamas and dressing-gown, had brushed her hair, how it had grown, the sweet honeysuckle smell. She's used my hair conditioner.

Eleanor crouched beside her mother and Kitty shut her eyes.

'Are you cold, Mum?'

She was so quiet. I don't know what to say to my daughter.

'I'll make you warm.' And up went the doona over Kitty's body.

She heard Eleanor walk to George's side of the bed and crawl in beside her and her arms hugged Kitty, those growing bones, and she heard, 'It's going to be okay, Mummy.' And she felt her child's breath on the back of her neck, her heartbeat into her mother's shoulder blades, and all she could think about was the way her daughter had picked her brother up from the floor, like she was contemplating a great mystery.

Eleanor said, 'Can you hear me?' And she held tighter, and whispered over and over, 'I love you, Mummy.' It was too much to hear. 'I love you, Mummy.'

Her child begging. I just want her to stop. In that moment Kitty wanted to die, wanted to be with her son, be a memory, a once-was. Why stay when life is always going to hurt?

'I love you, Mummy.' These words Eleanor had been saying her whole life. Kept saying despite everything.

Kitty was sobbing now, couldn't stop, wanted to turn to her daughter but didn't know how, wanted to tell her daughter that she hated her, that she loved her, that she never wanted to see her again, that she never wanted her to leave, wanted to tell her that it was never too late to begin again, wanted to tell her, I don't know how to mother you, but words didn't form. Kitty closed her eyes tighter, kept her back to Eleanor, went to sleep.

———

It was midnight when George woke her. 'I'm going to take him to the mountain like we said we would.'

Kitty glared at him.

George climbed into bed beside Kitty, put his arm over her body. She didn't want him but she didn't push him away.

The absence of Eleanor's body; that emptiness inside. 'Where is she?'

'She went to stay with Ruth's family.'

Another child gone.

'It's just the two of us now,' she said. The disappointment.

He told her, 'You don't have to come if you don't want to, but I'll take Eleanor with me.'

'George, he's scared. He was everywhere. He won't know what happened.' Let me protect him. The compulsion to mother her son. Would it ever go away?

'Kitty . . .'

She whispered, 'Please put him somewhere safe and sing to him.' The ache in her mouth.

George folded into the back of her neck and she let him cry into her.

'It hurts, George. It hurts so much.'

'I know it does.' And he kissed her and she closed her eyes, said, 'George, I don't want to wake up in the morning. I don't want there to be any more days,' and he told her, 'Some mornings when the sun shines bright you'll remember how warm everything can be.'

Eleanor

1973

A SUICIDE ATTEMPT had brought him back from Vietnam. She barely recognised him when she opened the door to him.

'Leon.'

'Eleanor.'

She'd forgotten the sound of his voice. Had forgotten everything. Had prepared for his death. She looked at his wrists, couldn't help it, and he said, 'I'm sorry,' and he cried, a side of him she hadn't known existed, and she opened her arms, let her husband come into them. 'I thought I'd never see you again.'

She walked him into the house, sat him on the sofa, and they held each other, the sweat-stink rising from his black polyester shirt too much for her to handle. Eleanor looked the other way,

263

said, 'I can't believe you're here,' and he pulled her face into his, clamped his mouth over hers, as if he were eating her alive, and she endured the touch of his skin against hers, waited for him to need air.

She didn't know what to say to him and so they barely spoke and they sat together on the sofa, sat with the separation of war between them.

———

She was in the backyard hanging out nappies and bibs on the line when he waltzed onto the grass, came up behind her, held her hips, said, 'Show me who she is.' It took her a moment to realise he meant Amy. What a way to ask about your daughter. Why not ask to see her immediately? She'd sent photos of Amy to Vietnam, had selected shots she could bear to part with, the small rough-cut photos she'd orchestrated at a photography studio that specialised in rendering screaming children scared of studio lights into family keepsakes. The speed of the shutter over and over until one frame could be passed off as a smile. It had been Kitty who had convinced her to have the photos taken. 'Imagine how it'll lift his spirits to see his month-old daughter.'

He didn't deserve to see how Amy had grown without him. 'You'll frighten her.' It came out before she'd been able to register what she'd said.

The smell of muscle tightening; the same scent that dripped from him when he clenched his body around hers at night. He stared at her, lip curled.

'I just meant she might mistake you for a stranger. She's not used to them. She'll get to know you, though.'

'You're killing me, Eleanor. I've just been through hell.'

'I'm sorry. Let's go see her then.'

In her daughter's room: baby powder in the air, the cocoon Eleanor and Amy had made together. Leon completely out of place, as if he'd fallen from the sky. It was like watching a stranger break into their home and search for items to claim for himself. Everything about him was bigger: he had to duck through the doorframe. He held on to the cot railings, peered in, and Eleanor felt like she was watching the world collapse around her daughter. Mine. That girl is mine. It didn't make sense to share her with Leon. She'd delivered herself through pregnancy, through fifteen weeks of constant morning sickness; delivered herself from the edge of non-existence, through birth. He'd been gone Amy's whole life. He didn't even ask her what the birth was like when she told him Amy had arrived. He'd missed all the work Eleanor had done to turn Amy from an abstract idea into a being that was hers. And now he wanted to own her.

Leon stuck his pinkie finger in Amy's mouth and Eleanor winced. Unwashed salted skin. Amy's mouth closed over his fingertip; her face soured.

Leon smiled at Amy but it was more a smirk. Maybe he's tired, she thought. Maybe this is all he can muster for anyone right now. Amy thrashed about, tried to remove him from her mouth. He wouldn't. Amy cried and Eleanor said, 'Stop it.'

'I'm just trying to give her something to chew. Isn't that what babies do?' He leaned towards Amy, sugared his voice. 'I'm your father. Look at how much you've grown. Your daddy's been away fighting people.'

'Leon, don't.' The sight of him standing over her child using war as a lullaby. Her stomach churned.

———

She'd noticed the small black box when he was unpacking his duffel bag. The way he smoothed the wood, as if it were a precious gift.

'What's that?'

He held it close and Eleanor noticed a small lock. 'It's just something from over there.'

'Do you want to talk about it?' She eyed the box, considered the memento mori inside: bullet, flower, relic, photos of men he'd fought alongside who wouldn't make it home.

He smiled gently. 'I'm not sure I can explain it properly.'

'Why don't you try? I'll listen.'

'I've kept this with me ever since . . .'

They'd told her about the incident when they'd called her. *There was an ambush. Unfortunately there was a child casualty and it would seem this is what precipitated the suicide attempt.*

'It's okay. We don't have to go there if you don't want to.' She couldn't imagine what must've happened that day. Eleanor wrapped her arm around him, felt the difference between pre- and post-war muscle. 'Maybe you've got a few mates at the barracks you can talk to?'

'I don't know if I can.'

'Wouldn't hurt just being around them.'

Later, Leon went out to visit friends and Eleanor was folding clothes in the bedroom. The box caught her eye. She picked it up. It was slightly heavier than she expected. She tried the lock but it wouldn't open; shook the box but there was no great movement inside. 'What are you?'

She put it back on the dressing table, went back to her chores, and a little while later Leon came home reeking of beer, of men shouting loudly, of someone returned to life. He almost tripped over his feet in the hallway and she helped him regain his balance, said, 'Let's get you some rest.'

He kissed her, said, 'I'm glad our life turned out how I wanted. Look at us. We have a baby.'

'Yes.'

'And I came back. Just like I promised.'

She patted his shoulder. 'Okay, why don't we talk about this in the morning when you're sober.'

Eleanor sat him on the bed, pulled his boots off, tried not to breathe in the stink of his feet.

'Have you been in my things?' A sharpness to his voice.

'Sorry?'

'Have you been in my things?'

'No. Why?'

He grabbed her head with both hands, swivelled her neck to the dressing table. 'The box. That's not where it was. You moved it.'

His fingernails dug at her skin, made her suck air through her teeth. 'I'm sorry. I was dusting and . . .'

'You have no idea what I had to do to bring that home. Don't ever touch it again.' He wouldn't let go of her head.

'I won't.'

'Promise.'

'I promise.'

He let her go, fell backwards onto the bed, and she sat on the floor at his feet.

———

For weeks they tried to get to know one another again and she tried to forget all that had happened in the past. Every time she remembered, was upset that he had come back, hadn't died like she'd hoped, she forced herself to look at his wrists, at the box that he kept on their dressing table, reminded herself that he'd tried to take his own life. She thought of George, all his years in and out of hospital, and she tried to summon empathy for him.

Leon ran his fingers over her breasts and she recoiled from his touch.

'What's wrong?' he asked.

'Sorry. I'm just not used to this. It's been a while.'

He kissed her forehead. 'Maybe we can make you used to it again.'

'Maybe.'

The next afternoon she went to the weekly gathering of new war wives, wanted to know if they felt the same as she did.

'Leon told me he shot someone.'

'He told you that?' Her friend, Justine, sipped gin.

'Why wouldn't he? I asked him about his suicide attempt and he told me a little bit about what happened. But I just can't stop thinking about it.'

'Well, of course he's going to shoot at someone. It's war.' Justine took another sip.

'Mine did too.' Pippa tried to soothe her, patted her hand.

I'm no dog, she wanted to say. But she didn't and they sat in a semicircle and they sipped their stiff drinks and Eleanor nodded as they assured her that things would get better.

That night, in bed, he huddled into her, said, 'I feel tense.'

'I've got my period,' she lied. He had always been squeamish about this. Maybe he'd leave her alone.

'I just want to have a pull. Will you do it?' He kissed her cheek, and his hand gripped her breast, like ripping tree root from earth, and then he took her hand in his, guided it to his penis. She stared at the ceiling. 'Tell me to pull on my cock,' he said. These animal names we give human parts. She thought of talons, of long green and brown tail feathers, of a crow with a beak full of morning, and she said, 'Pull on your cock.' The distaste of herself with his words on her tongue. The sickening heat that came from him made her head spin, and he said, 'This feels good,' and he said, 'It was brutal over there,' and he said, 'I thought about you all the time,' and he said, 'Pull harder. Hurt me.' And she did, was humiliated when he came in her hand.

———

He'd been home a month when he packed Amy's pram with toys, told Eleanor he wanted to experience real fatherhood. 'It's about time, don't you think?'

'Where would you like to go?'

'I don't know. I was hoping you'd be able to come up with something.'

'Amy likes walking through the gardens and the bush . . .'

Leon scoffed. 'Bit boring, don't you think?'

She shrugged. It was exhausting having to make everything entertaining for him, to compete with the adrenaline rush of war. Returning to domesticity must be difficult, she reasoned. She could relate. 'We could have a picnic?'

He gave her the thumbs-up, put on a record while Amy crawled around the lounge room.

Eleanor made sandwiches: brown bread, butter, ham, alfalfa sprouts, grated carrot, mayonnaise. Next she sliced pieces of chocolate cake, made sure there was enough for seconds. It had been a while since she had to make his lunch; she couldn't remember his preferences.

She stuck her head into the room to check on Amy, saw Leon wearing headphones, could hear the faint tinctures of a drum solo. He was sprawled on the sofa, listless limbs. Amy crawled across the rug to the stereo, pulled herself to her knees and twiddled silver knobs, giggled to herself.

'For fuck's sake.' Leon threw his headphones onto the floor. 'Get Amy away from the stereo, will you? She nearly blew my ears off.'

'She's a child, Leon. She has no idea what she's doing.'

'Amy. Naughty. Get away from there.' His voice boomed and Amy wailed. The sound of an angry man; Amy had never experienced it before in her life.

Eleanor ran to her daughter, lifted Amy into her arms. She stared at Leon, at his too-long body, at the way his feet overhung the sofa. He reached for his headphones, pulled them back over his ears, closed his eyes. 'Get the fuck away from me.'

Amy pointed at Leon, howled, and Eleanor said, 'It's okay, sweetheart. It's going to be okay.'

But even then, she knew things were not going to be okay.

Eleanor

Present

AN HOUR OUT from the mountain town and she needs to refuel, edges closer to the petrol station, watches two large crows land in the middle of the road, hold her gaze for a moment, two moments. Eleanor brakes, clenches her arms straight, determined to keep the car as still as possible so she doesn't hit them. She hears Amy slide forwards in her seat, says, 'Sorry, sweetheart, there are birds. I'd hate for us to run them over.' The car idles. The larger crow opens its beak, makes caw-caw noise, and she caws back until it is silent. The crows don't move, aren't done with her yet. She shakes her head, knowing she is starting to come undone. She is beyond tired, beyond anything she's felt for a very long time. In the distance behind her a Mack truck forges towards them and Eleanor wills the crows to fly off but they don't. 'Move,' she says to the windscreen. 'Move!' The truck thunders along and she screams at the top of her lungs, 'Jesus! Why can't you see what's coming for you?!'

The crows lift into flight as the truck passes the Belmont. Eleanor's bladder swells, tightens against her jeans.

Into the petrol station: out of the car into the night. She refuels, locks the door to keep Amy safe, pays, goes to the toilet. The relief of urination, of letting go. Wind through the bathroom window chills her thighs, makes goosebumps, and she welcomes it. At least I can still feel.

On the way back to the car she passes a pay phone, feels the urge to call Leon, to call home; a habit. But what will you say if he answers? Eleanor opens the booth, lifts the receiver to her ear and pushes in a coin. She feels a pressure inside her head so intense she sees double and she leans against the phone booth glass, shivers in the cold and the phone rings, it rings, it rings, it rings, it rings and she forgets to breathe.

He's not going to pick up. Eleanor slams the receiver onto the cradle, bursts out of the booth, notices a couple of truck drivers standing nearby, chatting. She'd often wondered what it might be like to be a truck driver, to spend that much time on your own. She'd told Ruth once and Ruth said, 'If you want to be alone just go live in a bloody forest somewhere. But I won't be visiting you.'

'You aren't even invited.'

To lose a friend when you're not looking; not doing enough. Maybe when we get to the mountain, when I feel better, I can find her again.

In her last phone conversation with Ruth, Eleanor told her, 'I feel like I get tricked into things.'

'Do you, though?'

'How do you mean?'

'Get tricked. In my opinion you always seem to know what to do before you do it.'

So why don't I feel that way? 'Am I being tricked? Is Kitty offering to help me and Amy a trick?'

'The problem is you're scared to make people in your life uncomfortable when that's exactly what you should be doing,' Ruth said.

'So you're a psychology expert now?'

'Well, maybe not a complete expert but definitely a psychologist.' Eleanor heard Ruth pull a cork from a bottle, pour herself a drink.

'You're infuriating sometimes,' Eleanor said.

'So are you.'

They laughed.

Eleanor paused, wanted the truth. 'Do you think I'm weak?'

Ruth took a sip of wine. 'I think you're scared to be your whole self. That's all.'

To be fragmented: pieces fall through the smallest of spaces. And Eleanor knew there'd come a time when she'd have to choose to be whole.

Eleanor walks past a truck driver who tells her, 'Miss, you've got something on your neck.' He points to her, is sincere, and she touches both sides of her neck and feels the outline of a scratch on the left side, something swollen. 'Thanks,' she says. In the car she turns on the overhead light, checks herself in the mirror, sees the bruising. 'Little one, we really have to get to the mountain.' She twists to look over her shoulder at her daughter, and there next to her on the back seat is the small black box. 'How did that get there?' Amy isn't interested in it, looks straight at her mother. Swamp movement in the pit of her stomach, bowels heavy, the way fear fills you before rushing out. Eleanor reaches over and lifts the box, is relieved it's still locked.

Eleanor places the box on the front passenger seat, puts on her seatbelt and starts the car, flees down the road.

———

It is darker than she expects it to be when she reaches the town but they are here now, have come so far. Eleanor can't see Amy when she glances in the rear-view mirror, and for a moment she travels back to the prehistoric years when there was no daughter to look at. The idea of it. Nausea boils from the middle of her stomach again, reminds her that this is the feeling from childhood when someone isn't where they ought to be. Eleanor slams her palm against the steering wheel, wants to scream into the windshield. Now is not the time to cry about empty spaces. She wants out of the car, wants to sleep, wants to set fire to the earth. 'It's almost over, bubby.'

The car follows the road ahead and the slight movement of her body following the curve of the corners makes her head sting. Her fingers ache into her face, tease into skin, into skull. She goes to soothe her eyes but they aren't where they're meant to be and instead she is rubbing at her lips. Her breathing quickens and she reaches for her ears to make sure they're still in place, but when she pays closer attention to the sensations in her body her fingers are stroking along the arch of her eyebrows.

Has my face rearranged itself? Why can't I find myself where I am meant to be?

'Pull yourself together,' she hisses at herself. But it's getting harder to hold on. It's been such a long drive.

Eventually headlights are haloes on the Kellerman's Motel sign and the Belmont turns into the pebbled driveway, small stones crunching underneath tyres. The place the Turners have always stayed. This place she has been desperate to get to since she and Amy left home. The motel is two rows of brick buildings surrounded by plastic potted plants. The Turners always stayed in the second building on the ground floor, room five. Relief at reaching her destination makes her body tremble. The red-brick marker reassures her that tomorrow when she wakes up the mountain will be there to greet her.

Relief gnaws at muscle. The way they begin to tighten and relax is exhausting. All she wants to do is sleep. Eleanor parks the car and carefully lifts Amy from her seat, nestles her daughter into her chest while she attaches the baby carrier to her body. So many hours since she last held her child like this. She gently pushes Amy closer into her stomach and chest to see how much of her daughter she can absorb. She kisses Amy's forehead, tries to ignore the way her body shakes. No, not now. Please not now. Let me at least get into the hotel room.

Bags in hand she enters the motel reception and the woman behind the desk, Candy, drops the key to room five in Eleanor's hand, tells her, 'Darl, you need anything whatsoever, you let me know.' Candy, her sweetness, reaches for Amy, rubs thighs for welcome. 'You both must be exhausted! You look like you've been through a hell of a time.' The comfort Candy has been trained to provide. Eleanor takes it.

Candy looks over the reception desk at Eleanor's small pile of belongings. 'Do you need help with that?'

'I'm okay.' I've carried it this far and I can keep going.

Candy steps out from behind the desk. 'It's perfectly fine to accept help when it's offered, darl. Doesn't make you weak.'

Eleanor considers the baggage she has brought with her, changes her mind. 'Actually I could do with some help. Thank you.'

Candy reaches for the blue suitcase, smooths her hand over Amy in the baby carrier with the other hand. 'Mine are grown now. Happened way too quickly for my liking.' She strokes Amy again, addresses her directly: 'You be good to your mum, won't you? She loves you. Yes, she does. Yes, she does.' The coo of her; night song.

The way strangers assume feeling and thought. Had someone said this to Eleanor about Kitty she's not sure she would have believed them. What does a child convey to a stranger that suggests they need to be told they are loved?

Eleanor kisses Amy, kisses her again, and Candy smiles at her. 'Bless you.'

The urge to kiss Candy on the cheek, to thank her for her care, for her patience, for not making her feel as if there were fault in her, as if she were broken. The gratitude is overwhelming.

'Okay, follow me.'

Eleanor shadows Candy's washing-basket hips across the gravel towards room five. Four cars are parked in corresponding room spaces.

Eleanor unlocks the door and steps into the room. It's as she remembered: a double and a single bed, cream wallpaper, a kitch-enette, bathroom with a bath, a duck-egg blue vase filled with hydrangeas on a bedside table, beige rotary phone, a notepad and pen under a bedside lamp. Eleanor breathes it in, knows they are closer to the mountain.

'Alright, love. You get your rest.'

'Thank you.'

Candy leaves; Eleanor is alone. 'Let's have a little sit-down together, Amy. Just you and me.' She lowers herself onto the medium-firm bed, sinks into the people who have come before her, feels the weight of her own tiredness. 'Amy.' Gentle is her voice. 'We're here.' Eleanor kisses her daughter's crown, can't bear to take her lips off her daughter as she reaches into the front of the carrier, into the space between their stomachs where it is warm.

Eleanor unhooks the carrier, untethers their connection, and her shoulders relax as she lowers Amy onto the bed, begins to lift her woollen jumper above her breast, and there is that feeling of standing on the edge of a mountain, the rushing of a heart, of blood flowing out through toes.

Amy on the bed, her tiny mouth open. Eleanor's breasts are full and sore and she carefully lifts Amy, cradles her body in the crook of her arm, and in this light Eleanor sees now how pale Amy is, how this trip has made her skin so quiet.

'Amy.' She whispers it.

Eleanor

The day before

SHE WOKE KNOWING this would be the day she left him.
I should have moved out of here so long ago. He was next to her
in bed, mouth wide, white teeth, diamond shine under his lip.
All those times she'd held him during the night, believing that he
had come home like her father: war-weary, something breaking
inside. But he was nothing like George. He was only violence,
like he always had been. The way he spoke to her and Amy. The
way he stayed away from home most nights and days. The way he
raged into her, demanded from her when he was home. She was
going to put an end to it.

Up from the bed and she went to Amy, and while she fed her
baby, stroked her eyebrows, Amy gummed her nipple, that way

she did now that she was teething, and Eleanor took stock of her daughter's room, all the things she could pack that wouldn't give the plan away. The essentials only. Nappies, a few changes of clothes, a blanket. Just enough to get through a day, a night, until she reached safety.

After feeding she put Amy in the cot, told her, 'Just a minute, sweetheart. Mummy needs to get something,' and she went to the hall cupboard, quietly slid a small blue suitcase from the top shelf, listened for movement from Leon, heard none. The medication he'd been given took him deeper and deeper into sleep, into the place where sound couldn't follow.

Into Amy's room and in went belongings, and then she snuck outside to the car, put the suitcase in the boot, made sure no one was watching.

Back inside, she took Amy in her arms. 'You and Mummy are going on a little adventure today.' Her daughter pulled at Eleanor's hair, said, 'Mum mum mum mum mum,' rested her hand at the back of Eleanor's neck. The way Amy touched her: my body your body. Still unaware that they were two separate people. She decided the best time to go was when Leon went for a run in the afternoon. She kissed Amy on the chub of her cheek. 'Let's just pretend everything is fine until then, okay?'

———

They were in the lounge room on the sheepskin rug, rolling onto stomachs and backs, when Leon padded down the hall into the living room. 'Good morning,' he said.

'Hello.' She rubbed Amy's feet, made her giggle.

'Haven't you made breakfast yet?' He scratched his stomach, went to the kitchen counter.

'No, it's almost lunchtime and I've been busy with Amy.'

'I guess I'll make it then.'

He turned the radio to talkback chatter, began making porridge, banging through the saucepans to find the right size.

'I was thinking of taking Amy to the park again.' He said it casually, an offering of some kind.

'When?' This was not part of the plan.

'Soon. I thought it would be nice to get to know her on my own.'

The idea of it. She thought of him holding her baby. If she said no to him it would ruin everything.

'Okay,' she said. 'But don't be gone too long. She gets hungry really quickly lately.'

He stirred his porridge, the metal spoon scraping against the bottom of the pot making her skin crawl.

'Are you feeling alright? You sound like something's the matter.'

'I'm just tired.'

Leon ate his porridge and they said nothing to each other and she played with Amy and then before she knew it he was putting Amy in the pram and leaving the house.

———

She packed her own belongings while he was gone, made sure to hide them deep inside the Belmont. Then she sat on the sofa and waited, didn't know what to do with idle hands, considered going to look for him, decided against it. She made pumpkin soup, ladled a serving into an earthenware bowl, put the rest into a Tupperware container to take with her later on.

Time slowed: one hour, two hours, three. She pulled on a pair of sneakers, decided to go looking for them: all the ways a mind creates horror when a story is incomplete. What if he's done something to Amy? She was still on the driveway when Leon came into view: a lopsided swagger up the footpath, his face slack, Amy howling in the pram.

He was drunk.

Eleanor bolted towards her daughter. 'What the hell is going on?' She grabbed Amy from the pram, cradled her in her arms.

'What?'

'Where have you been?'

'Out.'

'Doing what?'

He laughed, shoved the pram into her legs. 'I had a drink with a mate.'

'And you took Amy?'

'I wanted to show my kid off.'

Eleanor turned back towards the house, told Amy, 'It's alright. Everything will be alright.'

Leon yelled out at her, but she blocked out his voice, didn't want to hear what he had to say.

She was halfway up the front steps when she heard him run towards her. She bolted inside, tried to close the door against him, but he barged in.

'Get away from us!'

'Don't be fucking stupid.' Leon tried to grab her, pulled at Amy's arm instead; a small crack sounded, and her child screamed.

'Let her go!'

'I only had a few drinks.'

'You were gone for hours.' Anger sweltered from her pores and she began to cry. She tried to push past him to get her car keys from the hall table.

'Where are you going?' he demanded.

'I'm taking Amy to the hospital and then I'm leaving.'

It was his body that slammed into her first, then his words. 'If you leave I'll fucking kill you.'

Everything a bruise. It went on like this: she couldn't get past him. She ran into Amy's bedroom, put her daughter in the cot. 'I promise I'll come back for you in a minute.' She shut the door to muffle her crying, tried to think of what to do next.

Eleanor ran to the kitchen, picked up the phone, but Leon ripped it from her hands. They stared at each other and she didn't recognise him at all.

———

Late afternoon and the kitchen counter was a barrier. She heard Amy cry out for her from her room.

'You want to know what I did?'

She swallowed. 'You told me already – you went for a drink.' But she knew then. There was more.

'You have to understand, Eleanor. I was desperate. You stopped fucking talking to me before I left. What did you expect me to do? I was lonely. I started seeing a woman over there.'

'I don't care about you sleeping with someone.' The idea that she'd be jealous. It was almost laughable.

He wiped spit from the side of his mouth. 'I fucking had to deal with her. And I will deal with you too.'

'What did you do? What was her name?' Eleanor needed to make him talk, needed to give herself time.

'What fucking difference does it make?' He screamed it, these different sounds of war filling the house.

She could see him more clearly than she'd ever seen him before.

Leon sprang forwards, grabbed her wrist, held it so tight she thought veins would burst. 'I told that woman that if she didn't behave I'd kill her.'

His mouth so close that she could feel his words unfold into action on her skin. What had he done to her?

'The thing is, Eleanor, war makes you do things.'

She began to shake, needed to sit down. 'Please let me go, Leon.'

'I did what I needed to do.'

'No one needs to do anything . . .'

'That whore spat in my face. I had no choice but to teach her a lesson.' He tightened his grip on Eleanor's wrist, yanked at her arm. He whispered, 'So I shot her in the head and then I shot her girl.'

None of it made sense in her head. Her body surged, became too hot. I need to get to Amy. She tried to walk away and Leon yanked at her arm again, and pop went her shoulder.

Amy howled from her bedroom and Eleanor tried to push Leon away from her. 'Let me go to her.'

'Why? So you can leave and take her for good?' It stung when he slapped her across the head with the back of his hand. 'Don't think I won't do to you what I did to the other one.' He slapped her again.

Her daughter cried again and she watched him raise a fist above his head, watched the way bone and skin became a truncheon and everything went dark.

———

She woke in the night. In the house: a sound of skin against skin, of breathing; rushed. 'Amy?' Where's my baby?

She pulled herself up, went to her room, opened the door. Leon was standing by the cot. The house was quiet. 'Where is she?'

He looked into the cot. 'She's here.'

A sharp shock signal pulsed through Eleanor's head, and she hurried over. There was Amy, flat on her back, eyes to the ceiling.

'She wouldn't be quiet, so I picked her up.'

She barely heard his words.

'What did you do to her?' The whimper of her. She reached into the cot, carefully lifted her baby. She couldn't feel her daughter inside. 'Amy?' She turned to Leon. 'What did you do?' And he stood there and she screamed it louder: '*What did you do?*' And she held Amy tight to her chest, tried to find her pulse. There was none.

———

Eleanor rocked her daughter and the house was quiet. Leon had left her alone; she'd heard him go to their bedroom and shut the door. She rocked her daughter and the house was quiet.

'What am I going to do?' she said into Amy as she kissed her, kept rocking her, couldn't let her go. 'What am I going to do without you?' She rocked her baby, thought of the mother in Vietnam rocking her child. This thing Leon had done to them.

It was cold in the house. Eleanor stood from the rocking chair, put Amy in the cot. 'I'll be back, sweetheart. I just have to take care of something.'

She left Amy and walked down the hall to her bedroom. Leon was passed out, snoring, half-naked. Once she had loved the way his body filled their bed, expanded towards her so she could have him all. But now. 'You don't deserve to live.' Careful not to wake him, she leaned over, felt his warm breath. All the things he could breathe in. 'It's cold, don't you think?' Whispered it, this quiet mouse.

She went to their wall heater, turned on the pilot light and there was the first hiss, the first taste of gas; bitterness on the tongue. Eleanor stood away from the heater, waited for the gas to seep through the room, and she shut the bedroom door, taped up the crevices, blocked gaps with wet towels. The slow hiss of carbon monoxide calmed her; a lullaby.

On the way back to Amy's room she noticed something on the kitchen counter. The black box. The black box was unlocked. He'd put it there for her to see.

Open it.

Hands smoothed the top. She lifted the lid.

She screamed before she vomited, her body unable to control itself. She screamed again, and she sobbed. The inside of the box was lined with red silk. A long piece of matted, black hair was wound tight around photos. She untied the hair, a strand stuck to her fingernail. There: dozens and dozens of polaroids of injury, sections of bodies, of women, of all the ways skin could discolour, be torn apart, marbled flesh of purple, green, of yellow, blue, of red. Most photos were close-ups of the centres of bruises, of the intricacies of blood vessels weeping across a thigh, a torso. The idea of her husband leaning close to see the way their bodies reacted to his touch. She dry-retched and her hands shook but she kept looking, saw a bruise the shape of a crescent moon, the way it curled from dark blood-red into a hook of green-hued yellow; the hellish night sky closing in, this painful mark of fingers then palm strangling an arm.

He did this.

This black box, a hidden world: all the ways humanity had been reduced to acts of his violence, reduced to teeth-marked breasts, bitten necks. Bruised cheeks, bruised thighs, buttocks, hips covered in blue knuckle-sized reminders of all the ways this man, this invader, crossed boundaries, crossed bodies.

He had done this.

Some of the photos were taken from a few feet away, captured the ways in which a body had been positioned into his version of a woman: an arm above a head, long trails of red-raw fingernail scratches along chests and shoulders, as if someone had tried to dig away her skin and remove evidence.

Her hands shook but she couldn't let go. She thought of all the times he'd told her in letters home that the others wouldn't sit with him, left him alone, that he didn't fit in. But here. This was what her husband did when other men had looked away.

Eleanor flipped the photos over in her hand, noticed small, handwritten numbers in the bottom right-hand corner.

What was this? She flipped the photos again, looked closer. This catalogue of lives. Her body made a strange yelping sound, but she couldn't stop looking. I need to know everything he has done.

She found herself then, right near the bottom of the box. Her teeth up close from the first time they went camping; the night on her childhood bed; the night before he left for war. There: the leftovers of him on her body, a close-up of her inner thighs and ribs, the places that were so easy to mark, so easy to cover up. She flipped the photo over to see what number he had given her.

But instead of a number there was another photo stuck underneath her body: a pair of legs, bare and bleeding from a place she couldn't see, a grazed knee from a fall; the way skin opens up when it can no longer keep itself together.

She thought of the time he'd mentioned in a letter that he often had to help pull children up from the ground, the way a father rescues a child before hurt and tears take hold. Eleanor unstuck the photo from her body, turned it over. She sobbed, thumped her hand against the kitchen bench. These things he did to children too: he'd made them scream.

Eleanor closed the lid. These women, this child. She thought of Leon.

It was clear to her then what his suicide attempt was actually about: a diversion, a way to come home. He didn't want anyone to know what he had done, who he was. But she knew. And she knew what he had done to Amy and he would not get away with that.

She returned to Amy's room, lifted her daughter from the cot, shrouded her with the blankets, and they sat in the rocking chair, and she heard sleeping Leon, how he coughed, coughed again and again and again, and Eleanor rocked. I'll wait this out. She rocked and she told her child, 'I'm going to take you somewhere safe. I'm going to take you to the mountain to be with Badger.'

Eleanor

Present

SHE UNDRESSES HER baby in small movements. When she removes Amy's onesie, when she peels off the small lavender singlet and white socks, she sees the bloat of Amy's belly, her small veins. Amy's legs are the colour of gravity: dark blue-purple blood pulled to the underside of body; a new-coloured sky she didn't have a name for.

Here is the accumulation of all the changes her body had made since they left home, since she found Amy lifeless in the cot. She tells herself decomposition begins when cells are deprived of oxygen and gradually lose their structural integrity. She stops.

Eleanor looks at Amy, touches her belly then face, this small body in front of her, this small body that is part of her. She wants to scream but nothing comes out. She doesn't want to scare her daughter with what lives inside her. *If I let go of myself will I ever return?*

She thinks of the last time Amy made a sound, cried out, and it is there in her mind: Leon in the kitchen, the way he'd held Eleanor by the throat, how he scratched the right side of her neck before biting her, how Amy cried out in a way that was indescribable; how she tried to go to her daughter but he wouldn't let her. How can this be the last sound she gets to hear from her child?

———

In the dark she remembers how she always called for her mother when she was frightened and how, despite herself, Kitty would come and attempt to soothe, and her mother would say, *There, there, child*, and her mother would say, *It's all a bad dream*, and her mother would say, *None of this is real*, and her mother would mother. These night-time animal instincts; they always revealed their true selves.

Now it is dark again.

Here is the child asking for care and help and love. Here is the child running to her mother's bedroom in the middle of the night, asking her to kill the monsters that come. Here is the child running towards her mother after not seeing her for a week. Here is the child stroking her mum's legs while they listen to records, hoping that the music will distract her from the fact that they are closer than they have been for months. Here is the child coming home from school after the older boys have thrown a bottle of

Coke at her head. Here is the child excitedly showing her mother the small bones of a chick that fell out of a nest in the backyard, the child who asks, 'Did you know wings needed this many bones to fly?' Here is the child inching towards adolescence who tells her mother, 'I got my period,' and receives no response. Here is the child who at sixteen asks her mother to play with her hair because she is afraid of becoming an adult. Here is the child who promised herself to stop chasing the love of her mother.

Here is the child asking why women have to bleed, why it feels nice when you touch yourself, whether Jesus was a real man, if ghosts can see you when you go to the toilet, why her father screams so much, what her mum wanted to be when she grew up, how far she's ever walked in a day. Here is the child wondering why she can't understand herself.

Here is the child in a motel room dialling her mother to beg her to come be with her while she holds her dead baby's hand. Here is the child begging her mother to please, please, please tell her what to do because nothing makes sense. To tell her that life will go on, to tell her that her desire to return to the beginning of everything will not change what happened, to tell her how to get through this night without her daughter, to tell her how it's possible for the past to keep coming back. The phone rings once, twice, five, seven times. 'Mummy, can you hear me? I need you,' she whispers. But Kitty doesn't answer.

She hangs up the phone and all the air in the room is sucked through the cracks under the door and everything becomes tight and dark and sharp and Eleanor feels like she's about to explode.

She rubs the small bloat of Amy's stomach, lies down next to her; someone's child with someone's child.

Their heads on the same pillow makes it easier for her to kiss Amy's forehead, easier to find the last traces of her smell, the way she was before they left in the car: there's milk, there's cooked carrot, there's the honey-sweet of her neck. Easier to hold on for a little longer before the end comes. This is how they used to sleep in the beginning: Eleanor would wake in the middle of the night to Amy inching closer and closer to her, to her mouth. She couldn't stand how close Amy was, how she could feel her own breath radiate off Amy's skin. Why won't you leave me alone? Eleanor moved away but Amy followed and she knew she was defeated, let her daughter come as close as she needed to know that she wasn't alone, that she was safe. Eleanor breathed out, Amy breathed in; this new supply of oxygen.

Eleanor closes in on her daughter until their lips touch and she breathes out and out and out, the way she had when she found Amy in the cot, how she had tried to bring her back from the place her father left her. Eleanor had never felt so useless in her life.

'Amy, I'm sorry he hurt you.' Her flat-toned tongue, the sound her body made when she couldn't navigate out of it, couldn't find herself. Why can't I show you exactly how I feel? Kissing Amy's mouth it is all there: those early days of skin-to-skin contact, this way she had tried to bond with her child so she could find herself, express what it was that she was feeling. I want to breathe all that I am into you but nothing is coming, Amy.

Amy in lamplight, Amy so quiet: just like those first few seconds when she was born, the pause before life begins. Why is it that I only want to return to the beginning?

Eleanor caresses Amy's forehead, the way that always sends her to sleep, kisses her cheeks, kisses and kisses, holds Amy's cold hands, uncut fingernails sharp against Eleanor's thumb, and she whispers, 'Tomorrow you'll be with Badger and you'll finally be safe.'

She kisses Amy and her heart skips a beat, feels the first time she ever saw her daughter come to her from the pit of her stomach. 'Amy.' She says it soft in her daughter's ear. 'The time will come when I am nothing but old-growth skin, a forest of years, and should I live to the moment where I have whittled down everything that made me who I was and I am left with one last memory, I would want it to be this: those seconds after you emerged from the darkness of me, you on my chest, your sun-heart against my lungs, your eye seeing first light, your eye closing, opening, your tourniquet fist around my finger, me kissing your forehead, your eye into my eye, me kissing, me whispering, "I'm so glad you're here," and you blinking, you breathing like a tornado, your eye into my eye and those first seconds of us alone together before life started. Let that be my last.'

She pulls Amy into her chest, holds her tight. Amy is crying, I am sure of it. But the room is quiet.

Still nothing inside her. What point is there in going on when I can't feel anything, when there is nothing for me? I don't want to wake up.

———

Breastmilk leaks towards her armpit, the swell of herself an ache. My body keeps going on. Outside: a dawn crow sound then the thunder of car doors slamming shut; these two sounds together pretend it's a normal day. She heaves onto elbows, cotton under her skin makes her teeth snap tight and she gently lifts Amy to her chest, guides her daughter's mouth to her breast, the way of all mornings, and Amy stares at the ceiling and Eleanor breathes her in. She watches milk run from Amy's mouth, sobs, wipes Amy clean with the back of her hand, absent-mindedly licks herself away.

What do I do now? Follow a ritual, try to make it through the day. Get her ready one last time. And the alarm clock on the bedside reads 8 am and she calculates when she needs to be on the mountain. It seems so long. Rubs her face then lays Amy back down on the double bed and goes to the bathroom, fills the bath, throws a handful of bubble bath pouches into the water, watches the bottom of the bath disappear.

She lowers herself into the water, Amy firm against her breasts, and tries not to think of the way her daughter is slowly slipping from her skin. At least the water is warm enough to diffuse the pang of cold from Amy's body. She remembers the moment she birthed Amy, how the pain was so great she wanted to die. I want to die now too. But there had always been reasons to survive. She shook herself. Maybe not this time.

Eleanor circles soap into Amy's skin, washes her shoulders, the three little freckles there. How she'd miss this. 'I wish I hadn't rushed through my days with you, bub. I wish so many things.' Eleanor marvels at what she had created, all the skin that grew inside skin. She is all mine. The early years of parenting are dangerous, make you believe that you deserve the entirety of your child because they wouldn't exist without you. But now Eleanor knows the real danger: the inability to register that the new version of yourself can't exist without them. The cruelty of ownership. She washes her child and water laps, tide against ribs, neck, against small toes curling towards the soles of feet.

'Who am I without you?'

Amy: eyes open, blue and blacked skin floats. For a moment Amy is alive in the water, brings with her the sound of beach play, how she laughed eating sand, how she smiled as a wave carried her over its small peak. Eleanor tilts to smile at Amy, gags at the sight of her daughter's gaping mouth filling with water. She closes her eyes. This can't be real. But just because you look away doesn't make something untrue. A howl storms from the centre of her stomach and she opens her mouth, feels the first stipple of anger rage through, but as it hits the bathroom tiles she remembers the way she screamed at Leon, at the horror and incredulity of knowing his hands shook Amy into silence as if she were nothing more than a doll. She stops the sound of herself and instead sinks under, feels the way her eardrums itch from the weight of water, her throat sore from clamping tight. She holds her breath. Above: her daughter is an ancient landmass rising in the tide. I am already drifting from you. She tries to tether Amy back to the shore of her own body but panic knocks against her lungs, begging her to breathe, and she lets go of her daughter. Amy falls onto her stomach, her small face just above Eleanor's. This horror. She opens up, swallows water, a sharp pain crisscrosses cheek, throat then chest. I didn't know it would be this painful. Keep living, Eleanor. You have to keep living. And she nods her head, rises from the water, holds her baby – I don't want to let her go – feels the small trickle of water from Amy's mouth fall on her chest.

———

What does it mean to mother? Eleanor performs the last act of caring for Amy's body. She pats her down with a large white towel, soft touches till dry, and pulls out a bottle of body lotion from her suitcase. She squeezes the bottle, rubs the soft pink lotion between palms and massages her daughter's legs. Eleanor clicks her tongue, sings 'I Only Have Eyes For You' into the room, that old-time mother song, presses palm and fingers into skin, tickles her, imagines Amy's laugh, and Eleanor pokes her tongue out. This way of being together. I am not Kitty, I am not Kitty, I am not Kitty. I don't want to bring her back from the dead. I just want to feel myself do this with her one last time.

After she dresses Amy in a clean jumpsuit, says, 'Mummy's going to change now,' and rubs the same lotion into her own skin, she notices the bounce of fire in her stomach and thighs, these differences between the touch of life and death. She keeps her eye on Amy, pulls on her jeans, is struck by the smallness of her daughter, how far away she seems, like looking through a telescope at a planet being born. She shakes her head. I am not Kitty, I am not Kitty.

Eleanor leans over Amy on the bed, her small cave mouth, as if she's about to say something. What would our first conversation have been? This version of their life that has been taken. All that they had was mime talk and laughter, was learning the vowels that shaped the world, was Eleanor saying, 'I love you,' and Amy responding, 'Mum mum mum!'

She lifts Amy, cradles the base of her head as she straps the baby carrier to her body and fits her daughter into a sleep pose one last time. She scrawls on a piece of paper, *Gone hiking to the second lookout. If not back by evening, send help*, places it by the phone, exits the motel room, leaves the door wide open. This habit George had taught her that was so hard to break.

'Sweetheart, it's time to go to the mountain now.' It's time to let go.

———

Stand. Walk. And the trudge up the steep paved hill pulls at the back of her calves, at the cramp of long hours of car travel, of holding too tight to her baby. The damage that has been done. Cars barrel down the hill, brakes grind to slow.

She walks on, passes a playground, sees a smattering of winter-clothed adults watching torn-kneed children, a vigil of silver thermoses on picnic tables. Lower eyes to Amy, a beanie on her head to cover discolouration, Eleanor's arms aching involuntarily from the memory of pushing her daughter to great heights. She walks on.

The base of the blue mountain is brown-leaved, a crunch under shoe, is feathered with nectar-yellow wattle. Knotted tree trunks steady their wisping limbs, arguments between wind and earth; these ways we fight what's inside. She says, 'I still have so much to tell you,' and three hikers pass Eleanor, point above and tell her, 'Bit blowy up there. You two better hold on!' They smell of sweat and wet, of pushing a body past comfort. This is living.

Eleanor tucks Amy closer to her and it is like before, when she and George brought Badger here to leave his remains in a cave. Then, too, a group of men stopped to tell them about the winds, that they ought to be careful. 'We know what we're doing,' George had said. But Eleanor was happy to hear of a mighty wind; Badger would have no difficulty flying as high as he could.

Amy, we know what we're doing. The hikers pass out of sight and Eleanor takes to the mountain, a reunification with all things past. Here are the small steps chiselled out of rock, the rusted signs directing hikers to great heights. In her ear now: George explaining constellations in the sky, the familiar stories he's told each time they walked this same track. In her ear now: Kitty lamenting mosquito bites, the last summer she came with them to the mountain. All of them here now in some form, the Turners swarming inside each other's radius. 'How did our family become so distant, Amy?' Her breath shortening. This is the way things happen.

Eleanor continues on, sweat down her back, neck, sticky and damp; this labour from laying children to rest should never be easy but it's slowly breaking her. She wipes her jumper across her forehead, wool lifting off the tiny scabs of healing sores, her old nights of scratching at her skin to stop the anxiety from another day with Leon.

'Amy, there are very bad people in this world. I'm sorry to say your father was one of them.' The way it came out, passing fact.

Whiiip-whiips call in trees, birds communicating the arrival of strangers, and crows circle above. For a moment her stomach lifts towards the flight surrounding her. The summoning to be higher then higher, to see everything clearly below, makes her woozy, and she bites her tongue to fight the feeling of wanting to lift off and disappear. When she was little she used to ask George if what he saw in the planes was the same as for a bird and he would laugh, rasped metal, a torn tin can. 'I hope not.' Why keep what you see to yourself? I wish he had explained more of his world to me. Things could've been different. I could've been different. Kitty and George could've been different.

'Who are we if we don't say it out loud?' This into the mountain, this out loud to her daughter, to herself. Her heart is erratic, erupts with all her past losses. All the ways she hurts now. I don't know how much further I can carry this weight. Comforting Amy she slowly ascends the mountain, one muscle pushing the next along. She makes sure Amy isn't moving too much as small steps become large, but the rocking of their movement is inevitable and she remembers how they've been like this before, the days before Amy's birth, how nothing she did could stop the baby from her ferocious kicking. Soothing her asleep, soothing her awake: she could never be sure which. But now I am soothing you into peace, Amy.

Sound of wind, of crows flying above, of trees crashing against each other. The sky threatens rain and on she goes and everything hurts now, the way it does when nightmares crawl out of the night, sit on your chest and scream into pupils, into your heart, whisper, *I am real.* So hard to breathe. She concentrates on the pain in her thighs, the pain in her breast, her abdomen, her heart, the pain of having to labour your child into life and then into death.

Eleanor struggles with the weight of it all. Amy's arm falls out of the carrier and hits her mother's arm. Eleanor feels herself begin to dislodge from the places she's kept herself hidden and she bites her hands in order to focus on something else, just enough to make it to the mountain altar where Badger rests. She hears herself say, 'Amy, I think the price we pay for living in fear is not that we aren't our full selves – it's that we don't let other people see us for who we truly are. Fear robs us of our humanity.'

She wants to tell her daughter all the things she wished her mother had told her. All the things she'd been frightened to:

Amy, when I held you for the first time I thought I would die. To love someone is to prepare for the pain that comes from not knowing what happens next. For the longest time, I was so afraid I'd become Kitty that I forgot to be myself. All the things I could've told you, should've told you, had I just allowed myself to show you everything that I am. I don't have words to convey what it is to have a heart, what it is to pass that on to someone else. I don't know enough about the world to tell you all the mysteries that are yet to be discovered.

I have done bad things. I have done good things. I have been ashamed of myself, been proud of myself. I have made many mistakes. Mostly I've been a person. I wish I'd done so many things differently. I wish I'd left your father sooner, wish I'd seen him for who he really was. I wish I hadn't convinced myself to stop listening to my intuition. I wish I hadn't given up on myself so easily. I wish I hadn't looked to others for validation, to let myself believe that if I couldn't make them happy I was nothing. At the lowest points of my life I have wanted to disappear, haven't wanted to be around others, haven't wanted to be around you. I have wanted to return to the dark matter that everything has come from. I have questioned many times why we should live and what living is. But I can never find an answer and I don't think there is one. This is all I know: we are here. And at the end of our lives we will need to tell ourselves the story of who we were and what we did. In my story I am most afraid of knowing I didn't tell others how I felt. I didn't love enough people, didn't demonstrate enough love to strangers, to myself. People talk about hope as the thing that brings you through the hard times. I don't know about that. What is hope? The only thing I found was that I kept looking for something new in the world, something that would take my breath away, to make me stay. And one day you came along and my breath was gone. When it came back I'd never felt so alive. Amy, I never wanted to be a mother but I loved being yours. One of my worst fears has come true: I will continue to be here when you are not.

The wind is wild, is cold on her face, legs charging with pins and needles. The sky is arching into the afternoon, is black with crows, the distance hazy from eucalyptus oil, from tiredness. Eleanor pinches her cheeks to stay awake; I know this feeling: I am a bird in unihemispheric slow-wave sleep, and there in her head is Kitty. The two of them on her parents' bed on the day Badger was knocked over, her arms wrapped around her mother. How had I forgotten this? Kitty was warm and it was getting darker outside. She lay next to her mother, pulled the blankets up over them both, and then she burrowed into Kitty's back, hips, legs. Kitty sobbed, a sound so painful that Eleanor thought they were both dying, and the only thing Eleanor could think to do was tell her it would all be alright. How do you describe the feeling you have for someone before you were born? She clung to Kitty, whispered, 'I love you, Mummy.' Kitty squeezed Eleanor's fingers but she didn't say it in return and they stayed like that, a daughter clinging to her mother, telling her over and over that she was loved until her mother fell asleep and Eleanor stared into the back of the woman who made her and she whispered, 'Maybe one day you will say it too.' And she didn't let her go because she knew they'd never be like this again.

———

At the small cave she is an ache, is a wreck. Eleanor climbs onto the ledge where she last saw Badger, remembers how when they scattered him he flew onto birds, onto rock, into air, onto her and

George's shoulders, how they let him land on them before shaking him off and letting him go, and she saw the relief in George's smile before he cried, before he took her hand and told her, 'This is the best place for him to be.'

She makes sure not to scrape Amy along the rock as she unhooks the carrier from her body, cradles Amy in her arms. She kisses Amy, watches dozens of crows fly and land in trees. Yes, come and watch and remember her too. Outside the cave the sky is closing in. Almost time to let go, Amy, and she places her daughter on the rock and lies beside her, listens to the wind, to the murder of crows sing, tastes the bitter metallic blood at the back of her throat, the peat smell of old water on moss in her nose, and the mountain roars open and there is the smell of Amy disappearing. It is peaceful here; it is everything she promised her daughter it would be. There's nothing to run from anymore. Eleanor kisses Amy, says, 'I wish I could stay here next to you.'

She wraps her arm around her daughter's body, looks out into the sky. 'I want to spend one last moment with you. I want to tell you how much I have loved and love you.' But it doesn't feel enough. Love doesn't feel enough. How do you describe an experience you cannot see?

She tries to slow her breathing, tries to slow time, to stay with Amy as long as she can, but it is cold and water drips inside the cave, and eucalypt limbs moan, a parrot darts through the sky, a plane flies above, the wind whips into white noise, sharp tingles spread across her face, a rock falls a great height, an apocalyptic lavender and peach sunset begins to make way for the blue hour and her insides atomise, an inferno of primordial dark. Eleanor slows time to make way for the end of things, the beginning of things. How do you describe an experience you cannot touch? And it comes: the howling that is inside her, everything that she has been holding on to has arrived. She screams into the mountain. It hurts. It is rage. It is love. It is the past and it is now. She's never heard a sound like it. It frightens her. Off go crows. She can't stop. She screams and she cries and she screams until her face is red, until she coughs blood, until there is nothing else to come out. Now she's given what was inside her to Amy, to the mountain, now she's silent, she kisses her baby one last time and as the blue hour begins, something bigger than love has been made and she leans into Amy's ear. 'Long ago humans used to see something so rare in nature they didn't even have a word for it. Then they called it blue. Blue is the rarest colour in nature but I see it everywhere and you are blue.'

Acknowledgements

MY LOVE AND gratitude to the following people for advice, long conversations, and dealing with *Blue Hour* in all its guises (and everything that came with it) over the years: Felicity Gilbert, Susan Johnson, Stephanie Convery, Justine Hyde, Kylie Boltin, Lefa Singleton-Norton, Jane Rawson, Tom Saras, Andrea Parker, Joshua Schmidt, Emma Miller, Cassandra Austin, Lucy Roleff.

To all my family and friends: I am so glad I have you. To anyone who ever listened to me prattle on about this beast and my anxieties: thank you. Special thanks to Simon and Chris: some of the dreams I had in your house helped fill these pages.

My wonderful agent Pippa Masson: your wisdom, support, opinions, and utter patience with me continues to astound me.

I cannot do this without you. To Dan Lazar and Gordon Wise: thank you for everything. Thank you, Kate Cooper. Thank you to everyone at Curtis Brown Australia.

My publishers and editors Vanessa Radnidge, Mary-Anne Harrington, Ali Lavau: what a brilliant dream it has been. You all saw the things I couldn't see, didn't want to see. It's been an utter privilege to work with you. Karen Ward: your insight and care meant so much. Thank you, too, to Fiona Hazard, Louise Stark, Emily Lighezzolo.

Everyone at Hachette Australia and Tinder Press UK: your hard work and dedication means the world. I am forever grateful that you took me and these characters.

My dear friend, Robert Watkins: not only did you see this book through the difficult conception and first draft but you held me up through some of the most difficult years of my life. I love you, friend.

Andreia: thank you for the years of therapy.

To the creative life changing wonder of long-form improv comedy and all those who I met and befriended at Melbourne's TIC: thank you for teaching me how to fail properly and to have no shame in the way we choose to lean into gut-reaction.

My love to Sim: you, a piece of gold delivered at the right time. Thank you, thank you.

And to Alice: the time will come when I am nothing but old-growth skin . . .